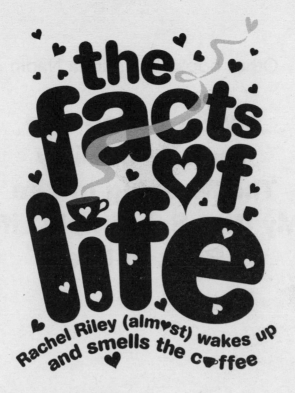

the facts of life

Rachel Riley (alm♥st) wakes up and smells the c♥ffee

Other books by Joanna Nadin

My So-Called Life
The Life of Riley
The Meaning of Life
My (Not So) Simple Life
Back to Life

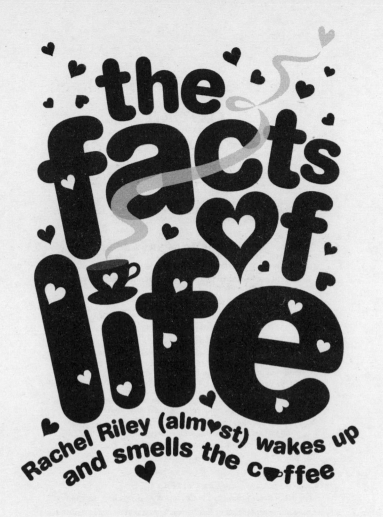

the facts of life

Rachel Riley (almost) wakes up and smells the coffee

Joanna Nadin

OXFORD
UNIVERSITY PRESS

OXFORD

UNIVERSITY PRESS

Great Clarendon Street, Oxford OX2 6DP

Oxford University Press is a department of the University of Oxford.
It furthers the University's objective of excellence in research, scholarship,
and education by publishing worldwide in

Oxford   New York

Auckland   Cape Town   Dar es Salaam   Hong Kong   Karachi
Kuala Lumpur   Madrid   Melbourne   Mexico City   Nairobi
New Delhi   Shanghai   Taipei   Toronto

With offices in

Argentina   Austria   Brazil   Chile   Czech Republic   France   Greece
Guatemala   Hungary   Italy   Japan   Poland   Portugal   Singapore
South Korea   Switzerland   Thailand   Turkey   Ukraine   Vietnam

Oxford is a registered trade mark of Oxford University Press
in the UK and in certain other countries

© Joanna Nadin 2010

British Library Cataloguing in Publication Data

Data available

ISBN: 978-0-19-272923-1

1 3 5 7 9 10 8 6 4 2

Printed in Great Britain by CPI Cox and Wyman, Reading, Berkshire

Paper used in the production of this book is a natural, recyclable product made
from wood grown in sustainable forests. The manufacturing process conforms
to the environmental regulations of the country of origin

july

CORNISH FLAG

Sunday 13

4 p.m.

OMG. Am actually weak at knees. In fact think may need to lie down for a bit. Is unprecedented. Is utter revelation. Am happy! Not just 'thank God it is chocolate sponge instead of povvy yoghurt for pudding' happy, but when Baby does the lift at the end of *Dirty Dancing* happy. Or when James got a laminator for his birthday happy. Oh. Am actually going to have to lie down as think may swoon, Jane Austen-like, in my delirium.

4.30 p.m.

OK. Am temporarily unswooned and can confirm that am in love with Jack Stone. Oh, even writing his name makes me feel breathless and dizzy. Although that could be dog, who has eaten Glade Plug-In and is emitting overpowering scent of hyacinth every three minutes. Or possibly low blood sugar as have used up all joules of energy snogging. Will stop for bit again.

4.50 p.m.

Have had replenishing Marmite on toast. But only one slice. As am in love, cannot eat properly, it is well-documented fact. But is enough to be able to write coherently, if only for brief moment. Am likely to hit wall of pain any minute, i.e. start pining and panicking as have not seen him for more than an hour.

Cannot believe I feel like this. Have been utter fool.

True love has been staring me in face for years but was blinded by shiny but hollow bauble, i.e. Justin Statham and his halo of blond hair, small nipples, and ability to play 'Stairway to Heaven' on guitar. These trappings are meaningless to me now. Jack is my true destiny. He is my Paulie and I am his Juno. Except not pregnant and with better dress sense. We are inseparable. Or at least we would be if he hadn't had to go home for Sunday lunch (at 4 p.m. in Stone household due to various issues involving tantric yoga classes, biorhythms, and scheduling on T4). But I will see him again tomorrow after school. Point is, we are soul mates, i.e. we like all the same things, for example The Doors and Waitrose hummus. Plus I can tell him anything. Like the time I ate sheep poo because I thought it was a Malteser. Or when I got my hand stuck down a drain trying to reach a Sylvanian something.

Except fact that am actually in love with him. Am going to build up to that. As *a*) do not want to appear like overkeen stalker type; *b*) am waiting for him to say it first, and *c*) declaration needs romantic setting, e.g. sunset, or beach, or balcony in unspoilt peasant village, i.e. not John-Lewis-decorated bedroom contaminated with odour of hyacinth-scented dog and within earshot of eleven year old singing 'Nessun Dorma'. Which is obviously why Jack has not told me yet either.

Also have not told him what actually happened on the night of prom, obviously. He did ask me where I went

when I left the party. I said was depressed about wonky portrait mix-up and had gone for refreshing walk. Which is not a total lie. Have not added bit that walk was to meet Justin and that ended up naked in his bed and possibly only narrowly avoided doing 'It' because Justin did snakebite sick and passed out on racing car duvet. Jack does not need to know silly details like that. Justin is a closed chapter, or paragraph even, in the foreword of my life. Oooh. Who would do the foreword? Maybe Julie Burchill. Anyway. Book metaphor is excellent as life is officially a fairy tale and Jack is my knight in shining armour. Or shining skinny jeans. Anyway, he is totally my Darcy.

This is it. This is my happy ever after. I just know it.

Ooh, doorbell. Maybe that is him. He cannot bear to be apart from me and has sacrificed his nut roast in order to gaze once more on my features.

5.30 p.m.

Was not Jack. Was Sad Ed, who has already eaten (two helpings) and is engulfed in gloom, as usual. It is because his mojo has decided to fall in love with our best friend and Jack's sister Scarlet, who is oblivious to Sad Ed's (admittedly not many) charms and is still pining after bat boy Trevor. I said surely my happiness could lift the veil of tears that is strapped permanently to his head but he said, *au contraire*, it is nauseating, and if I want to help I can tell Scarlet asap about me and Jack, and then she

might be inspired to reassess her friends, i.e. Sad Ed, for potential boyfriend material. I said would think about it.

6 p.m.
Have thought about it. Am not going to tell Scarlet yet. She is just too judgemental. And sometimes plain mental.

Mum is also in a bad mood. Do not know why. She should be delighted about me and Jack. He is clean, brainy and has never worn a Kappa tracksuit.

6.30 p.m.
Apparently Mum's misery is not in any way related to Jack, as James has pointed out, as part of his well-practised 'the world does not revolve around you' lecture. It turns out that was in such bubble of bliss that have made grave error in judgement and forgotten that today is Mum's birthday. That is why I only got one roast potato at lunchtime and the soggy Yorkshire pudding.

7 p.m.
Have solved birthday dilemma and given Mum Jack's portrait of me as present. And pointed out that this was yet further evidence of Jack being such excellent boyfriend as he has painted picture that can adorn her walls and remind her of me for ever. Mum said 'hmm'. And Dad said, 'Why would a picture of Princess Margaret remind her of you?' There is no pleasing some people. It is because they have forgotten what it is like to be

consumed with passion. Or possibly never knew in first place. Cannot imagine habitual vest-wearers Janet and Colin in heated clinch. Or rather do not want to imagine it. Ick.

Nothing can dampen my good mood though. Jack's portrait has saved me from domestic abuse. It is like magic talisman. Will text him to tell him that.

7.30 p.m.
And to tell him that had four fishfingers and peas for tea.

11 p.m.
James has just been in to demand an end to texting. He has counted no less than sixty-three beeps in five hours and has calculated that so far today my love has cost £7.56 plus several pence in battery recharging electricity. He is right. I do not need to text Jack. We are so in tune I will send my thought-waves out of window and he will telepathically know what I am saying.

11.45 p.m.
Just got text from Jack checking am still alive as had not replied to previous text. Think thoughts ensnared on Clive and Marjory's leylandii. Have texted back. But is last one of night.

12.05 a.m.
Is new day. So can text again. Have sent him message to say cannot sleep.

1.30 a.m.
No reply. Maybe he is dead. Maybe should ring and check. Yes will do that.

1.45 a.m.
He not dead. He asleep. Or rather was. Will do same. So can meet in our dreams. Plus James has confiscated phone.

. . . .

Monday 14

8 a.m.
Am still in utter bubble of bliss. Love, as effete Tory Bryan Ferry says, is the drug. Mum did ask if 'crack marijuana' was in fact the drug due to my uncharacteristic perpetual smile and fact that did not get minty with dog when it coughed on my Shreddies. She is still in bad mood about temporarily overlooked birthday yesterday. I said inconsequential matters such as dog spit and birthdays are of no interest to me since I now operate on a higher plain. Which made her suspicious again. So pointed out higher plain was love, and that I do not need artificial stimulants as Jack is more than enough. But mention of stimulation and Jack in one sentence made her eyes perceptibly bulge and lips go thin so left house before either she or James could launch into anti-teenage pregnancy sex lecture. James is very much anti-sex. And love. It is because he is still reeling from the devastating union (in pathetic

8

eleven-year-old sense) of Mad Harry and Mumtaz. Though am not sure if he is more distressed at Mumtaz's choice, or at the demise of Beastly Boys and untimely end of his boy band dream. He says only the dog understands him. Which is possibly true.

4 p.m.
The saggy sofa is just not the same without Jack. I cannot believe his buttocks have graced Yazoo-stained cushion for the last time (except for annual last day silly string/ release the sheep ritual). I miss him. I miss the sweet sound of his voice shouting at Fat Kylie to stop microwaving Wagon Wheels. I miss the thud, click of his boots with the drawing pin in the toe chasing rogue Retards and Criminals along B Corridor. John Major High is an empty shell without him. Yet just a few weeks ago I barely noticed him among the crowd of pasty faces and Arctic Monkey hairdos. Oh, it is utterly poetic.

Plus his head boy replacement, i.e. Sad Ed, is clearly not up to the job. He is too busy being consumed with lust over his self-appointed Chief of Staff/Director of Communications aka Scarlet to enforce any kind of control. Scarlet, *au contraire*, is consumed only by power. She has already been to see ineffectual headmaster Mr Wilmott three times to demand *a*) a ban on Dolphin-unfriendly tuna in the canteen, *b*) a ban on pupil-unfriendly Mrs Brain in the canteen, and *c*) an overhaul of the fruit and nut dispensing machine as there is a

packet of dried figs in there that is potential chemical weapon. He says they will not be able to implement any changes until September, and possibly never in the case of Mrs Brain. Scarlet is unperturbed and says it will give her time to draw up a manifesto for lasting change. Asked what I got to do in the new regime. She says I can be Peter Mandelson. Normally would be utterly peeved at weird-voiced and potentially evil role but luckily am too busy being in love. Am going round to Jack's house now. Ostensibly to visit Scarlet in her war room (aka the den), but mostly to gaze at Jack.

9 p.m.
Have done several hours of gazing, four minutes, thirty-three seconds of snogging when Scarlet went to the toilet, and some minor under table footsie while she comforted Suzy over birth of Jolie-Pitt twins (Suzy boiling with jealousy at vast and multicultural family when her own ovaries are withering on vine). Jack said maybe we should reveal our new relationship to cheer her up but I said this was further proof why we cannot, as our young and potentially fruitful union might push Suzy even further over the edge. Plus think having secret love is utterly literary. Is like *Romeo and Juliet*. Our families are from opposite sides of the tracks, well, Debden Road anyway, and might fight to keep us apart. Jack pointed out that my mum already knows what is going on and has not forbidden anything except closing of the bedroom door at

any time so that she can see into every crevice to make sure we are not doing 'It'. But I said she is only not declaring war yet because she is gloating in her superior position of knowing something before Suzy. Jack rolled eyes, but luckily at that point Scarlet came in to demand my immediate repatriation to presidential headquarters to take tea orders.

In contrast, Mumtaz and Mad Harry's love is very much not secret. Apparently they were all over each other on the St Regina's junior log (official territory of Years Five and Six) in first break. James says it is disgusting and he is minded to inform Mr Mumtaz who is not a fan of snogging, or Mad Harry. The only reason he is holding his tongue is because he gets his SATs results tomorrow and is confidently expecting them to be so high that he will be instantly admitted to Eton, and thus avoid having to go to substandard John Major High, which not only has a broken locust tank and unhygienic toilet facilities, but is where the Mumtaz and Mad Harry love nest will be ensconced come September. He is heading for certain disappointment.

. . . .

Tuesday 15

As predicted, James's SATs results have not magically opened the doors of Eton, Rugby, or Hogwart's. In fact, according to official statistics, he is utterly not as boffiny as everyone thought. Mum says it is the influence of

deadly Keanu O'Grady who is ruining not only his own life, with his endless consumption of Peperami and Capri-Sun, but the lives of those around him. James says it is not Keanu, it is that no exam can do justice to his unique intellect, and is begging to be sent to private school. Dad says we cannot afford it in these austerity times and we are all going to have to make sacrifices in the harsh months ahead. I asked what his were. He says he has been using the same golf balls now for several months.

I suggested we could move to Hull, i.e. potential new home of Jack and utterly cheap, according to Phil and Kirstie. But Mum says she would rather move to the Whiteshot Estate than north of Watford, i.e. not at all. James says there is nothing else for it then, and is demanding to be home-schooled. He has clearly had some kind of emotional breakdown. I can think of nothing worse than being trapped in the dining room with Mum for seven hours a day while she bangs on about osmosis.

· ·

Wednesday 16
10 p.m.
The home schooling dream is over. Mum says if the credit crunch continues, then come September she will not be available for tuition as she will be looking for a job. It is because she is worried we will be forced to shop at Lidl or give up Cillit Bang for own-brand substandard cleaner.

James warned her that we will become latchkey children, and get obese on microwave meals and that the house will go downhill and we will be festering in discarded Pot Noodle cartons and Mars bar wrappers within weeks. Which sounded excellently tragic. But Mum has put paid to any dreams of Dickensian squalor. She says she will only work part-time and we will continue to consume a balanced diet including liver once a week and oily fish on Tuesdays.

Also Granny Clegg has rung. Apparently Grandpa Clegg is up in arms about the curfew in Redruth, i.e. all menacing local youths have to be inside their houses by nine p.m. He says it is anti-Cornish and wants it imposed on anyone who eats olives, wears coloured wellies, or drives a 4X4, regardless of age. Granny says he is showing no signs of giving up his allegiance to the Cornish Liberation Army and that she does not know how much longer she can take it. This morning he claimed his blood ran black like the Cornish flag, and said if he ever needs a tranfusion, it has to be from someone born within the county boundaries. Granny is now sleeping in the spare room with Bruce. Said did that not compromise 'relations'? She said they hadn't had 'relations' since Boris Becker won Wimbledon in 1985 (no idea) so there is no change there. Plus Bruce does not sing mining songs and his breath is less deadly.

It is utterly sad. Jack and I will never end up like that, i.e. locked in political conflict. Or wearing elasticated

trousers. We will be at one for eternity. Even though he is at band practice, I feel utterly connected to him. In fact, can feel him telling me to call.

10.15 p.m.
Think maybe he was just telling me NOT to call him. So just marginal error. He had left mobile at home and Scarlet answered and demanded to know why was ringing him 'out of hours'. Said *a*) needed political advice relating to inbred Cornish relatives, and *b*) did not know Jack had official office hours. She said *a*) to tell Granny Clegg to embrace life and possibly join match.com to find a like-minded pensioner who does not think the Health Secretary is someone who types up prescriptions; and *b*) after ten is reserved for head girl (i.e. smelly Oona) business, band business, or girlfriend business, and I am none of the above. Said will bear that in mind in future. There is no way am telling Granny Clegg about match.com though. She has had a hip replacement. Plus am still holding out hope for a Clegg reunion. She may have forsaken her racist and generally moronic tendencies for newfound left-wing feminism, but she still thinks *Doc Martin* is real so all is not lost.

· ·

Thursday 17
There has been another relationship breakdown. Wonky-jawed Welsh Lib Dem Lembit Opik has been dumped by

the Cheeky Girl. It was obviously not true love. He should have stuck to his own kind, i.e. the wide-mouthed weather woman, also from Wales and also habitual shopper in Marks & Spencer's 'sensible' department, instead of being seduced by hot pants and exotic Transylvanian accent. James says it is utterly like his own situation, i.e. Mumtaz has been swayed by Mad Harry's bottom and has ignored James's superior intellect and interest in chess. Although he is visibly less despondent today. It is because Keanu has taken James's side and has banished Mad Harry from the gang. I said it was an empty gesture as in a week neither of them will be in the gang anyway as they are leaving St Regina's and Keanu will have to recruit a whole new set of idiotic minions. James says, *au contraire*, it is replete with symbolism, as it means he will enjoy the protection of the O'Gradys at John Major High. Said O'Gradys are not the mafia, they are just over-large family of helmet-headed mentalists. And that includes the girls. James said exactly.

Friday 18

Scarlet is getting more suspicious of me and Jack. It is because had to offer apologies for non-attendance at saggy sofa summit this lunchtime (to discuss potential ban on kettle on environmental grounds, i.e. it is giving off odd fumes since I tried to heat milk up in it for Ready Brek) because was meeting Jack for romantic walk down

Battleditch Lane (aka snoggers paradise aka dogshit alley). Obviously did not say was going for romantic walk, said was going to help head boy round up escaped lower school snoggees. Luckily Sad Ed came to rescue by saying he had a few things he needed to run by her in private. Do not think he meant strategy though. He is still hoping she will suddenly develop interest in his pants area. Thank God she is out tomorrow (on PA duty for Suzy, attending lubricant convention in Ipswich ('Sliding into the Future')). Which means Jack and I can spend entire day enjoying secret love. It is utter serendipity (new favourite word) that we do not have Saturday jobs any more. We do not need money—we can live on love alone. Think Mr Goldstein (hunchback, Fiat Multipla, proprietor of lentil-smelling wholefood outlet Nuts In May) must have known this when he sacked me.

. . . .

Saturday 19

10 a.m.
Hurrah. A day of love beckons. Am glad to be alive. Unlike Sad Ed, who has already texted to say he has only been herding trolleys for half an hour and is already suicidal and if he does not unite with Scarlet soon he will have to revive untimely death plans. Asked him how fellow herder Reuben Tull was, i.e. was he not cheered up by his seemingly endless ponderings on whether God is a

dog-headed lizard with lasers for eyes? But apparently
Reuben has other withdrawal symptoms (crop failure,
and not the wheat kind) and is 'on a total downer, man'.
As is Scarlet. Though is not drug- or Sad Ed-related. It is
because she is stuck in traffic on the A14 and Suzy is
insisting on playing her hypnotic anti-smoking CD, which
is not at all conducive to driving. Or giving up smoking,
as Suzy has been listening to it for three years and still has
a packet of Silk Cut permanently stuck down her bra.
Told her to call Sad Ed, as will be busy for rest of day. She
said 'doing what?' Said charity work. Is not complete lie.
Is utterly kind to Jack to snog him. And anyway, lie is for
good cause. Is essential she does not find out. Or secret
love will just be normal run-of-mill love. Which is not at
all literary or tragic. Will be OK. Convention does not fin-
ish until five and traffic clearly awful, so she will not be
back until six at earliest. If leave by half five she will be
utterly in dark still.

5.45 p.m.
It is all over. Scarlet very much not in dark any more but
bathed in 100 watt polar ice-cap melting light, i.e. she
knows about me and Jack. She burst in on us in den and
said, 'Oh God, it is true. Ugh, ugh, make them stop, Suzy,
make them stop.' Which was pointless as *a*) Suzy in
favour of all sex and *b*) were not actually engaged in any
nakedity, were in seventies loveswing watching *Scrubs*,
but was clearly in non-just-good-friends way as one of his

17

hands was twirling curl of hair and other was hovering dangerously close to left breast. Said I had thought she wouldn't be back and had not intended for her to find out like this and it is fault of unusually favourable traffic conditions rather than my fault per se. But Scarlet said in fact is Sad Ed's fault as he confessed on phone what sordidness was going on in her absence and is why she made Suzy ignore speed limit and traffic impediments in order to stage utter bust. Jack said it is better that it is all out in the open and that Scarlet should be happy for us. But Scarlet not in agreement. She demanded that all non-Stones (i.e. me) depart forthwith so she can lie down in darkened room and meditate in bid to calm mind. Jack said not to worry, and that he will talk her round and all will be fine by tomorrow. I said he had better as do not want to be forced to choose between best friend and lover. Although then realized that, actually, would be good as is utterly Shakespearean. But Jack said, 'I know what you are thinking and you are wrong, it would not be good, or literary, or tragic. Just annoying.' Oh, I love him even more. He is in tune with all my innermost thoughts and feelings.

Unlike Sad Ed who is utter traitor and in tune with nothing, as his misguided mojo only serves to testify. Rang him on way home to demand to know why he had spilt proverbial beans. He said he had hoped it would win him points for being loyal and also that she would collapse into his arms in either *a*) face of our horrifying

forbidden love, or *b*) realization that he is her Jack, only not her brother, and with slightly 'more developed' (aka fat) upper arms. He is utterly disappointed though. Not only did he miss the crucial revelation moment, but he is on overtime untangling a nest of trolleys that Reuben jammed behind the pay and display machine. Which, frankly, is divine justice.

Sunday 20

9 a.m.
Am racked with torture. Every second I do not hear from Scarlet is another potential nail in the coffin of our sixteen-year alliance. Is excellent. Am totally living in episode of *Skins*.

11 a.m.
Still no news from Stone household. James says whatever happens, I am my own person, and do not need the approval of my friends. I said I was glad to see he has for-given Mad Harry and is moving on in his life. He said on the contrary, Mad Harry is a treacherous villain and he is hoping to wreak revenge by going solo and securing five-album deal thus showing Mad Harry what he is missing by breaking up Beastly Boys. He wandered off singing 'The Promise'. Which was ironic as it did not show any. Plus the glory is never the same after the band has split. Look at Duncan out of Blue.

2 p.m.
Scarlet has texted. She is coming round now for a peace summit. Have texted Jack to come over too but he says is better if we sort this out together and not to worry, Scarlet is calm and has no discernible weapons on her. He is right. I will be brave and face my fate alone.

2.10 p.m.
Have texted Sad Ed for back-up. Calmness is worrying and Scarlet has been known to cause injury with only a strawberry bootlace.

4 p.m.
Hurrah. Am injury free, and still officially best friends with Scarlet. (Sad Ed permanently downgraded to second best friend due to betrayal, and also presence of penis.) Scarlet said it was an extremely difficult decision for her, as it compromises all her beliefs, i.e. snogging only weirdy bat people or oddballs you pick up at Glastonbury, but that, on reflection, it is not friendship-ending stuff, and is probably only a phase as Jack is going to college in a few weeks. So as long as I do not mention Jack's genitals then she will accept it. As have not actually seen Jack's genitals yet, cannot discuss them, so agreed. She is wrong about it being only a phase though. He is my ONE. Am sure of it.

Sad Ed is not happy though. It is because Scarlet said she hoped no one else was harbouring weird and unnatural lust secrets as she could not cope with any more

20

horrifying revelations. He pretended to be lost in musical reverie, but as was Snow Patrol on radio at time, was not utterly convincing as he is renowned for thinking they are mawkish sellouts.

. . . .

Monday 21

And as one fledgling relationship begins to soar, another is mired in the bird poo of life (could not think of other bird-related metaphors except dead seagulls or swivelly owl heads). It is the Cleggs. There has been more Cornish Liberation Army related hoo-ha in St Slaughter. Grandpa, Pig, and Denzil are now under curfew along with unsavoury youths. It is for picketing the sundried tomatoes and pesto shelf (aka the tourist section) in Spar. Maureen said she had no option but to call the police after Pig started telling customers he had injected the olives with contaminatory urine. They are now forbidden to walk the streets of St Slaughter, Redruth or surrounding conurbations at any time after nine p.m., and are instead holed up in Pasty Manor (aka Belleview, aka Chez Clegg) drinking Pig's potato wine, eating pickled eggs, and singing sea shanties. Granny says sound and smell is overpowering and she can bear it no longer. She is demanding that Mum comes to retrieve her immediately or she may well be under curfew for murder. Mum suggested she could stay with Aunty Joyless, or with Hilary (former boyfriend of Scarlet, future first-ever black Prime Minister, home

help to Cleggs), who is partially responsible for all the hoo-ha, having politically educated Granny above and beyond her place in life. But Granny says Aunty Joyless has a house full of zealots on exchange from a church in Bodmin and the Nuamahs are having their spare room painted (something called Dead Salmon, despite Granny suggesting a nice roll of lupin-printed Sanderson). Mum has given in and is going on Saturday. But not to collect Granny, to broker peace as a matter of emergency, as she does not want a Clegg here getting under her feet, even a newly politicized one. Dad is in agreement. He says it is bad enough having to endure that level of idiocy once a year, let alone 24-7. Although I think he secretly would welcome the addition of Viennetta to the Riley household. The credit crunch has hit puddings hard and we are on fruit or plain yoghurt only.

. . . .

Tuesday 22

5 p.m.

James has drawn up a list of pros and cons of housing a Clegg at 24 Summerdale Road as follows:

GRANNY CLEGG

FOR	AGAINST
Enlightened opinions on minorities.	Will bring Bruce, thus initiating almighty battle
No longer thinks hummus	of the moronic dogs,

is 'spit of the devil'.

with inevitable ensuing mess and shouting.

GRANDPA CLEGG

FOR	AGAINST
Will not bring Bruce.	Does not like: black people, gay people, tall people, ginger people, or anyone born east of Tamar. Is still not talking to Grandpa Riley (although Grandpa says this is a positive thing).

It is in case Mum's peace-brokering fails. I would offer Jack's services, as he is excellent negotiator (saggy sofa accord is still holding, admittedly by a thread since Mark Lambert showered sofa aka Jerusalem with a can of Vimto) but Saturday is beginning of our utterly romantic first summer holiday together, and do not want to spend it in contraceptive atmosphere of Pasty Manor, i.e. confined space with Grandpa Clegg (anti-romance) or Mum (anti-most things). They are both guaranteed to dampen desire.

6 p.m.
Not that am planning to do 'It' yet. Not until love has been officially declared by both parties, and not just in

sexual lubricant manner, but in true, non-pants-based Jane Austen-type way.

. . . .

Wednesday 23

It is utterly frustrating to be finally immersed in fairytale-style love but unable to share details of passion with best friend. I have tried but every time I mention Jack's lips (soft and taste of peppermint)/eyes (smouldering)/shoulders (broad and smooth with scar on right one where Scarlet stabbed him with a Bill Clinton figurine) Scarlet covers ears and says, 'La la la, I can't hear you.' Even Sad Ed has shut up shop. He says it is more than his frustrated mojo can bear at the moment. Have even broached the Um Bongo cushion to speak to Thin Kylie in my desperation (she is renowned for being interested in all things love-based (or sex-based anyway)) but she just said, 'I can't believe you, like, dumped Davey for that knobbrain. Are you, like, blind, or mental?'

. . . .

Thursday 24

Tomorrow is the last day of school. It is utterly poignant moment as is officially Jack's last day at John Major High, i.e. end of an era. Scarlet says it is not the end, it is the beginning, i.e. of her and Sad Ed's new and improved regime. Reminded her that she is locked in power-sharing government with Thin Kylie, but she says Kylie will lose

interest by October and be back in the West Bank microwaving cola cubes and fiddling with Mark Lambert's sherbet lemons, leaving her free to impose absolute rule. She is sounding more like Hitler every day. But have not told her that as do not want to alienate her further. She said she has had to ban Jack from talking about me at breakfast as she is struggling to keep her muesli down. Which sounds bad, but in fact is excellent as it means we are being gagged like political prisoners, trapped by the love that dare not speak its name.

6 p.m.
James says the love that dare not speak its name is 'boy-on-boy love' which ours is most certainly not. Said how did he know. He said Grandpa Riley told him. Asked how did Grandpa know, as was worried he might turn out to be closet Oscar Wilde or Graham Norton, thus throwing Baby Jesus's life into even more Jeremy Kyle-style turmoil than it already is. But James said Grandpa read it in *Take A Break*.

. . . .

Friday 25
Last day of school.
8 a.m.
Am too sad to even chew Shreddies. Have been forced to consume porridge, which takes no effort, but is now sitting in stomach like leaden ball, adding to my misery. In

contrast James has had two slices of toast and an under-ripe pear and is dancing to Leona Lewis on Radio 2 with dog. I said historic nature of occasion, i.e. last day of primary school, will hit him later like giant rounders bat, and he will collapse in heap of sorrow. He said not likely as Mumtaz is going to Pakistan for six weeks and it will be the ultimate test of devotion for Mad Harry, who has attention span of gnat and will be begging James to reform Beastly Boys within a week, and then James can spurn him to give him a taste of his own medicine. I said that was a bit harsh. He said 'harsh is as harsh does'. Which does not make sense and suspect he has been talking to Granny Clegg on phone, who is renowned for inventing crap proverbs.

4 p.m.
Sadness has been dispelled. Not by joyous atmosphere of silly string and stray sheep (exceeding all expectations this year by getting trapped on top of Mrs Leech's biscuit cupboard), but by Jack's tongue. Have made up for wasted years by snogging all over school including: common room, library, and against nut dispensing machine. Would have gone for Mr Wilmott's office but Fat Kylie in there with Davey MacDonald (Mr Whippy on Donkey Dawson's (weird shaped head, allegedly large thing) stag do in Clacton). We have left our indelible mark on every inch. Metaphorically-speaking. Now every time walk down C Corridor will be struck by memory of his hands

pinning me against sky blue walls while sheep milled around us like slightly smelly clouds. Notice that some- one, possibly Mark Lambert, has left actual indelible mark, i.e. stubby pen picture of genitals. Lou (caretaker, former Criminal and Retard, once ate school rabbit) was at it with a damp sponge when we left. He needs to have lesson with Mum. He will never get it off without at least a mild abrasive. It would be easier to turn it into a sort of erupting, though hairy, rocket.

Upper Sixth and substandard Year Elevens are not only ones leaving though. There is to be another departure from hallowed, albeit sheep-poo-strewn, halls. It is Mr Vaughan (head of Drama, lover of Sophie Microwave Muffins, proud owner of supersize nipples). He has got a new job in Bath. Scarlet said he will regret it as it is full of upper-middle-class Boden-wearing blonde airheads. Saw Sophie by nut dispensing machine while Jack having essential wee break from snogging. To show did not bear grudge over whole Justin/Jack thing, and that empathize with lover moving many miles away, said, 'It'll be OK, you'll see.' She said whatever, she will be glad to be out of this smalltown hellhole and get to uni. Asked where she was going. She said Bath.

Saturday 26

Hurrah, it is the first day of the holidays, and the long, hot summer stretches ahead of me. Except without hot bit as

is raining, as usual. But is still excellent as Mum is going to Cornwall this morning, plus she is taking mini menace James. He says his absence will only fuel Mad Harry's desire to rekindle their friendship. Mum was not at all happy about leaving me behind as she says Dad cannot be trusted to make sure I am 'controlling my urges'. Ick. But James has told Mum not to worry, he has given Dad a lesson in surveillance. Am unperturbed. Dad is renowned for being utterly lax when it comes to Mum's many and varied rules and regulations. Is lucky she is not leaving next-door neighbour Marjory PI in charge, with her ear for gossip and arsenal of digital spyware. Hurrah, will commence contraventions by inviting Jack, Scarlet, and Sad Ed round later to play loud music and take drugs.

10.30 a.m.
Or at least drink alcohol.

10.35 a.m.
Or possibly Ribena.

10 p.m.
Do not need Dad to meddle with urges as Scarlet is contraceptive enough already. Was only giving Jack minor snog (partial tongue, but no hands) when Scarlet started screaming 'My eyes, my eyes!' And squirted us with apple juice (near sell-by so possibly fermenting and cidery). Sad Ed just sighed and ate another Pringle. He is still waiting

for her to realize what is standing right in front of her, i.e. not largish son of Aled Jones obsessives with flabby upper arms and a stained Smiths T-shirt, but towering god of love. He will be waiting a long time. To make matters worse, the dog has eaten the volume knob on the CD player and it is stuck on 'barely audible'. Which is not at all edgy or law-breaking.

Sunday 27

10 a.m.

It is utterly poetic. Am being forced by Mum to stay away from Jack. She is Mrs Capulet, i.e. blind to my needs and desires. Mum said it is not poetic, and she is not Mrs Capulet, it is just that Dad cannot be trusted to cook Sunday lunch without burning or exploding it, so she has arranged for us to go to Grandpa Riley's. I said she was risking my love life, if not actual life, with this rash decision but she says she has given Treena a copy of Delia's complete cookery course and strict instructions not to let Dad or Baby Jesus or dog suck frozen sausages pretending they are Cuban cigars. Asked her how Operation Clegg was going. She said not entirely according to plan. Granny is still refusing to leave the spare room, Grandpa is refusing to leave the broken Parker Knoll and Bruce is refusing to leave the cereal cupboard. Said this must be very disappointing as is almighty blip in her record of imposing military rule, but she says she is hoping to

29

achieve small victory by corralling Grandpa into bath in minute. He has been on 'dirty protest' for a week. Then could clearly hear sound of someone singing 'Blow the Man Down' and James shrieking 'No more, Pig, no more,' and Mum hung up.

5 p.m.
Was wrong about lunch. Was excellent as Treena forgot rule about leaving dog unattended in room with unsecured meat and it ate two packets of mince including the polystyrene trays so Dad took everyone to pub instead for prawn cocktails and scampi (banned on myriads of grounds including hygiene, fat content, and so-called thousand island dressing). I bet James is regretting his choice of parent now. He is probably trying to digest several pounds of health-giving vegetables in the company of dirty-protest Grandpa Clegg, plus a man who smells like pig (Pig) and one who looks like one (Denzil).

At least Grandpa Riley is relatively fresh-smelling. And utterly understands me. Had forgotten he is very much au fait with matters of the heart. It is all the glossy magazines he is reading. And *Hollyoaks*. He said if feel it in my toes when Jack kisses me then is love for sure. Said feel it everywhere. He said then options are pill, condom, or femidom, but he wouldn't go for that as is like wearing plastic bag in chuff, according to seventy-six per cent of readers who have tried it. Said was not at that stage yet. Grandpa said I was in thirty-eight per cent minority and

had better not wait too long, as Jack is hot-blooded male and eyes, and hands, might start to wander—look what happened to Britney.

He is wrong. Jack would never leave me. Even if took vow of chastity. Though will not do that as am not anti-sex. Just worried will be rubbish at it. Like hockey, all over again. Think might be time to tell him I love him though. Because is true. Utterly utterly do.

. . . .

Monday 28

Mum and her demonic assistant James are jubilant. Not only are Grandpa Clegg's many orifices clean and lemon-scented (James says he used washing-up brush and bottle of Fairy Liquid and kept eyes averted at all times to pre-serve dignity, and contents of stomach), but Pig and Denzil have left the building, i.e. Pasty Manor. Asked if they had gone voluntarily. James said no, they had fallen prey to one of his expert 'hustles'. Apparently he used phone box outside Spar to call Chez Clegg pretending to be Trelawney, symbolic patron of Cornish Liberation Army, demanding Pig's and Denzil's presence at anti-Jamie Oliver march from the 24-hour garage (shuts at 8, on Mum's to-do list of complaint letters) to Watergate Bay. Said that Trelawney was dead and had been since 1721. James said clearly they are unaware of that fact.

James is right, it is excellent victory. Now they just need to persuade Grandpa Clegg to perform romantic

31

gesture in bid to win back heart of true love. Like paint over Hammerite Cornish flag on cladding. Or cut toenails.

12.15 a.m.
Or climb silently up *Dawson's-Creek*-style ladder for illicit midnight snog! Which is what Jack did fifteen minutes ago. Was excellent, although did have panic when heard knocking at window, as was having dream about Dracula at time. Although think it could just have been Trevor Pledger in full winged costume. Anyway, Dad is none the wiser. Hurrah, our love is utterly like mid-90s TV series, i.e. tragi-comedy, with clever postmodern script and big hair. May suggest *Dawson's Creek* idea to James. Although the Cleggs' record of injury through misadventure is quite high.

Tuesday 29
Dad has warned me that he will confiscate *Dawson's Creek* ladder if I continue to abuse its presence. As it is, he is fighting a losing battle with Mum, who claims leaving it in the side return is tantamount to an open invitation to burgling O'Gradys everywhere. Will have to tell Jack to be more careful. Clearly his drawing-pin boot tapped too loudly on the rungs. Though is odd as usually Dad sleeps through anything, including Mum changing the bed linen.

Also James has rung with grave news. Pig and Denzil

are back in Pasty Manor. Asked if they had realized the very dead nature of Trelawney and got wise to James's substandard hustle. James said, *au contraire*, he is Lord of the Hustle (which sounds hideous), but that they got hungry waiting at not-at-all 24-hour garage and decided to have armchair, or broken Parker Knoll, protest instead. Mum and Granny Clegg are now both in spare room having lie down.

11 p.m.
Oh my God. There has been another bedroom intruder. But horrifyingly, was not Jack this time, was Justin Statham—former boyfriend, future rock god, and possessor of small nipples! Worse, he has informed me that he bitterly regrets post-prom snakebite sick incident, as being mostly naked in bed with me was in fact opposite of vomit-inducing. I said he should have thought of that before he dumped me for Sophie Microwave Muffins Jacobs, especially given she had dumped him for Mr Supersize Nipples Vaughan. He said, 'I made a mistake.' I said, 'Yeah, well, me too, i.e. going out with you in first place. But I'm with Jack now, and we are in like. Possibly in love. We are soulmates and can tell each other anything. Unlike me and you, who had more secrets than episode of *Miss Marple*.' He said, 'Have you told him about mostly naked prom night?'

And then had complete panic and said 'yes'. Which I know is utter lie. But do not want Justin to think there is

33

chink of possibility we might still have chance. He just nodded blond Kurt Cobain hair and said, 'OK, Rach. I cede the battle. But not the war.' Which is very poetic for someone who only got D in English lit GCSE. And also somewhat ominous.

This is typical. Have waited years for a boy (i.e. not Sad Ed, who is boy, but only in loose sense) to ascend sacred *Dawson's Creek* ladder in bid to snog me, and now has happened twice in two days. At least Dad does not seem to have noticed this time. He is too busy enjoying Mum-free home and has been in living room since 6 p.m. with two cans of John Smith's Extra Smooth, a box set of *The Sopranos*, and a bag of Doritos. Is like when Berlin Wall came down and deprived communists went mad for Western excess.

· ·

Wednesday 30
11 a.m.
There has been weird and worrying incident chez Riley. Was enjoying Mum-free breakfast at Shreddies table (aka Crunchy Nut Cornflakes, Nutella, and doughnut table) and trying not to think about *Dawson's Creek* ladder hoo-ha, when Dad said, 'I hope you are not thinking about engaging in hanky panky with Justin Statham. Jack is bad enough but I do not like the cut of Justin's jib.'

Is terrifying. Dad has developed an all-seeing eye in Mum's absence. Is contagious, like measles. He does not

need to worry anyway, as am not fan of Justin's jib either (ick). Plus Mum is back in seven hours so there will be no hanky panky of any kind. Like Justin, she has ceded the battle and is bringing Granny Clegg back to 24 Summerdale Road. But she also of opinion war is not lost. She says is only temporary arrangement as she is hoping our noughties 'wayward living' will be too much for Granny, who will realize that she is best suited to Grandpa Clegg and the environs of St Slaughter, which are both still stuck somewhere in the 1970s. Mum is confident Granny will be packing the Spar bags in days. She clearly has a skewed concept of wayward living though. The last time anyone did anything wayward here was when Dad tried a can of Red Bull. He paid for it later though when he lost a four-ball because his chip shot was caffeine-compromised.

Have emptied Nutella and Crunchy Nut Cornflakes in preparation for return of austerity rule (i.e. fed contents to dog). They are high on banned list for double whammy of contravention, i.e. sugary evil masquerading as nutritious by involvement of protein-based nuts.

8 p.m.
Granny Clegg is here and is installed in the spare room with Bruce, who has been chained to radiator until he can learn to follow simple instructions like 'sit' and 'stay' and 'don't eat the stairs, you moron'.

Plus Mum wants to know why father of Bruce, i.e.

dog, is having apparent sugar rush (it has been running round garden in circle for ten minutes). Said it is just excitement at return of supreme leader, a feeling also shared by her loving and obedient daughter. James snorted and said my 'hustle' was inferior, as give away signs were fiddling with ear, refusing to look at subject, and use of word obedient. But luckily Mum too busy questioning Dad about suspicious orange powdery residue on remote control to notice.

9 p.m.
Bruce unchained from radiator, having also engaged in dirty protest. Though hope Grandpa Clegg did not poo on carpet as part of his.

Thursday 31
Hurrah, tomorrow is my birthday and is set to be historic occasion. Not only will turn 17, which means will be fully-fledged provisional driver—but will also mark highly anticipated joint declaration of love. Hopefully.

Have decided am going to do it tomorrow night during party. Which will not be usual childish affair, involving rogue O'Gradys, Bacardi breezer or shaving the dog, but will be intimate dinner soirée involving fine wine, haute cuisine, and me, Jack, Scarlet, and Sad Ed. Had hoped not to have to invite latter two, but Sad Ed says romantic candlelight will be aphrodisiac overload and Scarlet is bound

to lunge at him over the lobster thermidor. Said he was making quite a lot of assumptions, not least presence of candles, which, as well he knows, are banned from Riley household on grounds of fire and melty wax mess risk. As are lobsters, on grounds of them being *a*) overpriced and *b*) eating poo and therefore at high risk of harbouring life- or bottom-threatening disease, and *c*) having tappy legs and feelers (me not Mum on that one). Plus Scarlet will not eat them as she is strictly vegetarian. Caved in any- way. Cannot forsake friends just because am in love. Will kick them out after pudding and do declaration then.

Amazingly Mum has agreed to arrangement, including request for her to vacate property for evening. Think it is because she is already struggling with perpetual presence of Clegg. She has issued several caveats though:

1. She will do cooking (Delia's wild mushroom stroganoff) and we can warm up in low oven later.
2. Granny Clegg will remain in the house. But will be installed in own bedroom with audio CDs of Mary Wesley and individual Fray Bentos pie.
3. Bruce and dog will remain in house. But in down- stairs and upstairs toilets respectively, with doors to remain closed at all times.
4. There will be no alcohol, bar one can each of Dad's Shandy Bass (pseudo-alcohol and less potent than Benylin).
5. There will be no swinging, or 'sexual play' (Mum's horrendous words, not mine).

Will still be excellent night though. Do not need alcohol. Will be drunk on utterly heady mix of stimulating conversation, sparkling wit, and potent love of Jack. He has already given me my present. Do not know what it is, as is in envelope, with strict instructions not to open until tomorrow. But is probably poem he has written inspired by our love.

10 p.m.
Although can feel something jangling, in unpoetic way. But will not open. Am grown-up. Not seven year old who prises open flap of paper to check that all gifts are up to standard (James), or rips them open on Christmas Eve, thus instigating the Riley 'no presents under tree until Shreddies have been consumed' rule (me).

10.30 p.m.
But is not wrong to hold envelope. Am not actually opening it. Just using telepathic oneness with Jack to determine contents.

10.35 p.m.
Or maybe just feel outline of jangly thing.

10.36 p.m.
Is key. Oh my God. Is symbolic key to heart. Is poetic after all. This is it. It is his boy-way of saying he loves me! Have texted Jack to say also have gift for him (i.e. love) and will

be unveiling tomorrow night, privacy pending. He said, 'Can't wait to see them.' Texted back to say, 'Is not breasts. Is more metaphysical. Breasts later.' Grandpa is right. Even under exterior of progressive political and musical genius lurks oversexed *Nuts*-reader. But do not care. He is The One. And anyway, does not read *Nuts*. He is more *Guitar Monthly* man.

august

BABY MONITOR

THE HIGHWAY CODE

Friday 1

9 a.m.

Have opened Jack's envelope. Was not key to heart. Was actual key—i.e. to non-sick-smelling car of the people, i.e. Jack's Beetle. Envelope also contained note, which was not love poem, but declaration that he is giving me driving lessons for my birthday, starting this afternoon. BUT, if he goes to Cambridge University, he is giving me custody of car as he is going to use traditional bicycle power instead as is economical (plus is very *Brideshead Revisited*)! Is excellent thoughtful gift. Plus tension over gearstick is renowned for inducing atmosphere of love. Look at Mike Wandering Hands Majors (bouffy hair, driving instructor, rumoured to be father of five children by former pupils in Saffron Walden environs). Dad is jubilant that am not going to be driving one of his fleet of Ford Fiestas. Not only is he saving £25 a week, Mum will not get to ogle Mike's vice-like grip on the faux leather steering wheel from the dining room window.

Have also had somewhat less thoughtful presents from family i.e.:

- Copy of *Highway Code* (Mum and Dad—credit crunch clearly affecting presents as well as puddings);
- Feu Orange car deodorizer (James—affected not so much by credit crunch but by fact that he is addicted to odd smell);
- Bar of Dairy Milk (Granny Clegg—also not affected by crunch, just habitually povvy);

- Driving gloves (dog and Bruce—not crunchy but unwearable as make me look like mentalist);
- Stack of glossy magazines (used and in some cases stuck together with suspicious substance—Grandpa Riley, Treena, and Baby Jesus);
- Kernow car sticker (Grandpa, Pig, and Denzil).

Do not care, as am about to take flight in Jack's winged chariot of love. Hurrah! Am not at all worried about doing as told, as am used to following strict instructions (17 years of experience), plus how hard can driving be?

6 p.m.
Driving is impossible task. Every time look in mirror, swerve into kerb. Plus gear stick hand apparently has invisible thread connecting to accelerator foot, which is apparently not at all good for health of *a*) car, *b*) approaching pedestrians, and *c*) Jack. No wonder Sad Ed is still struggling, with his oversized fingers and flat feet. Jack says next time we will concentrate on the basics, e.g. turning engine on. Asked when next time might be, but he deferred question with kiss. So even though chariot not winged, is still one of love. Cannot wait until tonight and historic declarations. The wild mushroom stroganoff is warming in oven, the four cans of Shandy Bass are chilling in fridge and the best tablecloth is out of quarantine, but with a severe warning that any spillages are to be tackled immediately with a damp sponge and appropriate

Stain Devil. As predicted candles have been banned, but Mum has agreed to using Dad's emergency camping light to give appropriate mood lighting. Thank God they have gone out and have taken James with them. They are round at Malcolm from IT's and Mrs Malcolm's. Mum is hoping James will bond with Alastair (10, squint, entire *Lord of Rings* Panini sticker set collection), elevating him out of the circle of devilment that is Mad Harry and Keanu for good. Granny Clegg also safely out of way in spare room with steak and kidney pie and audio version of *The Camomile Lawn* (as read by Joanna Lumley), and dogs shut in toilets with Radio 4. Being watched while weeing is small price to pay for avoiding colossal idiocy that hovers over dogs at all times. Now all I have to do is wait for my guests in utterly glamorous hostessy manner, i.e. sipping wine (aka lemon barley) and playing classical music (aka Glasvegas), which is utter modern classic, according to Jack.

6.30 p.m.
Have had minor setback. Had to go to toilet (oversipping lemon barley) and was not quick enough with lock. Bruce made bid for freedom and threw itself at upstairs bathroom door having established that mortal enemy, i.e. dog, was inside (trying to dig tunnel through lino). Which sent dog into frenzy of door butting and then strange silence. Further investigation revealed dog to be concussed, possibly through mistaken butting of sink so had

to give it reviving shower. Am now slightly moist all over, and emanating odour of wet dog, which is not at all love inducing. Have sprayed self liberally with Mum's Tweed. Plus have shut dog in James's bedroom where any damage will be a blessing. Bruce is in with Granny Clegg, listening to Joanna Lumley and eating congealed kidneys. On plus side at least will be able to wee in private from now on. Bruce worryingly interested in wee and potential for drinking thereof.

7.30 p.m.
Oooh. Doorbell. This is it. In just a few hours, relationship with Jack will have shifted up a gear (without hitting kerb), plus Sad Ed and Scarlet will possibly be entwined in mojo-satisfying love. Hurrah!

10 p.m.
Oh God. Horrifying thing has happened. Have not had night of love at all. Instead think may have been dumped. Am too shocked to write now. Will go to bed in hope that either *a*) am wrong or *b*) overnight, body will block traumatizing memory from brain and will be in state of ignorant bliss.

- -

Saturday 2
8 a.m.
Body not blocked traumatizing memory at all. And think

am not wrong. Think am definitely dumped. According to annoyingly disobliging brain, events occurred as follows:

Friday 7.30 p.m.
Guests arrive and hostess takes coats etc. upstairs in professional manner. Scarlet demands that hostess also take self upstairs and wash as odour of dog/Tweed is overpowering and could cause hives.

7.45 p.m.
Hostess returns refreshed and slightly less odorous and announces dinner is served. Menu as follows:
Canapes: Twiglets and Frazzles (as purchased by Dad, in contravention of several rules of state, as birthday 'treat');
Mains: Delia's mushroom stroganoff (as made by Mum);
Pudding: Apple 'snow', as made by James or cheese (Cathedral City) and biscuits (cream crackers not Jacob's, but Waitrose, so not totally povvy);
After dinner mints: Matchmakers (as brought by Sad Ed for light snack).
Party consumes canapés and mains but rejects pudding and mints on various grounds (meltiness of snow, nonorganic nature of Cheddar, Nestlé's buyout of Rowntree Macintosh).

8.15 p.m.
Party finishes allocated Shandy Bass. Scarlet opens bag to reveal two bottles of Merlot donated by Suzy for occasion

(she is cutting down to five bottles a week in case she has to have medical for adoption interview). Jack opens Merlot. Hostess tackles ensuing stain according to instructions.

8.30 p.m.
Party opens second bottle of Merlot. Hostess refuses second glass, citing fact that Mum is recent purchaser of portable breath test gadget, and is likely to use it without provocation on her return, in less than three hours.

8.45 p.m.
Sad Ed decides Nestlé not so evil after all and consumes entire box of Matchmakers.

9.30 p.m.
Discussion on guitarist out of Franz Ferdinand (scary or just unfortunate positioning of instrument) cut short by ominous crashing sound upstairs. Hostess goes to investigate inevitable Granny Clegg/Bruce/dog misdemeanour.

9.31 p.m.
Hostess discovers cause of crash is, unbelievably, not any of usual suspects but in fact Justin Statham falling through open bedroom window having slipped on last rung of *Dawson's Creek* ladder due to ill-advised wearing of flip-flops in rain.

9.33 p.m.
Justin declares he is not giving up in fight for Rachel and cannot believe Jack's kisses as potent as own. Hostess says Jack's kisses indeed more potent. Justin demands kiss-off experiment. Hostess says Ick. Justin says he is not leaving without test results. Hostess gives in for betterment of science and snogs Justin. Earth does not move. Hostess informs Justin this is case and demands departure forthwith. Justin says 'Then if am not potent love god then why did you get naked in bed on prom night and at one point touch small nipple, before did sick everywhere . . . '

All of which would have been fine had this schedule not been going on simultaneously in dining room:

9.31 p.m.
James Riley and Colin Riley arrive home having had *a*) argument with Alastair over the latent heat capacity of toluene and *b*) argument with Mum over whether or not two helpings of rhubarb crumble constitute a breach of dietary regulations. Both demand to know whereabouts of hostess. Party informs rogue Rileys that hostess upstairs with dogs and Clegg sorting out 'incident'.

9.32 p.m.
Instead of going upstairs, James Riley reaches behind love talisman portrait of hostess and pulls out baby monitor (which had been informed was in attic in pieces after Mad

Harry tried to get dog to eat it in bid to project his voice from bowels of animal, but has apparently been revived and now has pride of place in James's anti-Marjory arsenal of surveillance equipment).

9.33 p.m.
Baby monitor switched on and party witnesses entire chemical kiss experiment.

9.37 p.m.
Party, plus rogue Rileys, burst into hostess's bedroom. Scarlet manhandles Justin to floor. James is caught in crossfire by flailing flip-flop and is removed by Colin Riley for first aid.

9.38 p.m.
Jack says, 'Yes, Rachel, why did you get naked in bed with him and touch small nipple, when had just rung me and declared that were in like.'

Hostess says, 'Because was high on fake herbal aspirin aka psychedelic mushroom stuff and thought you had done wonky portrait because thought I was wonky minger.'

Justin says, 'Thanks a lot.'

Jack says, 'Ditto.'

Hostess says, 'Sorry. Was huge mistake. Is not fault. Is fault of Reuben Tull. And possibly Justin as he is one who said would be good revenge to do "It".'

Jack says, 'You were going to do "It" with Justin?'

Hostess says, 'Yes. I mean, no. I don't know. Point is I didn't.'

Justin says, 'But only because I had whitey.'

Sad Ed says, 'Yeah, man.'

Scarlet hits Sad Ed with sticky copy of *New Woman*.

Jack says, 'Great, so every time we have a row or you have too much to drink, or take mushroom-based drugs by mistake, you're going to go running back to Mr Small Nipples.'

Hostess, who is having flashbacks to Mum and her lecture, says, 'No,' in very quiet voice in practised manner.

Jack says, 'You said you could tell me everything but you didn't tell me this.'

Justin says, 'You're such a liar, Riley. You said you'd told him.'

Hostess looks at floor willing it to swallow up. Floor does not oblige.

Jack says, 'You know what, I can't do this.' And descends dramatically down *Dawson's Creek* ladder.

Justin says, 'Me too.' And descends less dramatically due to limp, bare feet, and getting Foo Fighters T-shirt snagged on boiler overflow pipe.

Scarlet declares need to lie down in darkened room. Sad Ed offers his own bedroom. They exeunt, stage right. Leaving villainess alone, clutching flip-flop, and fighting back snotty tears.

(Saturday 8.30 a.m.)

Oh God. Have fallen for classic baby monitor scam. Life is not fairy tale. It is cheap ITV drama. Why, oh why did I not drink too much Merlot? Punishment from Mum would be welcome as would have bonus of either *a*) being too drunk to conduct conversation with Justin in first place, possibly even to get up stairs, or *b*) at least mind would be blank at moment.

Unless, maybe is all bad dream. Or at least exaggeration in own mind. Am prone to overactive imagination. Will text Scarlet to check.

8.45 a.m.

Have sent text: AM I DESTITUTE ONCE MORE?

8.47 a.m.

Scarlet has texted back: YES.

Oh how can one small word be so utterly life destroying?

8.48 a.m.

What if actually is life destroying? Must text Scarlet again. HAS JACK KILLED SELF?

8.49 a.m.

NO HE IN ROOM DRUMMING TO DEEP PURPLE. AND STOP TEXTING. AM NOT TALKING TO YOU. YOU ARE SMALL NIPPLE FANCYING LOVE CHEAT.

It is worse than I thought. Well not worse than death. But almost. As know for a fact that Deep Purple is emergency-only music. Plus now have potentially lost best friend as well. Am going to sob into pillow for a bit.

9 a.m.
James has been in to inform me my presence is required at the Shreddies table to explain several suspicious matters. Said was too depressed to consume food as am love reject. (Love, and lack of, is entirely compromising nutritious needs. Will get scurvy if carry on at this rate.) James said *a*) Mum's lips are very thin and *b*) at least he fought for his love instead of falling at first hurdle. Said *a*) how thin and *b*) he did not fight for love, he got clouted by Mad Harry for referring to Mumtaz as cheap. James said *a*) thinner than the time Dad let the dog drink two glasses of Marks & Spencer cognac, *b*) whatever, and *c*) I can either i) wallow ii) fight for Jack, or iii) follow James's lead and rise triumphantly, stronger and more manly from experience.

He is right. (Not about rising more manly from experience. He is utterly not manly. He is weedy weirdo.) But about fighting for Jack. Is totally unliterary to allow rubbish baby monitor incident to ruin love. That is sort of thing that happens in *Coronation Street* (I imagine, as have never seen due to double ban for being *a*) Northern and *b*) common). Whereas my life is utterly high-class BBC in-house period production and only thing that can

separate me and Jack is dose of consumption. Will go round Jack's immediately for fight and ensuing snog-filled reunion.

Once have eaten slice of toast. Cannot fight for man on empty stomach.

11 a.m.
Have had two rounds of toast and Marmite, a bowl of Cheerios and an apple (for vitamins) and am going to get my man. In metaphorical and hopefully physical sense. Have texted him to meet me on common ground, i.e. the common.

4 p.m.
Have not got man. In any sense. Was catalogue of disaster.
1. Jack thought I meant bench next to car park (aka Barry Island) not bench next to slide of death, so spent an hour watching Whitney O'Grady hurl herself into oblivion whilst Jack was on other side of common getting mintier by minute.
2. Once had established confusion (and vacated to Jack's bench as O'Gradys quite distracting), then spent another twenty minutes sitting in gloomy silence.
3. Then wished was still in gloomy silence as words that finally came out of Jack's mouth were not at all complimentary, i.e. 'You're just not who I thought you were. No, scratch that. You're exactly

who I thought you were. I just hoped I was wrong. You've humiliated me, Rach. Again.' Said, 'Have humiliated self.' Jack in agreement this time. But then hit me with silver bullet, i.e. said, 'I think maybe we are just not meant to be.' Which felt like had pierced heart. As we are totally meant to be. Like Darcy and Elizabeth Bennet. Or the two fat ones out of Gavin and Stacey. Realized then that had to do love declaration immediately, before was completely too late. So followed James's Ninja advice, which was to close eyes and pull on reserve inner strength. But when opened them, Jack was gone, and had said 'I love you' to local madman Barry the Blade who was looking in the bin for kebab bits.

This is utterly the worst day of my life. I have lost my boyfriend and my best friend and have been given relationship advice by a man who has not changed pants in two years and is rumoured to have stabbed first wife to death.

On plus side, things cannot possibly get any worse.

11 p.m.
Dog has fused electricity by eating fridge cable. Am now in dark, with screams of small children (i.e. James) haunting me in my misery. Is utter metaphor for life.

Sunday 3

10 a.m.

Ugh. Am still engulfed in giant thundercloud of gloom. (Though is not actual gloom as fuse mended and all appliances fully functioning.) Have texted Scarlet to see if she has reconsidered her communication shutdown and wants to come over and comfort me in hour of need/ watch T4, but she says she is operating a period of official radio silence and cannot cross my threshold as would be betraying Jack. Plus she has to go to Waitrose to get some raspberry balsamic vinegar. At least Sad Ed is not so choosy. He says he is also depressed as Scarlet utterly did not take advantage of him in his darkened bedroom and several times demanded that he stop staring at her as was like horror movie when friend turns out to be mentalist zombie and eats you. So at least we can be united in our status as pariahs.

3 p.m.

Am in bedroom with Sad Ed listening to morose music and watching him eat peanut M&Ms. Love is afflicting him in opposite manner, i.e. he has gone into confectionery overdrive and consumed ten Crème Eggs, four Snickers, and half a pound of Galaxy in last twenty-four hours. He in agreement that Stones are unworthy of our affections and we should stop getting hopes up that they are key to our happy endings in life.

3.15 p.m.

Can hear something outside. Is familiar. What is it?

3.16 p.m.

OMG. Is unmistakable sound of rumble of non-sick-smelling car of people on pea gravel. Jack has realized we are meant to be. Hurrah. Any second now he will ascend perilous heights of *Dawson's Creek* ladder and fling me against John Lewis painted pine wardrobe in fit of passion.

3.18 p.m.

Or possibly use more traditional method. Doorbell has just gone. He is obviously trying not to upset Mum and general anti-ladder feeling. He is so considerate! Will await thud, click on stairs instead.

3.20 p.m.

Oh. Jack has gone. And did not fling me against anything. Did not even come upstairs at all. Instead James, i.e. portent of doom, has delivered note. It says, 'Have taken key.' Said is metaphorical. Is to heart. He has sealed it up and I cannot penetrate it any longer. Is devastating. James said is not metaphorical or devastating. Is key to non-sick-smelling car of people. Sad Ed said is devastating as he was hoping to use Beetle for untimely death once passed test. James pointed out he was more likely to die of old age. Which even Sad Ed agreed was true. Though

has made him more depressed than ever. And me. I could have been passenger and we could have driven over edge of Grand Canyon (or at least ditch behind Homebase) like Thelma and Louise. Instead have no car, no boyfriend and no hope of suicide. Will end up as withered old woman staring out of bus window talking to self and wondering where life and love has gone. Am Miss Havisham. Or Granny Clegg.

Am going to retreat into hermit-like hovel for rest of summer. Sad Ed and I have agreed is only way to minimize torment. We are going to stage bed protest. Against unfairness of life and vehicular access. Starting tomorrow.

. . . .

Monday 4

9 a.m.

Is Day One of bed protest. Have got supplies, i.e. bottled water (to be sipped slowly to minimize loo requirements), Kendal Mint Cake (for joules of energy, and fresh breath) and stack of Grandpa-soiled magazines.

11 a.m.

Mum not happy about bed protest. She says is bad enough having Granny Clegg malingering under the covers until gone nine but I am young and fit and should be out enjoying healthy walk in countryside, or at least lurking around bus stops. Said was not fit. Was sick,

i.e. heart is broken. Mum said, 'Oh for heaven's sake, not again.' And went off to delimescale the bathroom sink. Thank God. Now can go back to tormented sleep in peace.

11.15 a.m.
Or not. Granny Clegg has been in to offer remedy to cheer me up. Said what is remedy. She said Bruce—i.e. his happy face can make even the terminally ill feel vital. Looked at Bruce. Bruce wearing same hairy glare as usual. Plus was chewing pair of Dad's pants. Said am beyond any cure. She said would leave Bruce anyway.

11.30 a.m.
Have had yet more interruptions. This time was James with reviving cup of tea and invigorating talk. Which is better, but only marginally. He said he has 'been to that dark place and feels my pain'. But that I need to take a leaf out of his book and get over it. Said was not taking leaves out of James's book as book has also involved mysterious dancing in leotards and furry pants in recent past. And to please leave and take Bruce with him as his smell and perpetual burrowing in carpet are not all conducive to peaceful protest.

Have barricaded door (locks banned due to potential for *a*) underage sex and *b*) underage chemical experiments). Am alone now. Nothing can interrupt my hermit-like existence.

11.40 a.m.
Need loo. Should not have drunk tea. Was secret weapon planted by Mum to get me to cave in. But will not. Have weed in Pringles tube in times of emergency. Am practically Bear Grylls. Will just wee in cup. Is bound to fit as is only what went in one way.

11.45 a.m.
Have had slight wee spillage. Tea expanded inexplicably inside body to fill cup and had to divert into pencil holder. Wish had kept Bruce after all. He very interested in wee and would probably drink if let him. Have mopped up with odd sock. Will limit fluid intake and concentrate on reading instead to lift me above trivial bodily needs and on to more cerebral plain where words are my only sustenance.

2 p.m.
Have read *Vogue*, *Elle,* and *Take a Break* and am thirsty, hungry, and weirdly twitchy. Think must be getting cabin fever. Oooh. Am like James Cracknell and that one with the gigantic teeth off *Animal Park*. Except am not rowing around world naked. But is almost the same. Will just text Sad Ed to see if he also jittery. That is not official contact with outside world as Ed also on hermit protest.

2.05 p.m.
Sad Ed says *au contraire*, he is perfectly happy in his saggy

bed of hermitude. This is because it is utterly normal for him to stay under covers for days at a time (his record is seventy-six hours, during a *Buffy* marathon), whereas I am like fragile flower, and crave light in order to blossom. Curtains are my barricades (literal and metaphorical) trapping me in my torment until someone rescues me from my plight. Oooh. Is like Rapunzel. And Jack is my prince. Maybe if send him telepathic message he will rescue me from tower of imprisonment.

2.07 p.m.
Though will not let him climb up hair. Is wiry and quite long, but still patchy after claggy raisin/hoover haircut incident.

2.10 p.m.
OMG. The *Dawson's Creek* ladder is moving. Can hear it scraping along wall. Is knock at window. Hurrah! It is Jack, i.e. handsome prince, come to take me into his manly arms.

2.15 p.m.
Was not Jack. Was Mum. Who is utterly not handsome prince but wicked stepmother type. Said her SAS protest-breaking tactics did not wash with me and try as she might she will not get me out of the bedroom. She said, *au contraire*, she was conducting a thorough assessment of our security arrangements and was removing ladder as it

contravened several regulations, as she had informed Dad on no less than eight occasions. It is utterly unfair. Not only is my bedroom now non-TV style one with door as only egress (excellent word, gleaned from *Oxford English Dictionary*, along with tine (prongy fork bit), uvula (dangly bit in mouth, not genital as had thought) and merkin (pubic wig—ick)). But now Jack cannot rescue me even if he wanted to. Am stuck in prison of my own making.

4 p.m.
Oh God. Need poo. Should not have eaten fruit. Is Mum's fault for hammering home vitamin consumption message on daily basis. But is crisis as do not think even Bear Grylls would poo in pencil holder. Why oh why did I not think of chamber pot à la Grandpa Clegg. (Is not out of necessity, they have had indoor toilet for four years. He just likes convenience, and feel.) There is nothing else for it. Am going to have to use bathroom. But will be fine. Will do stealth poo. Like Ninja.

4.15 p.m.
OMG. Poo not as stealthy as thought. The picket lines have been crossed and my bed has been stripped of sprig-patterned duvet cover and pillowcases, plus the curtains have been pulled back and room thoroughly aired. It is an outrage. Nobody respects my beliefs. Or toilet requirements. Have demanded Mum's presence immediately, using non-hermit method i.e. shouting.

4.20 p.m.

Mum has ignored request but sent her minion of choice i.e. James. He says I made a fatal error in thinking I could mess with laundry day. Said thought laundry day moved to Wednesday, due to mid-week uniform emergencies relating to St Regina's 'cookery' lessons (chocolate crispy cakes and cheese on toast). James said is now extended to bi-weekly event for limited time only, in order to cope with excess Clegg-wear and dog-related spillages. Ugh. Is so unfair. Even laundry conspires against me. Plus is lovely sunny day. Is typical. Sun decided to show face when heart is immersed in darkness. Brightness is hurting eyes. Maybe bed protest has damaged retina. Am like wolf child emerging from cave. Will have to wear sunglasses for ever more.

Though now am up might as well have lunch and watch bit of TV. Will have sofa protest instead. Is comfier, although Granny Clegg has assumed full control of remote which means endless *Heartbeat*.

5 p.m.

Have taken sunglasses off. Cannot see sepia-tinted 1960s rural England properly.

9 p.m.

Am back in bed. Though is not protest as much as TV has been commandeered by Dad to watch *Top Gear*. Am being philosophical though (am excellent philosopher, as fast

approaching AS level result will testify) i.e. tomorrow is another day.

9.10 p.m.
James says that is not philosophy, that is stating obvious. And anyway, tomorrow never comes. Said it did yesterday.

Tuesday 5

9 a.m.
Tomorrow is here. Ha. And am still gloomy. But am out of bed, which is progress. Although is partially due to fact that dog is in it. It has seemingly followed my example and is on anti-Bruce protest. Bruce is not on protest. It is busy looking triumphant on the sofa while James serenades it with a medley of Take That hits. He is an utter traitor. James says he is not, but that Bruce may in fact be genetically superior to dog, due to its mother's pedigree DNA. Reminded him its mother is Fiddy Britcher, who exists on diet of Kraft cheese slices and chicken tikka sandwiches, which is far from intellectual. He said I will change my mind when Bruce sniffs out truffles or buried treasure. I said I would not hold breath.

2 p.m.
Oooh. Have forgotten to inform Sad Ed that bed protest is over and he can get up and pull back the curtains on his

life—actual and metaphorical. Will text him immediately. Then he can come over and resume normal moping instead.

2.10 p.m.
Sad Ed has texted back. He says he is quite happy where he is as Mrs Thomas has given him a bell to ring for assistance (one dong for sausage sandwiches, two for Jaffa cakes). It is so unfair. He is lucky to have a mother who understands his plight. Even if she is in the Aled Jones fan club. Will just spend day in normal summer holiday mode instead, i.e. watching TV and sighing a bit.

4 p.m.
Have stopped sighing. James said it was disturbing his police dog training with Bruce. They are hunting for dead bodies, i.e. Granny Clegg, using only the power of smell. I said it was unrealistic as any dog could find Granny Clegg, given her ingrained odour of beef pie, but James says it is the timing that is crucial and Bruce has got it down to forty-eight seconds. Said he should test it against dog in case dog is superior after all. He has agreed in name of science.

5 p.m.
Dog took thirty-seven minutes twenty-two seconds. It is back in bedroom in disgrace. Mum has ended police dog training for day. She says shock of seeing Granny Clegg

slumped on stairs with tongue lolling out gave her near heart attack. Plus the dog managed to pull the dining room curtains down during its hunt.

8 p.m.

Am not sure which is worse—Granny Clegg as murdered corpse or as live version. Now she has taken to doling out love advice. She says she remembers when she had her heart broken by her true love. She said she wept for weeks every time she saw a milk float. Said *a*) thought Grandpa Clegg was true love and *b*) milkman is cliché. She said, *a*) no, first love was boy from Praze-an-Beeble called Curly Collins who *b*) was not milkman, but did party trick of drinking pint of gold top in four seconds. Said so Grandpa Clegg was rebound man. She said no, he mender of heart. Said what with. She said a steady job with the gas board. Then she looked a bit wistful and sighed heavily. Which is a good sign. Her heart is not dead to the power of Norman Clegg yet. Shudder.

Wednesday 6

1 p.m.

Am going out. Cannot lock myself away for ever. Even Sleeping Beauty got up eventually. Am just going for fresh air. Possibly in direction of Jack's house. But is act of defiance, i.e. only to show him that am alive and that he

cannot break me. Although possibly if he sees am alive he may fling himself at my mercy and beg for a second chance.

1.05 p.m.
Or try to break me.

4 p.m.
Am back from walk of defiance. Which less defiant than hoped, i.e. Jack did not see me being alive and vigorous despite me walking past house twenty-seven times. Scarlet however did see me and sent me text saying she had called police to report stalker menace.

Bumped into Thin Kylie on way home. She was sitting on wall with Fiddy smoking a Benson and Hedges and chewing Nicorette. Said why was she not in kidney-shaped pool enjoying brief display of sun. She said there are two dead pigeons in it and Cherie and Terry are arguing over who fishes them out. Told her about love plight. She said that's what happens if you go out with nerds who think with brain instead of knob. Asked her how her fiancé, i.e. Mark Lambert, (definitely does not think with brain) was. She said the Lamborghini is in better nick than ever. Was about to point out that Mark Lambert did not own Lamborghini—he owned Toyota held together with No More Nails and parcel tape, and minibike (semi-crushed). But luckily at that point Fiddy started choking, possibly on Nicorette, so escaped without confirmation of

fear that Lamborghini in fact Lambert penis, i.e. centre of his thought processes.

· ·

Thursday 7

There has been contact from enemy headquarters, i.e. Grandpa Clegg has rung from Pasty Manor. Thought it might be to announce end of mentalism but was further confirmation, i.e. to ask Mum to ask Granny how does the cooker work as he has had some pig in there for four hours and it is still raw. Mum was worried he had turned into cannibal in desperation and was consuming fellow anti-curfew protestor but Grandpa said it is not Pig, it is one of Pig's pigs. Then he asked where does toilet roll come from as they have run out and are using *Daily Mail* which is not at all absorbent plus his bottom has gone a bit inky. Mum lost temper and told Granny Clegg she should go where she is needed, i.e. her own home, i.e. not 24 Summerdale Road, where everyone is fully aware of location of oven switch and provenance of Andrex. But Granny says she is not going anywhere until Grandpa renounces his allegiance to the Liberation Army, evicts Pig and Denzil, and trims toenails, which are actually clacking on floor now. Plus the Olympics starts tomorrow and our telly is much bigger. Reminded her that she was anti-China, due to their treatment of Tibet etc. etc. but she said that's as maybe, but they do know how to put on a good show.

· ·

Friday 8

Granny was right. The Olympic opening ceremony was fantastic. How do they get the thronged thousands to move in time like that? Saffron Walden Amateur Operatic Society struggle with a chorus of ten and one of them always falls off the stage. Is wonder of world.

Scarlet has texted to say is not wonder of world, is utter display of fascism, and all participants are probably facing certain death if they so much as blink off beat.

Which is weird, as had not texted her. Think oneness not with Jack at all but possibly with Scarlet. Which is not good as do not want her reading innermost thoughts. Especially when am thinking about snogging her brother. Oh. Have to stop thinking it. Have to empty mind.

8.45 p.m.

Mind successfully emptied of thought. Was not through meditation. Was through display of idiocy in front room, i.e. weeping and mental barking at telly. Not at prowess of Olympians, but at apparently devastating news that moronic TV Alsatian Wellard is dead. Pointed out to Mum that was mistake allowing Granny Clegg to break house rule Number 4 and watch *EastEnders* but Granny says is part of her education about real life beyond the river Tamar. On plus side, dog and Bruce seem to be united in their grief, which is good news as far as furniture destruction goes.

Also Sad Ed is still in bed. It is new record. Asked how he was managing toilet wise but he says he has en suite so in fact he can poo within eyesight of bed. Said did not need to think about that. Especially if Scarlet listening in. She will never love him if she has seen him poo. Telepathically or otherwise.

- -

Saturday 9

Sad Ed is still in bed. Went to observe him on trolley herding duty at Waitrose at lunchtime but Reuben Tull (giant afro, purveyor of medicinal mushrooms, apprentice herder) said he had called in sick. Said what with. He said 'weirdness'. Said I was sicker, i.e. had no man, no job, and no meaning in life any more. He asked if had tried God. Said thought he believed supreme being was in fact laser-eyed dog thing. He said 'affirmative'. So said no, had not pinned hopes of happiness on battery-powered Lassie. Hounds in our house are bad enough. The fighting is over, but now they are both 'helping' James with his investigations, i.e. they are trying to dig for murdered corpses in the compost heap.

- -

Sunday 10

Today has reached new lows in Riley household shouting levels and things being banned. Everyone has been sent to their rooms, one dog is in the garage and one is

70

having a 'holiday' at another location, i.e. the Whiteshot Estate, until all foreigners (i.e. Granny and Bruce) are returned to their places of origin. Have pointed out that it was Mum's fault for inviting Riley senior household (i.e. Grandpa, Treena, and Baby Jesus) over for lunch when house already contaminated with presence of Clegg. But Mum said it is not her fault, it is Treena's fault for telling Granny Clegg she needed a makeover, James's fault for giving Granny Clegg a makeover, Granny Clegg's fault for showing Bruce makeover, Bruce's fault for biting Grandpa Riley in panic, Grandpa Riley's fault for bleeding all over Dad, Dad's fault for bringing up time Grandpa Riley got him to feed his fingers to a Muscovy duck 'for a laugh' at lunch, and the dog's fault for bringing up its lunch. Said on plus side I am scot-free for once. She said, *au contraire*, it is also my fault that Baby Jesus ate a miniature Crabtree and Evelyn avocado-flavour soap, as I was in charge of taking him to loo, which is further proof that is good thing am single, as risk of pregnancy and child rearing, which am clearly not cut out for, reduced by several percentage points. Voluntarily went to room at that point before Mum could do more shouting/use of words like subnormal or fallopian tubes.

At least one person is out of their room. It is Sad Ed. Asked if was because he had overcome his broken heart or found alternative target for Scarlet-loving mojo, but he said no it is that his portable TV blew up. Said that must

have been frightening. He said it was as he missed the end of *Grey's Anatomy* and now he will never know if Dr McDreamy shaves his beard off or not.

8 p.m.
He does. James googled it.

· ·

Monday 11

Mum is mental with anti-social behaviour/criminal madman potential. Marjory has rung to warn her that someone is lurking outside the house. Reminded Mum of fatal error in judgement when she thought Al Qaeda were about to blow her up and it turned out to be Weirdy Edie ogling Dad but she is adamant that the perpetrator is male this time. He is currently hiding in a rhododendron. James is also in overdrive. He says it is his first real job as a PI, it is just a shame that he is down to one tracker dog, i.e. Bruce, now that dog has taken up residence at 19 Harvey Road for foreseeable future. It is not a shame. Bruce can only detect Granny Clegg and neither of them are stealthlike. James is undeterred though and is determined to beat Marjory in identification of criminal lurker. Is bound to be an O'Grady. Or Barry the Blade. Oh God, what if he has fallen for me after my accidental bin love declaration and has earmarked me to become Mrs Blade, so that he can marry me and then murder me in a crazed knife attack?

72

3 p.m.

Lurker is gone but James said is not Barry the Blade as Marjory has already phoned in with a field report and says he is outside Goddards eating a pork pie. Said I thought he and Marjory were PI rivals. He said he has duped her into acting as his mentor, but it will be him who revels in the glory as the young upstart. Said he could have solved mystery by just going downstairs and confronting lurker. But James says where is the challenge in that?

· ·

Tuesday 12

11 a.m.

Am racked by shocking news. It is that Peaches Geldof (who is totally me, except that she has tattoos, lives in London, and Dad is ageing muso type with cool hair and Crombie versus Colin Riley who is ageing accountant with short back and sides and cagoule from Millets) has got married. This is yet further reminder of what I have lost. I could have had Las Vegas wedding with own young upstart musician and spent rest of teenage years lounging in Brooklyn loft reading Bret Easton Ellis. Instead am in spare room watching bush with binoculars while James takes break from detecting for wee break and brain-stimulating snack (i.e. Omega-rich Flora on seedy granary).

11.05 a.m.

Oooh. What if lurker is Jack? What if he has been inspired

by Peaches Geldof true love too and has come to beg me to become Mrs Stone? Am going down immediately.

11.10 a.m.
Lurker was not Jack. Was Mad Harry! (So slightly mad, and criminal.) He is lingering around house in the hope that James will beg him to reform Beastly Boys. Said what about Mumtaz? He said, 'While the cat's away.' Said Mumtaz not cat, she girl. Mad Harry said whatever, he is bored rigid and she isn't back from Islamabad for five weeks. At which point James appeared from observation point number two (i.e. upstairs bathroom) and said he should have thought of that before he chose sex over musical supremacy. Mad Harry said Mumtaz's kisses cannot compare to the sheer joy of performing 'You Raise Me Up' alongside James. James said talk to the hand, and that he can lurk all he wants but Beastly Boys are dead, and their dream died with it. But Mad Harry said he still believes in Boy Power and went back to his lurking post. He is clinging to hope, like wreck of the *Hesperus*, clutching on for dear life. But James has already swum ashore and is reading magazine by the pool. It is utterly sad. Although on plus side will not have to witness any more renditions of 'Bleeding Love' in matching shiny T-shirts.

Wednesday 13
Mad Harry is still in the bush. He went home for tea and

sleep but was back at eight this morning with a carton of juice and a Harry Potter. This is what comes from being an only child. If your girlfriend and best friend desert you then you walk alone in the world, with just literature for company. At least I have sibling to take mind off trauma in hour of need.

3 p.m.
Sibling busy sifting tomato bed for bones. Think would be better off as only child. Or in bush with Mad Harry.

Anyway. Have more pressing and potentially tragic matters to concern self with, i.e. tomorrow is A level results day. Am not concerned for my performance (is AS levels so not even real exams) but is Jack. He cannot leave environs of Saffron Walden until have persuaded him that we are each other's destiny after all. Which may take more time than hoped. So either he has to get all As so he can go to boffiny Cambridge, i.e. only thirteen miles along A11. Or he has to fail completely so that not even Hull will take him. Am pinning hopes on him having had minor seizure in exam hall. Or Edexcel getting his papers mixed up with Fat Kylie's hairdressing multiple choice. Is feasible. Curse second-rate universities for setting low entry criteria.

* *

Thursday 14
8.30 a.m.
Feel sick. Cannot even eat Granny's Ready Brek (usually

banned for being too smooth). Is D-Day, i.e. will fate put 155 miles and the murky Humber between me and Jack, or will she deal him a hand of Fs and keep him trapped in non-fish-smelling Saffron Walden for another year? I hope so.

Mum is already pacing around the Shreddies table in anticipation (at my results, not Jack's). I do not know why she is so het up. As James has pointed out, I get a second go next year anyway. And, even if I do get an A in philosophy, there is no way she will let me take it for A2 in case it compromises my 'real' subject, i.e. English (drama and politics verge on BTEC bricklaying in her eyes).

9 a.m.
This is it. Am going to school. Have to face Jack. And my future. And also remember to get own results before Mum implodes.

2 p.m.
OMG. Fate has dealt me giant hand of Aces. Or a Royal Flush. Or whichever is good hand (poker banned in house under rules pertaining to gambling, fluorescent lighting, and green sun visors), i.e. Jack got As in everything. But isn't going to Cambridge, or Hull. Not yet anyway. He is deferring for a year. Did not find this out from Jack. He got results online as is still too angry to see me apparently, according to Sad Ed, who got it off Scarlet.

But do not care as means he will be within my clutches, aka reach of loving arms for another year. Hurrah!

Also Sad Ed and I got Bs in everything. Which would have been almost as excellent, had Scarlet not got three As, so is now eyeing me with superior brain anti-nipple love cheat stance instead of just anti-nipple one. (And Sad Ed with 'Cannot believe you are head boy and I am mere head of communications, is like Blair and Campbell all over again' stance.) Am rising above it. Now have another entire year to win back heart of true love. Will not give up. Will be persistent, like superglue. Or Mad Harry. He has moved on from lurking in the bush and is now on public display, i.e. is sitting on wall singing 'Back for Good'. Mum says if James doesn't hurry up and sort their relationship out she is going to hose Mad Harry down and will not spare the weedkiller attachment.

. . . .

Friday 15

Mad Harry is no longer lurking outside. He is inside, in James's bedroom, and I can distinctly hear the sound of scale practice. James is pathetic. He has no willpower. He claims he is just using Mad Harry and will dump him come September like the turncoat he is. He will not. Mad Harry is his destiny.

On the plus side, it proves persistence pays off, which bodes well for me and Jack. And me and Scarlet. Am going to commence campaign to win them back immediately.

Or possibly on Monday. As need to formulate plan. Plus Mum is out, Granny Clegg is asleep with Bruce on chest, and I have control of remote.

. . . .

Saturday 16

There has been a shock manoeuvre from Camp Pasty. Grandpa Clegg has rung and has surrendered and begged Granny Clegg to return to her rightful place! He says he cannot cope alone any more. Asked where Pig and Denzil were. He says they have gone to Pig's for a bath as conditions at Pasty Manor have deteriorated beyond comprehension. There is no hot water (Grandpa cannot work the thermostat), no food bar frozen Yorkshire puddings, no toilet roll (they have run out of *Daily Mail* and are on *Parker's Used Car Guide*, which has very small pages), and the sink has fallen off the wall. Grandpa says it is like 1950s all over again. Although personally thought it was like that before the whole coup thing.

Anyway, Granny is having none of it. She has told Mum she wants to have her pension book transferred to Summerdale Road as she is thinking of moving in permanently. Mum went pale and told her not to be too hasty. But Granny says she can see herself eking out her days on our sofa, with her loving family around her. Mum is now in emergency panic mode. She says she is not prepared to look after a Clegg on anything other

78

than a temporary basis. James pointed out the advantages of a multi-generational household, i.e. free TV licence, dog number one stays at Whiteshot Estate. But Mum said dog is picnic compared to Bruce. This is true. After Granny made her announcement I actually saw Bruce smile ominously. Think he evil, like Cujo.

· ·

Sunday 17

Multigenerational household tension is palpable. Granny is issuing a litany of demands, now that the spare room is to become her permanent abode, including:

1. New curtains. She says oatmeal (Mum's preferred hue, of everything—clothes, walls, linen, food) is too depressing and she wants a bold rose design.
2. Some nice Axminster carpet to replace current (oatmeal) shade.
3. And a portable TV in bedroom (worse than heroin in Mum's book, which as have pointed out before, is actual book).

Mum's lips have disappeared, i.e. is advisable to give her at least ten-metre berth. In fact, Dad has gone to play golf and James has volunteered to caddy for half his usual rate. Think will follow their example and exeunt to Scarlet's. Will be chance to rekindle our best friend status, and to initiate my year-long win-back-Jack campaign.

5 p.m.

Am also in emergency mode. There has been more shocking permanent residence news—this time from house of Stone. It started off well, i.e. actually persuaded Scarlet to let me in. She said are you here to apologize to me, or to moon around over Jack in hope he will change his mind and stick tongue in orifice again? Said to apologize to you, obviously. Do not even like Jack any more. Have accepted our relationship has run course. And orifices now hermetically sealed. But then she said, 'Good. And anyway, he too busy to be mooned over, even if wanted to, which he does not.' Said why he too busy. Scarlet said he is packing. Said for what? Assuming it was for brief post-A level celebratory holiday, e.g. yurting in Brecon Beacons. But it was not. He is going to build schools for impoverished and uneducated children. And is not even in Wales. Is in Guatemala! Bob is driving him to the airport in the sick-smelling Volvo tomorrow morning! Said it is awful. Sight of me so unbearable he is having to flee to war-torn third world country, where he will live on refried beans and possibly get that thing where a hooky fish swims up your penis and you die (Sad Ed saw it on *Grey's Anatomy*). Scarlet said I was overreacting and not all beans refried (why do they do that?), plus he knows better than to sway penis in contaminated water. And anyway, at least I had her back again as probationary best friend. Asked her what had changed her mind. She said she had thought about it and, on balance, even though utterly broke Jack's

heart, she preferred it when best friend not hovering near brother's genitals as is too ickky to contemplate. Said hmm. But was too busy thinking about Jack's genitals. And broken heart, obviously. Oh it is utterly romantic. He is selfless charity worker, as well as musical prodigy and political genius. I love him even more! Maybe he will become non-religious missionary, i.e. spreading the word of Keynesian economics. Oooh. Or I can go out there and work alongside him in a giant hat and khaki hot pants. Will be like Indiana Jones film. But without Nazis and giant rolling ball thing. Hurrah! Am actually happy again.

Monday 18

9 a.m.
Or maybe he will meet love of his life over a cholera-infested latrine pit and they will both catch leprosy and die in each other's arms. OMG. It is AWFUL. I have to stop him.

9.15 a.m.
Have had genius idea. Am going to do airport dash. Is utterly romantic and always works in films, e.g. *Love Actually* (although is eight-year-old boy, but all the same, is very tear-jerking). Am going to Scarlet's immediately. Or at least, in an hour. Want to ensure Jack actually departed before set off otherwise is not dash, is just drive in silence in same sicky Volvo, which is not at all

romantic or life-changing. Will text Sad Ed to come too. Is possible romantic airport atmosphere will aid in his plight, i.e. Scarlet will hurl self on him at boarding gate. Or more likely cake section of Costa Coffee.

10 a.m.
This is it. Am going to change the course of history! Or stop Jack getting a fish up his penis, anyway.

5 p.m.
Have failed. Jack has gone. And can hear the fish swimming towards his pant area as we speak. Events as follows:

10.05 a.m.
Arrive at Scarlet's.

10.09 a.m.
Sad Ed arrives at Scarlet's, despite having less distance to travel and having left five minutes before me.

10.10 a.m.
Sad Ed given pint of water and emergency pain au chocolat to revive sugar levels. Scarlet refuses to do mouth to mouth citing potential risk of 'cooties'.

10.11 a.m.
Rachel Riley points out 'cooties' not real but made up American thing like malt shops and bobby pins.

10.12 a.m.
Sad Ed says no cooties real. He has had them twice.

10.13 a.m.
Scarlet refuses to countenance airport dash on several grounds, i.e. *a*) she does not want to encourage me going near brother's bits, as is as bad as fish, *b*) it is utter cliché, *c*) she is boycotting Stansted due to kerosene melting polar bears etc., as well I know, and *d*) none of us can drive, except Suzy, who is still over limit from drowning sorrows at departure of first-born into wide world.

10.14 a.m.
Suzy declares that *a*) Jack's genitals are free territory, *b*) was not a cliché in *Love Actually*, was utterly tear-jerking, *c*) we are preventing Jack from flying so is pro-polar bear, and *d*) Sad Ed can drive and she will invigilate.

10.16 a.m.
Party gets into non-sick-smelling car of people.

10.26 a.m.
Sad Ed finds first gear. Non-sick-smelling car of people departs chez Stone block paving on eight-mile journey towards destiny.

11.26 a.m.
Car of people arrives at destiny, i.e. short-stay car park,

with only thirty-four minutes to go until Jack departs for certain fish-related death.

11.36 a.m.
Party dashes through airport in excellent cinematic display.

11.37 a.m.
Sad Ed crashes into herd of trolleys (oh, the irony), ruining cinematic effect, and costing several seconds.

11.38 a.m.
Party arrives at departure gates. Heroine (i.e. me) searches desperately for hero among crowd lining up for boarding.

11.39 a.m.
Hero appears behind heroine with copy of *Melody Maker* and Double Decker (not the same without raisins) and says, 'What the hell are you doing here, Rach?' Heroine says, 'Why you not in queue. Have you changed mind?' Hero says, 'No, flight delayed for hour. That is queue for Formentera. Look, there is Thin Kylie.' Heroine observes Thin Kylie with tongue in Mark Lambert's mouth and hand down back of trousers.

11.40 a.m.
Heroine says, 'Have come to change your destiny. Need to

tell you something. Um. Thing is. Um. Am in love with you.' Hero looks away and shakes head and says 'Rach' in way that does not indicate he in agreement. Heroine says, 'But have done romantic airport dash and everything.' Hero says, 'Life is just one big drama for you, Rach. You think you're Elizabeth Bennet or Bridget bloody Jones. But I don't want Bridget Jones. Or anyone from Richard Curtis style rom-com. I want you. The real you.' Said, 'But this is the real me.' Hero says, 'That's what I'm worried about, Rach.' Said, 'But will try harder. Honest. Will never snog Justin again. Even though last one was not actual kiss, was scientific, i.e. to prove you are better at it. So am like Marie Curie, if you think about it.' But Jack not in agreement with this. He said, 'There you go again. Jesus, Rach. You shouldn't want to be anyone else. You should want to be yourself. Life isn't a bloody film, or a book.' Said, 'But you are knight in shining whatever.' Hero says, 'No, am really not knight in shining whatever. And you don't need rescuing anyway, except possibly from self.' Heroine tries blackmail tactic, i.e. 'But I thought you cared about me. Was obviously utter lie.' Hero sighs and says, 'Look, I do care. That's why I'm telling you this. You need to give up on the fairytale stuff. You need to grow up, Rach. Otherwise we don't stand a chance.' Heroine says, 'Mmmmggghh', as is doing snotty crying. Hero kisses heroine on forehead (carefully avoiding snot-smeared areas), and departs in direction of destiny, i.e. Gate 12.

And now hero is several thousand miles away in war-torn and exotic Guatemala. And heroine is back in war-tornish but not at all exotic Summerdale Road, lying on bed, staring at poster of Ophelia drowning. Oh God. Am Ophelia. Going mad with grief. Am literally drowning in own tears.

. . . .

Tuesday 19

Have had revelation. Am not Ophelia. Am Rachel Riley. And do not care. Sad Ed and Scarlet have been round to comfort me in hour of need/point out that Jack is right, i.e. we should be proud to be ourselves, even if we are only seventeen, white, and from Saffron Walden, and is much more exciting to be black or drug dealer or lesbian. Anyway, point is, we do not need knights in shining armour. We are strong, intelligent women (and penis-compromised man) and can rescue ourselves from dragons, and selves. Sad Ed not entirely happy with that point. He has been planning for weeks to engineer situation whereby he has to rescue Scarlet from terrifying wild animal so that she is indebted to him for ever and will be forced to love him. But Scarlet told him he had better not be showing any signs of anti-feminism or she will be petitioning Mr Wilmott for a rethink of head boy appointment on sex discrimination grounds and their happy team will be split irrevocably. Sad Ed made pledge.

Scarlet is right. Basing life on books is utterly childish. Have taken down Ophelia poster and boxed up all false-hope-inducing romance-based books, e.g. *Pride and Prejudice*, *Emma*, and *Sugar Rush*.

From now on, am just me. Am going to grow up. And accept that, in this life, there are no happy endings. There is just tomorrow.

Wednesday 20

Unless your surname is Clegg. There has been news on the grand reunion/happy ending front. Granny Clegg has sustained a severe head injury, i.e. she tripped over Bruce and knocked herself out on a curtain cleat. Which is excellent as, despite the bloodstain on oatmeal carpet, which makes house look like set on *Crimewatch/EastEnders*, Granny Clegg is experiencing partial amnesia! When she came round she demanded to know where she was, and why house smelt weird (i.e. of hyacinth-flavour Glade plug-in instead of Fray Bentos and feet). Plus she has refused reviving cup of ginger and lemon tea as it was 'for lesbians' and has demanded the Spar bags and a return to Pasty Manor immediately! James said Mum was under moral obligation to tell her of her political awakening and her decision to move to Summerdale Road following the Pig and Denzil hoo-ha. But Mum says what she doesn't know won't hurt her. She is repatriating her first thing tomorrow. Hopefully the sight

of malnourished and soiled Grandpa Clegg will not effect total recall.

In fact, might go with her. Am utterly bored. Life is empty without romance-based books, TV, or films. Under current rules can only watch fact-based things, i.e. news (as long as do not imagine am Kirsty Wark) and documentaries (as long as do not imagine I am sex trafficked Russian being abused by criminal overlord). Even *Lovejoy* is banned as have been known to imagine was Tinker, under extreme circumstances.

. . . .

Thursday 21

Have changed mind. Utterly brilliant fact-based thing has happened, i.e. there is a wild beast on loose. It is an ocelot called Brian who has escaped from Linton Zoo and was last seen heading along B1052 towards Saffron Walden. Local news is mental with excitement. Granny Clegg says is old hat and ocelot is nothing compared to Beast of Bodmin, which she has seen several times including once when it did poo outside Hester's. (She has not, it was overweight cat from launderette.) Mum is jubilant as is proof Granny still mentally incapacitated/back to normal self. The Spar bags are packed and they are departing as soon as Bruce has had a wee.

James and Mad Harry are also mad with excitement. They have built up an arsenal of equipment to locate and capture beast. Though Mum has already confiscated the

Hoover. She says it is still recovering from its stint in 'Ghost Hustlers' when it was used to suck up ectoplasm (dog vomit/soup/Badedas bubble bath). They are going round to Grandpa Riley's in a minute to fetch the dog. They claim its anti-cat instinct will prove essential in successful ocelot capture. They will be lucky if they can persuade dog to leave 19 Harvey Road. I know for a fact it is enjoying low-protein high-crisp diet.

3 p.m.
Ocelot fever has also hit Loompits Way. Sad Ed wants to join the hunt so he can rescue Scarlet from its rapacious claws. Reminded him of ban on rescuing knights of any sort, but he says she will change her mind when its jagged teeth are sinking into her milky white thigh. He is mental.

7 p.m.
Have walked round town twice and there is no sign of ocelot anywhere. Am back home in safety of living room, watching alternative wild beast chew its own tail, i.e. dog. James and Mad Harry managed to get it away from Grandpa Riley but it did not in any way aid ocelot hunt as has put on several pounds in crisp weight, so it has been sacked and they are going to rely on their wit and cunning alone. They have no hope. Plus, according to news, ocelot is miracle cat, i.e. has been spotted in several places at once, e.g. savaging mole on fourteenth hole of golf course, stalking small children in Bridge End Gardens,

and looking at screenwash in Halford's. If ocelot has any sense it is heading for bright lights of city, e.g. Cambridge, where at least there is a McDonald's to scavenge.

. . . .

Friday 22

10 a.m.

Grandpa Riley has rung with an ocelot sighting. He claims it is at this very minute next-door in the O'Gradys' living room, he has seen it through the grimy nets. (Theirs, not his. His were confiscated by Mum for being common.) He thinks it has chosen them for their superior size and meat-based diet and has rounded them up. Asked him if he had rung police yet. He said no, as Mum had issued him with new rule that he was only allowed to ring police after checking with her first that emergency was actual emergency. (He is on blacklist for false alarms, e.g. 'cannot find can opener', 'someone has stolen BBC1' (aerial fallen out), and 'Jesus is stuck up a tree' (though this was actual emergency not Messiah-based fantasy as assumed by PC Doone).) James said he had done the right thing, and that it was best not to involve the police at all, and that he and Mad Harry are going instead. Is good job Mum is in Cornwall as she would be issuing several more bans.

11 a.m.

Have texted Sad Ed to tell him to lure Scarlet in direction of Whiteshot Estate for savaging.

2 p.m.
James and Mad Harry are back. So is Sad Ed. Was not man-eating ocelot in O'Grady living room. Was stuffed lion called Maurice. Stacey and one of the Liams stole it from the museum in a ransom bid. Is utterly disappointing. Had hoped someone would be minorly maimed. James and Mad Harry say *au contraire* is triumph as they have solved mysterious plot and are hoping to secure grand reward for endeavour. Plus they say it is the inaugural case for their new detective/safari agency Beastly Investigations. Said did not think there was going to be much call for wild-beast-related crime solving in Saffron Walden. James said, 'That's what you think.' He is moron. Sad Ed is depressed though. He has been pinning his hopes on seizing Scarlet from jaws of woman-eating wildcat. Instead she ended up fending off Fat Kylie who threatened to hit him with Mr Whippy's ice cream scoop for 'being twathead'.

5 p.m.
Ocelot has been caught. Was not on golf course. Or in Halford's. Was on common looking in bins with Barry the Blade.

. . . .

Saturday 23
Mum is back from Cornwall. She says Pasty Manor is restored to its former glory, i.e. both Cleggs are happily

inside it, arguing over who gets the broken Parker Knoll. Apparently scene was of utter devastation, i.e. toilet blocked with several Anne Leslie columns, suggested costs for 1985 Mini Metro, and a flyer for Bobby Helmet. Plus somehow Pig and Denzil had managed to get diesel oil, or possibly treacle, all over the spare beds. Pointed out that Mum lives for challenges like that. She said yes, it was a three-cloth job. Asked if she had had words with Pig and Denzil about staying away but she said apparently is unnecessary as newly unprogressive Granny is talking about joining them in the fight for independence. She even refused to let Grandpa change house name back to Belleview as gesture of surrender. Said was romantic. She said is not, is shameful. But at least is 300 miles away, as is Bruce, who apparently was utterly overjoyed at return. Although it took several washings before he recognized Grandpa Clegg. Mum said he looked like a tree protestor what with his matted dreadlocks, withered limbs, and haunted look of the perpetually undernourished.

Sunday 24
9 a.m.

Not only am I loveless, and trapped in small town without even romantic comedy to fill me with hope for the future, but also have no hope of getting out as Jack has ridden into sunset (on board DC10, as opposed to astride white charger. And not so much sunset as mid-afternoon

gloom, but you get the point) with key to non-sick smelling car of people. Is nothing else for it. Am going to have to beg Dad to pay for lessons.

10 a.m.
Dad says he absolutely cannot afford to pay for driving lessons in the face of economic gloom and that is waste of money anyway as he is perfectly capable of teaching me to drive. Mum says *au contraire* he is perfectly incapable, as his previous speeding fine/obsession with Jeremy Clarkson/inability to stick to the ten-to-two position proves, and that she will teach me, as she is known for her rigid abiding to all speed limits, as well as ferocious mirror, signal, maneouevring. Have got first lesson in four hours. Is like woke up in minor bad dream, but now has turned into full-scale nightmare with demonic homunculus thrown in for good measure.

3 p.m.
Dad is booking me in with Mike Majors next week. It is because Mum says she cannot be expected to teach someone who turns a simple request to turn right into a philosophical discussion. I said I cannot be expected to learn from someone who insists that I wear her brogues (not on-trend Alexa Chung ones, hideous Clarks' ones) as Converse might slip on accelerator and cause fatal accident. Especially when did not get above five miles an hour as Mum kept saying, 'Careful, careful, watch that

pedestrian', when *a*) pedestrian was several hundred yards away, and *b*) was an O'Grady so prime target for mowing down. Dad said he cannot be expected to listen to this nonsense any more, it is enough to make him turn to drink. At which point Mum turned her minty attention to him so could escape to bedroom to read fact-based books.

* *

Monday 25
Bank Holiday
Am so full of facts am turning into nerd. Is dangerous stance. May well end up repelling all members of opposite sex for good. Look at James. In fact do not look at James. He and Mad Harry are currently dressed as James Bond (black polo-necks, dark glasses, and swimming trunks (in case of water-based emergencies)) and are practising spy tactics, i.e. rolling across lawn whilst shooting dog with water pistol. Dog does not mind. Plus it is still too fat from the crisp diet to move if it did.

* *

Tuesday 26
Am beyond bored. Scarlet is away on economy drive ironic caravan holiday in Bognor Regis and Sad Ed is on unironic Aled Jones tour of Bangor. James says I can join Beastly Investigations if I want. Asked if he had any commissions. He said no but they are going to stake out Mr

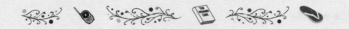

Hosepipe (aka Mr Lambert, father of Mark, former strip-per, current fireman) later as it is possible he is running white slave trade from back of fire station. He is not. He is running a crap lookylikey agency, e.g. PC Doone as Freddie Mercury (PC Doone looks nothing like Freddie Mercury. Looks like Bobby Davro with false moustache) and Mark Lambert as David Beckham (with cunning aid of sunglasses and cucumber down pants).

Will go for walk instead. Though will utterly not pre-tend am Elizabeth Bennet on wistful stroll around grounds of Pemberley. Or Cathy staggering to Wuthering Heights. Will be romance-free, fact-based walk. Will iden-tify wild plants. Or note locations of dog poo.

4 p.m.
OMG. Have bumped into man on walk. Literally. Was not even looking for one, and was utterly not pretending to be Tess of d'Urbervilles lowly-birth type but actually related to rich but evil aristo, when there he was, standing in front of me, rubbing bruise on nose, looking completely like Johnny Borrell, but with less tight trousers, and a packet of custard creams in hand instead of vodka bottle. Said sorry, was not looking where was going, was think-ing about important fact-based matter. Like, er, mortgage crisis. He said, 'No worries. Sometimes I go into another world when I get going on politics.' Then he walked off past Marjory's humming theme from Channel 4 news.

Is fate.

5 p.m.
No is not fate. Is pure coincidence. Am not going to fall at first romantic comedy hurdle.

7 p.m.
But he is older man, i.e. at least 22, judging by out-of-date Strokes tour T-shirt. And Jack told me I had to grow up, and what better way than by going out with older man?

Wednesday 27

Have walked round block five times but older man not in evidence. James says I can hire Beastly Investigations to track him down for one pound fifty. Said one pound twenty-three and half a packet of Polos? He has agreed. He and Mad Harry are behind the wall with the bin-oculars and aquatic disguises as we speak. Pointed out lack of water hazards in Summerdale Road environs but James said his namesake, Mr Bond, would never have lived to die another day if he had ignored water peril. And anyway Thin Kylie has a kidney-shaped pool and Marjory has an ornamental pond, both of which are utterly hazardous (and lower middle class) as verified by Mum.

4 p.m.
There has been a positive sighting of T-shirt man. To be

fair did not require binoculars or aquatic-wear, or even detective agency. He just walked past house and nodded and said hi. Which would have been good if had not been in full view of me in front garden trying to get dog to hurry up and poo by singing the 'poo song' to it (i.e. Kenny Rogers and Dolly Parton 'Islands in the Stream', which for some reason has laxative effect on dog). Plus Mum was hovering in background with rubber gloves, smelly Bob spade and poobag, ready to dispense with poo as soon as it made appearance. James is jubilant none the less. He says his services were essential as they now have him on camera and can trace him back to his lair. So he is fully deserving of his £1.23 and mint-based confectionery. Mum not so happy. She said hopes I am not having romantic urges towards strangers, especially ones who are old enough to be my father. Said *a*) am anti-romance and only interested in facts, which is why *b*) I know he is not at all old enough to be father as no one of Dad's age would know who Strokes are let alone have body to wear a figure-hugging T-shirt bearing their 2004 tour dates. And *c*) he does not live in lair as is not cartoon baddie or Osama Bin Laden. But then decided to exit to house as Mum was armed and dangerous, i.e. pointing poo-laden smelly Bob spade at me.

Thursday 28
James and Mad Harry have garnered further inside

information on T-shirt man. According to their investigations, he is possibly in league with Mr Patel of Mr Patel's fame, as he spent fifty-eight minutes in the shop this morning. So either they are running a black market ticket tout ring, or he has a porn/Pot Noodle/sticky lino fetish. Also he is not a vegetarian as he came out eating a Ginster's pasty (contravening Mum's many rules pertaining to Ginster's use of mince rather than cubed steak, and purchasing convenience food from corner shops where it is kept in unhygienic conditions and rarely warmed to required temperatures).

4 p.m.
Mum says he is none of the above. Except for foolhardy regarding pasty consumption. According to Marjory, who got it off Mrs Dyer (unconvincing dye job, fat feet, smells of Yardley), he is lodging at Chestnuts B&B (1950s semi, manky conker tree in garden, proprietors Les and Ying Brewster of sex bar and Siam Smile restaurant fame) until he finds a flat, which is why he was talking to Mr Patel as Mr Patel is property magnate (not magnet, have made that mistake before) and owns half of Saffron Walden. Also, he is 23, which, while not technically being old enough to be my father, is still utterly out of bounds. Also she has banned James from any more detecting/wearing of swimming trunks anywhere other than municipal pools/beach-based areas. She says *a*) he clearly has no talent in this area, and *b*) he starts secondary school in

four days' time and if doesn't want to get dragged down by the hordes of gum-chewing knife-toting O'Gradys then he had better start getting his head in the game. Said *a*) no one totes knives at school, it is banned, although gum is encouraged due to plaque fighting properties, but it has to be dispensed into bin, not stuck to desk or Mr Wilmott, and *b*) did not know she had seen *High School Musical*. She said *a*) I have had just about enough of your fact spouting, I think it was better when you read Enid Blyton all day and thought you were Darrell because you both had curly hair, and *b*) Operatics are doing it as winter show. Said *a*) is true, am quite like Darrell, and *b*) in that case hoped she and Dad are not auditioning after the *Grease* fiasco. She said no, but Clive and Marjory are hoping to be cast as Ryan and Sharpay. Said would not hold breath. She said nor would she as is bound to go to sadistic dentist Mrs Wong and Russell Rayner (closet homosexual, golf professional, once in an Erasure video).

* * *

Friday 29

James is in room with Mad Harry planning for school. They are sharpening their pencils, tying their ties and checking their trousers are regulation length. They are so going to get heads flushed down toilets on Monday. Will pretend do not know them. Cannot be associated with such levels of weirdness. Instead have done detecting on

own, i.e. wandered past B&B on pretext of poo trip. But to no avail. T-shirt man is very much not in evidence. Which is possibly good thing as dog bit Chestnuts sign off the gate and swallowed it before could prise it out of hairy jaws.

9 p.m.

Mum has banned me from taking dog on any more poo trips. She says it is exhausted. Plus it will lose the ability to control its bowels and start needing to poo every two hours. Like Dad. Did not ask. She is right though. I am wasting my time. It was not fate bumping into T-shirt man. Was just idiotic Riley-esque accident. I do not believe in romance or happy endings. I just believe in facts. And the fact is, he knows where I live, and hasn't been back. Although the sight of Mum with poo-spade could be deterring him. Not even Dad could find that pleasant. Thank God Scarlet is back tomorrow. She will reinforce my fact-based mission.

. . . .

Saturday 30

Scarlet is back. But is out of bounds. I rang to ask if she wanted to come round once Sad Ed has finished trolley herding but she says we cannot see her until her transformation is complete. Apparently she has had a revelation in Bognor Regis and will unveil all on Monday at school. Sad Ed says it had better not be Wicca again as he is

100

still sad after melting his wand, aka light sabre, in ritual sacrifice.

- -

Sunday 31

James is going mental with grown-upness, i.e. in anticipation of his first day at secondary school. He is already wearing his uniform (with full sleeve painting apron on top to alleviate potential porridge spillages). He is going to be severely disappointed. All he will do in first week is draw locusts, burn peanuts, and get chewed by the school sheep. A timetable that will continue for weeks, if not years. Real learning does not begin until Year Ten, as any fool know.

september

NAPPY

Monday 1

First day of school.

Hurrah. It is finally here. After several arduous years, am at pinnacle of career at John Major High, i.e. am Upper Sixth. Which gives me instant rights to barge to front in chips and beans queue, access top shelf in library (Usborne Pop-Up Guide to Body) and wee in superior A Corridor toilets. *Au contraire*, James is at bottom of food chain, i.e. Year Seven, doomed to tinned sweetcorn (ick), *Sweet Valley High*, and the no-seat loo. Have given him essential survival tips, i.e. do not look a Criminal and Retard in the eye, do not offer to find a valuable they claim to have dropped down toilet in exchange for reward, do not join maths club, chess club, science club, or farm club (double whammy of mentalism as not only is geeky but you smell of goat poo all day). Plus have warned him it can take weeks to make friends and, if he gets scared, then Mrs Leech (school secretary, too much face powder, biscuit habit) has a ready supply of bourbons and orange squash. Have also warned him that under no circumstances is he to lurk around common room or in any way reveal that I am related to him.

Mum has taken at least twenty photographs of him looking like Little Lord Fauntleroy. Asked why I was not allowed in picture to mark historic day, but she said my miniskirt and dog-chewed Led Zeppelin T-shirt did not reflect theme of academic prowess. Plus my hair takes up too much room.

5 p.m.

School was excellent. Me and Sad Ed are utterly imbued with Upper Sixth authority, i.e. Year Sevens stare in awe when we pass in corridors. Although that could be down to dog-chewed T-shirt which now reads 'Le Z'. Plus Sad Ed was wearing skinny jeans, which are not at all flattering to his 'unique build', as have pointed out on several occasions, but apparently his combats are in wash following incident on Aled Jones tour so he is limited wardrobe-wise. James has failed to abide by any of my rules though. Already he and Mad Harry are nestled in the cocoon of geekery that is the mathletes lunch table. Apparently they impressed the 'boss' (aka Ali Hassan) with their ability to sing the periodic table and correctly identify the valency of boron. As did Mumtaz. Though James says she is only there by default because she is related to Ali so it is totally like the mafia, or Nicolas Cage. Said mathletes not in any way like the mafia and anyway I thought he was going to dump Mad Harry come September once Mumtaz was back on the scene. James says Mad Harry says Mumtaz has been offish with him since her return and that six weeks in Pakistan may have restricted her, love-wise, so James is just biding his time to see which way the wind, or Mumtaz, blows.

There is other, non-nerd-related canteen hoo-ha. It is Scarlet. In shock fashion/lifestyle move, she has turned back into a goth, i.e. black fishnets, pasty complexion,

106

perpetual smell of patchouli. She says she had an epiphany in Bognor, which was not ironic at all, just wet and crap, so she spent entire week in bunk reading seminal vampire-based novel *Twilight*, plus several sequels, and has seen the light, or rather dark, again. I said this was potential breaking of pact as reading gothic romance utterly not OK under terms and conditions, but she said, *au contraire*, she has learned all sorts of important facts about vampires, Native American culture, and pick-up trucks, so it was educational, rather than emotional stimulation. She has lent me book to see for myself. But can tell she is lying. I can see suspicious glow on cheeks even under chalky sedimentary layer.

Anyway, rebirth has upset Goth Corners Mark I and II no end, as, according to official John Major rules, her age, seniority and ownership of vegetarian leather coat give her right to be declared Head Goth and sit on the Throne of Darkness (plastic chair with bats drawn on in chubby marker). But that position is currently occupied by Tamsin Bacon, former Wiccan novice, and current girlfriend of Trevor Pledger (former Head Goth, ex-boyfriend of Scarlet, currently on gap year in shuttlecock factory). Scarlet says this is a mere detail. She is going to get Sad Ed to impose head boy authority and take possession of the throne. Sad Ed is bound to do it. I caught him gazing at her ankles (only bit visible due to return of voluminous goth skirt) in English with utter boy lust.

8 p.m.
May just read bit of *Twilight* for research purposes. All facts are equal in eyes of education.

1 a.m.
Oh my God. Scarlet is right. Is totally seminal. Am in love with moody vampire Edward Cullen, and possibly with werewolf enemy. Plus am utterly heroine Bella Swan, i.e. cool, bookish, with father who can't cook. Although he not chief of police, and Saffron Walden not really at all like Forks, i.e. Forks is big wet forest with swirly grey clouds and Saffron Walden is leafy commuter town with Starbucks. God it is so unfair. Why can't we move to somewhere with vampire potential. Like Forks. Or possibly Leeds, which is wet, at least.

1.30 a.m.
Although obviously and most importantly have gleaned lots of good vampire facts, e.g. reason can't go out in sunlight is because they go all glowy and twinkly. See— would never have known important vampire-detecting fact if had not read romance. So is not breaking rules. Plus, is horror, so cannot have happy ending.

. . . .

Tuesday 2
Ramadan begins
There has been a goth-related fight in canteen. Sad Ed imposed authority, and weight advantage, by sitting in

Throne of Darkness, to reserve it for Scarlet. But four minigoths managed to topple him forwards into Mrs Brain's healthy soup of day (baked bean and sausage) and move chair to Goth Corner Mark II, instantly designating it as Goth Corner Mark I. So now there are two rival goth camps. And although Scarlet is leader of one, it is the substandard Mark II version. She says she is going to use plan B. Which is get Sad Ed to build a new and bigger throne, thereby outdoing the Throne of Darkness, and transferring authority back to her table. I said a) Sad Ed is not known for his carpentry, or indeed any, skills, and b) wouldn't it be easier just to settle dispute in traditional John Major High fashion, i.e. fight on sheep field. But Scarlet says a) he offered, and b) fighting is going to be banned under Sad Ed's new head boy rules, and they are going to introduce a system of heated debate instead. Plus c) (which came from nowhere, but is further proof that she is invading me telepathically) neither of us is anybody other than ourselves, but if push came to shove, she is Bella, not me. I said but Bella has car, and I am at least taking driving lessons, unlike Scarlet who refuses on various grounds (anti polar-bear, potential for road deaths, leather steering wheels). Plus her dad can cook vegetarian toad in the hole. Scarlet said it is not about cars or cookery skills, it is about essence de goth, which she has, and I do not. I said I can buy patchouli tomorrow if that is all that matters but Scarlet just said 'point proven' and ate another sesame snap.

Also, Mumtaz was noticeably absent from the mathlete table. Asked James if this was indicative of post-separation decline of her relationship with Mad Harry. James said potentially. Although mainly is because is Ramadan and she does not want to be around all those granary sandwiches. But that this is causing love-divide issues as Mad Harry is very food-orientated, and not so respecting of her religious beliefs as James, who has been known to observe Ramadan in past, albeit only for few hours, and ending in fainting on netball court. Said hoped James not thinking of embracing Islam again in bid to vie for affections. He said the only affections he is interested in are Mad Harry's. But not in a man-love way.

8 p.m.
Although thinking about it, James and Mad Harry do enjoy dressing up in leotards and fake fur. Plus they like Will Young. And *Hannah Montana*. Maybe they are gay. That would be excellent as not only would I be instantly cool, but Mum would go mental. Will tell him to come out of closet immediately.

8.30 p.m.
James still in closet. Though he claims there is no closet. He says he is 100 per cent heterosexual. Said not even just 90 per cent? He said possibly 99 per cent, if you count his admiration for the physique of young Kirk Douglas. Which he does not. And to stop bothering him as he is

'fagging' for 'the boss' tomorrow. Said aha, he is Ali's maths bitch, which is totally gay. He said it is not, he is just calculator monitor. So is just nerdy, not gay. How utterly disappointing.

* *

Wednesday 3

8 a.m.

Hurrah. It is drama today. And we have new teacher now that Mr Vaughan is ensconced in Bath, with his supersize nipples and Sophie Microwave Muffins. It is sad, because Mr Vaughan had excellent, forward-thinking approach to teaching, e.g. not minding if anyone was late for lessons. Or even showed up for lessons. Although he was potential pervert-in-school. Plus new teacher will possibly be RSC actor taking philanthropic sabbatical to pass on cavernous experience to the next generation of stars. Oooh. Maybe it is Dr Who!

9 a.m.

New teacher rumours have reached epic proportions. According to James, odds are 10–1 on Dr Who, 5–2 on Simon Cowell, and evens on Mrs Best from Burger King Sports Academy, who is vaguely related to someone on *The Bill*, and who Mr Wilmott has had his eye on for years, ever since her groundbreaking production of *Joseph* with actual locust plague. James is now fully entrenched in the mathletes illegal gambling ring. He and Mad Harry are

111

debt collectors, due to them being former gang members. I said I did not think a few months as henchmen to Keanu O'Grady was necessarily satisfactory qualification but James says it is the closest to menace any of the mathletes have ever been—they are like superheroes. How sad.

4 p.m.
Oh. My. God. New drama teacher is not Dr Who. Or even Mrs Best. It is Older T-Shirt Man from B&B! Who is not actually called T-Shirt Man but is officially Mr Pringle! On downside, he is not RSC actor, or even related to someone on *Bill*, but on plus side he looked utterly gorgeous sitting astride back to front chair in faded black T-shirt and position that says 'I am completely in charge, but in leftfield, maverick kind of way.' Now I know how Sophie Microwave Muffins must have felt when confronted with Mr Vaughan and his smoking habit and big nipples. Am utterly smitten. He is my handsome prince. Hurrah! Will have happy ending after all.

4.30 p.m.
Have had rethink. Am not smitten. Am not looking for romantic fairytale happy endings etc., etc. Am only interested in facts.

4.45 p.m.
And, obviously, he is teacher, which is out of bounds and illegal. In Mum's eyes, if not in actual eyes of law.

5 p.m.

Scarlet has texted to say is illegal in actual eyes of law. How does she do that? Anyway, am determined to enjoy only cerebral relationship with him. He can be my mentor, like Alan Sugar. We will not snog, but will have grown-up fact-based relationship.

. . . .

Thursday 4

Have demanded that Sad Ed use his head boy privileges to get school secretary Mrs Leech to divulge any facts (see, am sticking to rules) she may have on Mr Pringle's provenance, and preference, woman-wise. It will be cinch. She is anyone's for a cup of tea and a gypsy cream.

12 noon

Fact: Mr Pringle has degree in drama and media studies from University of Stoke on Trent.

Fact: He is NOT on sex offenders' register.

Fact: His first name is Patrick. But he prefers Paddy.

Hurrah. So now know he is pro-working class, i.e. chose Stoke (not too thick to get into Manchester, which is what Mrs Leech claimed), irony-embracing (Paddy, despite not being Irish), and officially NOT a pervert.

Said that was not many facts, really, but Sad Ed said apparently he over-sugared the cup of tea and his iced rings were stale. Plus Mr Wilmott came in to demand to know where his swivelly orthopaedic seat was. Mrs Leech

said is utter mystery, maybe the Criminals and Retards have borrowed it for corridor racing again. They have not. It is installed in Goth Corner, complete with velvet cushion, superglue bat attachments and Scarlet enthroned in it. She is like that supreme Dalek, Davros—half evil dictator, half chair. There is no contest with Melody Bean. Her chair has no wheels or orthopaedic back support and in fact only pretension to gothness is felt tip cartoon. She has been forced to concede defeat, thus avoiding splitting the Goths further (already suffering due to a difference of opinion on admitting EMOS and the Tim Burton freaks).

. . . .

Friday 5

There is fact-based hoo-ha at 24 Summerdale Road, which is threatening love-based hoo-ha (Mum and Dad's, not mine or James's. Or dog's. As he is still genital-free). It is Mum's new job hunt. She has been scouring the *Walden Chronicle* for suitable (part-time) appointments and has ringed two potentials:

- Trainee traffic warden (uniform and notebook included)
- Vice-Chancellor of Essex University.

Dad said, 'Fact, Janet: you are not qualified to be a Vice-Chancellor. Plus we can manage quite well enough on my salary, with a few minor cutbacks.'

Mum said, 'Facts, Colin: I can spot a traffic violation

when I see one. There are NO qualifications to be a Vice-Chancellor. Plus no one uses paperclips any more, so your job future is looking increasingly dubious.'

Dad said, 'Fact, Janet: Wainwright and Beacham is the county's top-ranking treasury tag supplier, so my future is assured.'

Mum said, 'Fact—' but at that point me, James, and dog left before we got caught in fact crossfire. James is right though, she would be excellent traffic warden. Although we would have to run away due to potential for O'Grady menace. I am still taking flak for her dog-poo-wars.

Saturday 6
9 a.m.

Hurrah. It is my first driving lesson today. Or at least first lesson involving properly qualified instructor, i.e. Mike Wandering Hands. Although hope he will not be doing any hand wandering with me. As, despite being older man, he is utterly ick-making. Given his taste in women, i.e. Mum, it is unlikely anyway. Hopefully will be triumph. As will not be distracted by either desire to snog him (Jack) or eject him from front seat (Mum). Plus must have inherited some of Mum's driving skills.

11 a.m.

Have inherited none of Mum's skills. Or charm, according to Mr Wandering Hands. He said is a miracle I was even

'born of her womb'. I said I had thought same thing. And in fact hoped it on number of occasions. But sadly all signs point to her being biologically related. He seized opportunity to discuss my shortcomings with owner of womb, who agreed with him, having watched proceedings from window using Beastly Investigations binoculars. He said it might be advisable for me to have intensive lessons. Mum said she would run it past Dad. Mike said he didn't think Mum was kind of woman to need permission (ick). Mum said she does not need permission, just satisfaction of proving why she is right to apply to be traffic warden in order to fund lessons. Then luckily Mike had to go to teach Ying Brewster (wife of Les, former sex worker, landlady of Mr Pringle) who has been having lessons for four years and has failed a record thirteen times. Though Mum says it is deliberate, and she is only doing it to be close to Mike, now that Les has had a vasectomy. But Mike has no interest in her as she is walking cliché (low tops, high boots, perpetual smell of Poison).

1 p.m.
Mum and Dad are not speaking. It is because Mum told Dad that Mike was supportive of her traffic warden dream. Dad said it is only because he wants to ogle her in a uniform and black tights. Mum said Mike was no admirer of uniform, purely of authority, and that anyway she will be opting for sensible trousers and lace-ups.

Cannot stand arguing. Is like love-kindling *Grease*

episode never happened. Although in fact do wish that had never happened. Anyway, am going to go and mope with Sad Ed on the trolleys for a bit. Now I feel his driving lesson pain. So far he has cost Mr and Mrs Thomas over £300 and he still cannot do a three-point turn without mounting the kerb or stalling or pranging several other vehicles. Or all three.

6 p.m.
Sad Ed says it is possible that it is the rest of the world who is wrong and that we are the only ones with natural driving ability. Though fact that at that very moment he crashed a herd of trolleys into car park exit barrier does not bear this out. Reuben Tull said maybe we needed to see beyond the steering wheel and white lines and chill about the whole driving thing. Said if that was an offer of drugs then the answer was no. Asked if he could drive. He said he doesn't need to, he soars above the people trapped in their tin boxes and travels in his mind. Case proven.

On plus side, am going for Sunday lunch at house of Stone, i.e. Scarlet's. Sad Ed is coming too. Scarlet says it is a power lunch, i.e. to discuss campaigning matters. Whatever. Suzy is vastly better cook than Mum, lets you drink wine at the table and her house is imbued with essence of Jack, so can osmotically ingest his aura. Plus glean essential info off Suzy as to his state of mind, and penis (fish-free, hopefully).

117

Sunday 7

Atmosphere at Shreddies table is decidedly frosty. Is the Mike Majors thing rearing its ugly head, or ugly wandering hands, again. Plus Grandpa Riley is coming to lunch with Treena and Baby Jesus. Which means Mum will be in preemptive strike mode all morning concerning spills and fighting. Thank God am going to Scarlet's.

Am utterly going to show off fact-based stance, so Suzy and Bob can report back that am grown-up and not happy-ending, fairytale obsessed child person. They do not need to know about Bella/vampire thing. Although finished second book in series last night and it is clear that Scarlet is mistaken as to who is who. Is obvious. Jack is Edward Cullen (mysterious and broody), I am Bella (brainy and misunderstood), and Sad Ed (or potentially dog) is werewolf boy (hairy but loyal). Scarlet is one of vampiric sisters, i.e. irritating and superior.

5 p.m.

Why oh why are my parents not sexperts and abortionists? Or at very least open to culinary experimentation? Not only was lunch at Scarlet's fascinating feast of canapés (Suzy nesting like mad pre-potential adoption by cooking entire Nigella party food book), but conversation at table was dynamic row encompassing the Gaza Strip (actual one, not carpet in common room), Jerusalem (saggy sofa in common room, not actual one) and which Miliband has better potential Prime Ministerial hair

(answer neither, although at least Ed's can go in more than one direction). Chez Riley, it is nutritionally balanced casserole or shepherd's pie rotated on fortnightly basis, with occasional roast thrown in to baffle everybody, plus conversation is limited to what the dog/James/Dad has/hasn't done.

On down side, Jack is having excellent time in Guatemala. Had secretly hoped he might be yearning to come back to my loving and very adult arms. But Suzy says he is embracing back-to-basics lifestyle and shedding all his Western trappings. Plus his penis is fine. Said maybe we should Skype him immediately so that he feels homesick for parmesan straws and aubergine dip but Suzy says there are no computers or mobile phones in Chichicastenango. She only heard by letter and he said that might be last as a goat ate the postbox last week.

Apparently lunch Chez Riley also vaguely successful, i.e. only one major spillage (Treena's elderflower cordial, though that could have been deliberate), two breakages (the freezer handle and Dad's nine iron, both Jesus), and one dog-related incident (it chipped tooth on nine iron). Plus, sexual/financial tension somewhat relieved by stunning announcement that Mum has got a job. It is looking after Baby Jesus. Apparently Grandpa can no longer cope with the trials of childcare (i.e. he cannot run fast enough to prevent Jesus escaping to Mr Patel's 2 or the O'Gradys' house, which he has taken a fancy to, it is all the junk

119

food and endless *QVC*—in both cases). Plus he says Jesus's conversation is doing nothing for his potential Alzheimer's as is limited to endless questions about Macca Pacca and where the Wattingers are (he does not have Alzheimer's, he has a Guinness habit). He is desperate to go back to Twilight Years Day Centre. He says it will be new lease of life. Which is possibly true, though from experience conversation tends to revolve around what happened to Lord Lucan and who is going to die next, so not entirely brain stimulating. Plus I have seen the communal TV tuned into *Night Garden* on more than one occasion. Anyway, he begged Mum to take Jesus in to save his sanity, and (in cunning, well-played move) to impose her excellent record of raising intelligent, socially-adjusted children. Mum has accepted. She is going to have Jesus on Mondays and Tuesdays, and over-time by prior arrangement. There has been some discrepancy over payment, as Grandpa thought reward of passing on cavernous knowledge of phonics should be enough, but he has agreed to hand over his magazine money instead. Mum is going to be minted—he spends at least £50 a week. Dad says she is going to regret her decision and wish she had waited for an office-based position, with perks, e.g. a pension scheme and Nespresso machine. As it is she is going to be up to her elbows in J-cloths and Cillit Bang. James pointed out that will be perk enough.

Monday 8

There was more hoo-ha at the mathlete table this lunchtime. It is Mumtaz. She has dumped Mad Harry. I said was inevitable, culturally, as she has probably been promised to a cousin in Pakistan. But James said it is not that, she has fallen for Damon Parker, who has memorized the dates of every ascension to the throne since Ethelred the Unready, and is in Year Eight. So she too is prey to the significant charms of the older man.

7 p.m.

Not that am going to fall for older man. Just am aware that there are attractions, e.g. experience of world, ability to purchase alcohol legally, no urges to let sheep out in 'hilarious' prank.

Tuesday 9

Had tour of new John Major High childcare facility today, i.e. The Camilla Parker Bowles Memorial Crèche (Camilla not actually dead, but Mr Wilmott has thing about her and is hoping naming in her honour will secure visit). It is being staffed by Mark Lambert and both Kylies, who have transferred from bricklaying and hair and beauty respectively. Asked if they were following burning ambitions to become Supernanny. But apparently it is not that. It is because it is warmer, and there is a television and endless supply of rusks. Plus the Kylies are hoping to keep

121

up their training by using the 'inmates' (Fat Kylie's word, not mine) as live models. They will have trouble keeping them still enough judging by the cupboard full of Capri-Sun.

. . . .

Wednesday 10

8 a.m.
Have slight sick feeling. Maybe ate dodgy sausage last night. I know for a fact the dog had licked one of them before it made it into the oven. Or possibly is because have drama later. With Paddy.

8.15 a.m.
I mean Mr Pringle. Obviously. And it is not that. I have no feelings for him other than age-appropriate ones.

8.30 a.m.
Still feel odd though.

5 p.m.
Oh my God. Sick feeling was hands of fate swirling around in stomach. I think Mr Pringle could be my ONE. It turns out he is utterly anti-fairytale too and has similar fact-based stance to my own. Although his involves cutting edge documentary drama and *Das Capital*, not *Richard Hammond's Blast Lab* and the *Usborne Pocket Guide to Birds*. But none the less, it is utter meeting of minds. He says

Hollywood endings are the opium of the masses and dupe us all into subordination, instead of fighting for social justice. And that only hard-hitting factual drama has the power to change the course of political history. Am going to educate self immediately so can prove I am utterly his Juliet.

5.15 p.m.
Not that he is Romeo, nor I Juliet, as that is not hard-hitting or factual. Although they both die, which is not very Hollywood. But maybe they should have just staged a hunger strike or got up a petition instead and solved the family feud that way.

5.20 p.m.
And also he is not ONE as Jack is ONE, which will prove by being grown-up and fact based and utterly anti-love.

. . . .

Thursday 11
Granny Clegg has rung in a panic. It is the Hadron Collider, i.e. giant machine to recreate the Big Bang. She is terrified that it is Armageddon and that we are going to be blown into a black hole and devoured by 'strangelets'. James gave her lecture on difference between science fact and science fiction (e.g. gravity and fire: real; ET and Mr Spock: made-up) but Granny Clegg says Auntie Joyless (God-bothering sister of Mum,

mother to badly dressed cousins Boaz Jehosaphat and Mary Hepzibah) says Collider is 'vessel of the devil and all his cloven-hoofed minions'. (She is just minty as it contradicts theory that earth not created by Big Bang but by God.) She is now getting Grandpa, Pig, and Denzil (now taken up semi-permanent residence at the Fray Bentos table) to build a nuclear bunker in the outside toilet and will be stocking it with tinned beans and anti-alien/Beelzebub weapons (aka Pig's pigeon pistol) immediately.

- -

Friday 12
There has been another victim of the impending economic meltdown. KXL airline has collapsed, trapping thousands of people on Costa Del Sol, including Cherie Britcher. Mum says it is natural selection and she will only start to worry if BA, with its roster of culturally superior destinations, starts to suffer.

- -

Saturday 13
Hurrah, have another driving lesson today and am anticipating leap in improvement. Have eaten brain- and manual-dexterity-stimulating breakfast of scrambled eggs. In contrast Dad very much not calm. He is determined that Mum will not be in when Mr Wandering Hands arrives and is making up spurious plans to lure

124

her away from Summerdale Road. He will have a hard time. She has already got the binoculars out. Though she insists they are to observe my parallel parking at close quarters, rather than Mike's manly gear arm. (She said manly, though not in earshot of Dad.)

If she has sense she will get out of house though as house is currently full of Mad Harry who is very much not mad but is moping in Sad Ed-like manner. It is Mumtaz. He says life is meaningless without her in it, solving logarithms and snogging during *University Challenge* (they are both stimulated by the boffiny presence of Jeremy Paxman). James is undeterred. He says a day of Beastly Investigations will have him restored to normal mentalism in no time. They are going to attempt to track down Archie Knox's (son of hairy librarian Mr Knox, also hirsute) lost guinea pig Cecilia, once Mum has repatriated the binoculars. Which is better than original plan, which was to dredge shopping-trolley-clogged Slade for alligators. It is hard to believe they are at secondary school.

4 p.m.
Driving lesson marginally improved on last week, i.e. did not mistake clutch for brake pedal, and remembered to manoeuvre after have checked mirror, not other way round. Although Mr Wandering Hands raised spectre of intense lessons again. Said not sure that Mum's new job would stretch to that. He said, 'Ah, so Janet is following

my, I mean her, traffic warden dream.' Said no, she is going to babysit Jesus.

Got him to drop me in Waitrose car park, which he seemed disappointed about. (Not least because Reuben came perilously close to the Fiesta with a record forty-seven conjoined trolleys (maximum allowed is twenty but he and Sad Ed are having competition to herd the most in one go).) But, anyway, was not to avoid love triangle issues, was because had important purchase, i.e. birthday card for Jack. He is 19 on Monday. Have chosen factual and political theme, i.e. picture of Saffron Walden Town Hall, and signed off 'yours truly', which is utterly grown up and anti-romance. Had to get his address off Mr Goldstein (former employer of me and Jack, hunchback, owner of lentil-smelling healthfood emporium Nuts In May). Which was totally like Mutya going back to ask favour from other superior Sugababes, considering he heartlessly sacked me (albeit for potential defecting to Waitrose toiletries aisle). But needs must, as there is no way Scarlet will hand it over.

Got home to find blood on floor in kitchen and Mad Harry writhing in agony at hands of Mum. Was not murder though, as first suspected. It was a Beastly Investigations wild-animal-related injury. He tripped over dog and cut forehead open on cheese grater. Mum was administering TCP in usual aggressive manner.

Sunday 14

Went round Sad Ed's today, following shepherd's pie (no surprises there, but bizarre inclusion of sweetcorn instead of habitual peas caused raised eyebrows all round, including dog). He is stepping up his campaign to win Scarlet's heart and mind and mojo, i.e. he is thinking of going Goth. I said he has advantage of pale complexion (he fears the sun, preferring to lie in bed watching *Angel* box sets) but that his build is not at all vampiric. Unless vampires also gorge on Toffee Crisps. He says he is minded to go on diet. Not of blood (unless in form of black pudding, which do not think is slimming), but cutting down to two packets of Nik Naks a day, and replacing Mars Milk with milk milk. I said was good idea. Though am not at all sure it will do trick with Scarlet. Edward Cullen can move with superhuman speed, whereas Sad Ed can barely manage a slow jog (he gets nipple rub and stomach chafing). Plus only twinkling he has done was when Mark Lambert entwined him in the school fairy lights in Year Seven and plugged him into the mains. He has never recovered.

Monday 15

Today is historic occasion in bipartite (good facty word) manner:

1. It is nineteenth birthday of Jack Stone—former love of life. And still future love of life, once have done requested growing up. Will be sending him facty

thoughts across the Atlantic. And hope that Scarlet does not intercept them with her spooky and militant sixth sense. Which have realized is further indication that she is not Bella but a Cullen, as they are ones with ability to read minds. And oddball dress sense.

2. Is Mum's first day as official carer for Baby Jesus Harvey Nichols Riley. She has already drawn up a pre-emptive strike list, involving Jesus and dog. Mostly concerning not allowing them in the same place at same time, and restricting all access to remote controls, as they have both been known to interfere with television by stealing/ingesting the indigestible.

4 p.m.
Oooh. Forgot another historic fact.

3. Is last ever *Grange Hill*. John Major High is awash with sadness. I wish I could join in but *a*) am unmoved by fictitious fayre, and *b*) have never seen *Grange Hill* due to Mum's ferocious parental controls.

Anyway, has been triumph on one count. Not Jack. Have heard nothing back, telepathically or otherwise. It is Jesus. Mum has declared her regime a success, i.e. there have been no major breakages and only a minor spillage (liquid soap, so self-cleaning). Jesus is not so jubilant at the arrangement. He is used to at least six hours of Cartoon Network, four Fruit Shoots, and several packets

128

of Wotsits a day. In stark contrast he got half an hour of David Attenborough, a glass of milk, and a wholemeal oatcake. He is currently looking glassy eyed in a corner clutching James's naked Will Young doll. James says it is like *Trainspotting* when that heroin addict went cold turkey. He says it is calm before the storm and Mum will have to lock him in the spare room tomorrow with a bucket. Mum demanded to know when James had seen *Trainspotting* (banned for glamorizing drugs, shaven heads, and Scotland) but luckily the dog fell down the stairs before he could reveal source (i.e. Scarlet, which means official shouting goes to me).

Tuesday 16

Mum is taking James's advice and taking Jesus out of house for afternoon. She says if he is going to get violent and messy then she does not want him within range of her oatmeal furnishings. She is taking him to soft play at the Lord Butler Leisure Centre. She says according to web-site it encourages physical and mental skills and will be safe and happy environment. It will not be. I have seen what can happen in an unsupervised ball pool. Scarlet is still traumatized by the sight of spherical plastic to this day.

4 p.m.

I was right. Mum has added Soft Play to her list of banned items on grounds of hygiene (three plasters and a

dead earwig in the ball pool), injury risk (woefully inadequate thickness of crash mat) and O'Grady count (Whitney and Mrs O'Grady both hurling themselves menacingly down the inflatable slide, which in Mrs O'Grady's case is potential manslaughter). She is having a lie down and Jesus is watching television. It is not Cartoon Network, is History Channel, but I can tell he is claiming a minor victory. He has same semi-smug look as dog when it has been begging for a KitKat and gets a custard cream.

More importantly, is drama tomorrow. Think may have wardrobe revamp in order to reflect new grown-up Upper Sixth status.

4.30 p.m.

Not that the two are related. Is just that need outfit that says 'am serious fact-based individual' rather than ironic Brownies T-shirt, gold lamé miniskirt (actually boob tube), and purple Converse, a look that only says 'am underage, colour blind, and possibly slightly retarded'.

Wednesday 17

8 a.m.

Am wearing black. Black is utterly grown-up and facty. Plus will win me points with Scarlet as is goth-friendly wear. Hurrah.

8.15 a.m.

But not points with Mum, who says I had better not be thinking of getting any of my nether regions pierced or tattooed. Have pointed out that am not actual goth, and that black is uniform of all serious minded academic types. She said she does not recall Moira Stewart (favourite helmet-haired multicultural newsreader) wearing lace gloves and a cloche hat. Do not know why she is so minty. It is a non-Jesus day today so she can focus on her leisure activities, i.e. hoovering the mattresses and scouring mildew out of grouting with a toothbrush.

4 p.m.

Scarlet also not impressed with pseudo-goth wear. She says I cannot pull the look off with my voluminous hair and freckles. At least did not look as bad as Sad Ed. He was wearing eyeliner and face had definite powdery white glow. He denies use of make-up but saw packet of Waitrose self-raising flour in locker at first break. Anyway, it does not matter what Scarlet thinks. Mr Pringle aka Patrick aka Paddy was definitely in approval. He says black is the blank canvas on which we can paint our characters and is uniform of his old drama group Clause 4, who did something called gorilla theatre. It sounds excellent and groundbreaking. Is probably about mimicking our base instincts and returning to nature. May try it for next week's practical lesson.

Thursday 18

8 a.m.

Mum is in vile mood. It is because she has got Jesus again today. It is not so Grandpa can go to Twilight Years Day Centre. It is so he can have hair cut. Mum pointed out the prior arrangement clause in the contract (which is actual contract, drawn up by James and countersigned by Mum and Grandpa) but Grandpa said he had given her two hours' notice. She is only in a mood because it will compromise her plans to realphabetize the CDs (following some confusion over whether the Nolans should be filed under N for Nolans (Mum), T for The (Dad), or C for crap (me and James)). Jesus is not at all alphabet-friendly. Or CD-friendly. He has tendency to file them in random manner, i.e. by inserting them into small cracks.

5 p.m.

As predicted Mum's day not entire triumph. It is her own fault. She should never have let Jesus be in charge of dusting the cases. At least only Kenny G and Crystal Gayle are missing. And, personally, would have said this was a blessing.

Friday 19

Granny Clegg rang again to tell us that the world is not going to end after all. It is not her hip of doom (previous allegedly fortune telling hip, now replaced with metal

one) or any other portentous body parts telling her this. It is GMTV. Apparently the Hadron Collider has developed an electrical fault and so there will be no Big Bangs and we will not be eaten by strangelets any time soon. Granny thinks they probably got it from Dixons in Truro. She says she got her hairdryer from there and it has a mind of its own. It does not. It has Bruce-related damage. Mum is jubilant at latest idiotic missive from Cornwall, i.e. there is still no sign of Granny Clegg's memory reactivating. Mum does not believe in elevating anyone beyond their station in life, even if that station is Hammerited terrace called Pasty Manor replete with a man called Pig.

Saturday 20

Ugh. Have got driving lesson this morning. Is odd how have been awaiting this seminal moment for years, yet now has arrived, wish was 16 again and limited to walking or sick-smelling Volvo. Is utter disappointment. Like being tall enough to go on Waltzers at fair and then you realize is just electric roundabout being spun by halfwit.

5 p.m.

As predicted driving lesson entirely not good, i.e. am still having spatial awareness issues, i.e. think car twice width that actually is and have tendency to shut eyes and panic when approaching any other vehicles. Pointed out that at least do not think car thinner than is, which would be

whole lot messier. Mum says I am bringing shame to the Riley name. I said what about Dad. But Mum says at least he knows an inch is an inch. James told her not to worry as in less than six years he will singlehandedly restore the House of Riley to its splendour when he passes within a week of starting lessons. This is possibly true. Though he also thinks cars will be defunct by 2014 and that we'll all be wearing jetpacks and silver suits and eating fishfingers in pill form. Am going round Scarlet's to escape mentalism. She is not even learning to drive so at least will feel vaguely superior.

10 p.m.
Am not feeling superior at all. Is because Scarlet pointed out that she can already drive, including handbrake turns (illegal) and hill starts (impossible), as Bob taught her when she was ten. She just chooses not to on environmental and economic grounds. Also dinner was not usual hotbed of Nigella-based canapés and stimulating conversation (also frequently Nigella-based). Was beans on toast and row about Suzy's erotic art collection (aka filthy porn pictures). It is because Suzy and Bob got a letter from Mr Lemon at the council (formerly of housing and school admissions, now in charge of adoption and refuse collection) this morning. Their adoption interview aka interrogation is on Monday and Suzy is worried their normalizing measures may not have gone far enough. They are right. Do not think removing Kama Sutra and a

Gordon Brown mask even scratches the surface. Plus Scarlet is hardly a model of wholesomeness. She was wearing bust-revealing corset and reading *Your Vagina, Your Call* at the table. If only Jack was still here, with his intelligent aura and chest-covering outfits of choice. Mr Lemon would be begging them to take a horde of waifs and strays off his hands.

Sunday 21

Mum says Suzy is mad wanting another baby at her age. Pointed out that Suzy is in fact a full year younger than Mum and so may have more youthful invigoration, plus she is more lenient when it comes to stains, junk food, and Channel 5. Mum went visibly thin-lipped. She is showing classic symptoms of post-weekend deflation, in anticipation of day of hard grind tomorrow, instilling discipline and food groups other than crisps into Baby Jesus.

Monday 22

Mum is more determined than ever to sway Suzy away from having another child. It is because she spent the afternoon at 'Mummy and Me' aka tedious toddler group at Bernard Evans Youth Centre. James pointed out that, by rights, she was there illegally, as she is not officially Jesus's mum, but Mum says that was problem. Brenda Marsh (also runs Fat Busters, four foot nine, fifteen stone)

congratulated her on getting her figure back after birth. Mum says it is ultimate humiliation to be considered the parent of a boy dressed as a Power Ranger.

James suggested she should set up her own rival toddler group called 'Carer and Me' (i.e non-sexist, and non-ageist). James is idiot. Mum got sudden faraway look in eye, i.e. is now mental with anticipation at becoming Gina Fordesque baby guru, imposing strict routines and stain-free bibs. At happy-go-lucky and very stained end of spectrum Scarlet has texted to say Bob and Suzy's checks went fine, although there was slight mishap when Mr Lemon asked about the sex swing. Apparently Suzy said it was state of art baby bouncer. They are now confidently expecting the arrival of a Chinese or Malawian orphan (their stated preference) within a matter of weeks.

- -

Tuesday 23

4 p.m.

Have remembered have to do practical for Mr Pringle tomorrow. Will watch some monkey-based David Attenborough to get gorilla tips. Baby Jesus will not mind. He has taken to wildlife regime very well. There is more sex and violence than Nickelodeon.

6 p.m.

Will make excellent gorilla. Am totally immersed in

character. Plus know loads of gorilla facts, like they are utterly vegetarian, and they live in nests (who knew!— am amazed they do not fall through). Baby Jesus also demonstrating gorilla tendencies. Though Mum not so amused at him trying to nest on windowsill. Asked what he was still doing here anyway, as Grandpa usually picks him up before *Home and Away*. Mum says Grandpa and Treena have gone for a quick drink after work. James asked if it was by prior arrangement. Mum said yes, but only by five minutes. James shook his head and said it is tip of slippery iceberg. Mum said it is not, Jesus is going home after *Look East* and will not be back until next Monday.

. . . .

Wednesday 24

8 a.m.

Jesus is already at the Shreddies table. Grandpa dropped him off at half seven, with no prior arrangement other than shouting up at Mum's bedroom window. James raised practised eyebrow at Mum but Mum too busy trying to keep Jesus and dog away from the bran flakes. They are both banned following excess poo issues. Also, have texted Sad Ed to make sure he is in character for drama. Am already in gorilla mindset, i.e. admiring leaves on hydrangeas as potential nesting material. Although James says gorillas do not nest in hydrangeas, due to weight versus twig width ratio, as I would know, were

I to join him and Mad Harry as part of Beastly Investigations. Declined again. They are only offering me substandard position, i.e. binocular monitor, which is not at all befitting my superior Upper Sixth stature.

8.30 a.m.
Sad Ed has texted back. It says, 'Vy, yes, pretty maiden.' Have texted back to ask who the hell he is supposed to be.

8.35 a.m.
Sad Ed has texted back. It says, 'Is Dracula, duh.' He is idiot. As if anyone, i.e. Scarlet, is going to believe that. Whereas gorilla theatre is not only convincing, but is utterly left-wing. Though am not entirely sure how.

4 p.m.
Oh. Apparently gorilla theatre is not about gorillas at all. Or any animals. It is actually 'guerrilla' theatre, i.e. edgy underground maverick style drama, as opposed to monkey impressions. Mr Pringle said it was easy mistake to make and not to feel bad. I said was not mistake, was deliberate undermining of expectation. He said, oh, well in that case, I get *dix points*. Although think it may have been sarcastic. On plus side, my arm waving and hooting was nothing compared to Sad Ed's Dracula impression. Reuben Tull actually fell off a chair laughing (though that might also be the 'refreshment' he had partaken of at lunchtime).

Also, Jesus is still here. He is staying the night. James says it is like Granny Clegg all over again, and he will be a permanent resident by Christmas. Mum says it is not like Granny Clegg, as Grandpa is definitely repatriating him tomorrow after breakfast. Plus Jesus does not say 'hooge'.

- -

Thursday 25

8 a.m.
There has been a handover of power at Shreddies table this morning. Dad has been left in charge of administering nutritious breakfast and vitamins while Mum has lie down in darkened bedroom. It is because she was up fourteen times in night to attend to Jesus's many and varied demands including seven pickings up of 'Baby' (naked Will Young), two cups of water, one poo, one wee, one check for Wattingers under the bed and one removing him from top of chest of drawers. James said she should be thankful that we were never like that. But Dad said *au contraire* I had nightmares about falling off my unicorn and James used to appear ghoulishly at the end of the bed and demand to know how gravity worked. James said at least his showed burgeoning intelligence, whereas mine was early signs of living in fantasy world. Reminded him of time he claimed he was a hobbit. He said 'there's nothing fantasy about middle world'. He is moron. Anyway, on plus side Dad let us eat

139

marmalade out of the jar. Jesus was doing it anyway so was only fair.

4 p.m.
Jesus is still here. Grandpa and Treena have got food poisoning and have begged Mum to keep Jesus. James says they have not got food poisoning, as is impossible to get food poisoning from Frazzles, which they were apparently consuming in vast quantities in the Queen Lizzie last night. Asked how he knew. He says off Mumtaz, who got it off Damon Parker, who got it off his cousin 'Nosey'. Apparently Ali Hassan has agreed to secondary business activity (alongside illegal gambling ring) i.e. spy network. Their slogan is 'a geek in every corner'. Shudder. Anyway, Jesus's unholy presence is useful distraction tool as need to ask Mum's permission to join utterly excellent new non-geek-based school club. It is Film Club and is being run by Mr Pringle. He is going to show seminal documentary drama on Friday nights and then we will discuss films, like on *Culture Show* with Mark Kermode, but with smaller foreheads and less of look of giant toad. First one is *La Haine*, which is about disaffected inner-city French youths. Which I totally identify with. Except the French bit. And the city bit. But am disaffected. I think.

5 p.m.
Mum has agreed. Or rather, she said 'whatever'. Which is the same. But is also unprecedented as 'whatever' is on

banned list. But think fact that Jesus had just inserted raisin into wall socket possibly pushed her to limit.

. . . .

Friday 26

8 a.m.
Dad is wearing stubble and haunted look of crimewatch photofit. It is because Mum has found solution to having to get up for Jesus's demands. It is to let him sleep in bed with her and Dad. James said is outrage as it goes against all her anti-new-age-hippy ideals, and pointed out that we were not even allowed to get in bed for morning cuddles. Mum said it was not anti-hippy, it was to avoid bacterial cross-contamination. Dad also in agreement with James. He says he has been kicked, poked, and weed on in night and now has to go and spend eight hours chained to desk auditing the drawing pin department. Mum said he could always stay at home and childmind his brother, i.e. Jesus. Dad took box of Shreddies and spoon and shut himself in Passat before she could enforce idea. Jesus is utterly jubilant though. He is like devil child slowly turning host family against each other, before he eats us all alive. Possibly. Not that will be here to witness it as have seminal film club date tonight with Mr Pringle.

8.15 a.m.
And is not date. Is club. So there will be other people there.

141

8.30 a.m.

Although will be in dark, and French theme is utterly romantic, and possibly no one else will sign up so we will be alone in charged atmosphere of fact-based love. Oooh.

10 p.m.

Was not at all charged atmosphere. For a start was not even in dark, was in overlit 'audio-visual suite' aka the library, with strict instructions not to turn lights off as Mr Wilmott does not want teen pregnancy quota up as we are already lagging behind Burger King Sports Academy since Debs Donaldson in Year Nine had twins. Plus Scarlet, Sad Ed, Reuben Tull, Dean 'the dwarf' Denley (part-time meat mincer and full-time midget), Stan Barrett (once saw Paul Weller in John Lewis) and half of the music table (admission criteria: owning a guitar or an Arctic Monkeys CD) were also in attendance. Did not even get to sit next to Mr Pringle. Instead was wedged in between Sad Ed and Scarlet who argued over my head, or rather through my hair, about whether or not *Gone in 60 Seconds* is classic of modern cinema. (Answer not, unless you also include *Fast and Furious* and *Chronicles of Riddick* in canon. Which Scarlet does not.) Hair had definite powdery residue afterwards due to Sad Ed still sporting his self-raising corpse look. It is not winning him any points with Scarlet. Although the minigoths are definitely showing him more respect, i.e. they have stopped tripping him outside the fruit and nut-dispensing machine. Melody Bean

142

is still not talking to him though since their wedding fell through. She was also at film club, flicking carob-coated peanuts at his head. Have found several in hair. Have eaten them. Waste not want not, as Mum says. Or at least she would say if was not imbued with minty Jesus-based rage. He is upstairs in bed. Grandpa and Treena are now not answering their phone. Dad says he is going to leave Jesus on doorstep of 19 Harvey Road tomorrow morning like foundling child. Although Mum has forbidden this in case the baby-mad O'Gradys kidnap him and raise him as their own. She says wolves would do a better job.

. . . .

Saturday 27

Dad has issued a Jesus-related ultimatum. He says if 'the child' is not repatriated by *You've Been Framed* then he is going to move in with Grandpa Riley instead. Mum looked tempted for a minute, as Dad's sweat glands are high maintenance in the laundry department, but then Jesus reasserted his idiocy by trying to iron the dog. It is agreed. James (as second most authoritative Riley) has been sent round to Harvey Road to inform Grandpa. And also take dog out of house before it chews any more chair legs. It is showing signs of increased mentalism, also Jesus-related. Am not surprised. So far it has been dressed up as a Harboo (wrapped in coloured sheets), 'hidden' in airing cupboard (for four hours, necessitating decontamination of all towels), and had novelty troll-topped pencil

inserted in nostril, troll-end first. Am actually glad have got driving lesson. Three point turns and emergency stops are almost zen-like compared to trying to manoeuvre around living room.

5 p.m.

Dad is jubilant. Not only is Jesus out of the house, but Mum has given up her job as childminder. His manly position as main breadwinner is restored, along with peace. Apparently Grandpa actually cried when Jesus was handed over. He begged Mum to reconsider and said he was only just getting his life back, which was limited anyway as possibly he has fatal bowel obstruction. Mum said he does not have fatal bowel obstruction, he needs to eat more fibre and fewer Bird's Eye Steak Grills, and anyway, he should have thought of that before he got his care worker pregnant at the age of 73 (Grandpa not Treena, she was 28).

Sunday 28

Dad is less jubilant. Jesus is not back. But Mum and James have shut themselves in the dining room and are having a career assessment, i.e. James has got his highlighters and Post-Its out and they are listing pros and cons of various job opportunities. I said Dad should be happy that Mum is so keen to share his money-earning burden, but he says he is worried she will revive the ill-fated 2004

housework roster and make him share in that burden, which as we all know, will only end in tears and shouting when he uses the wrong sponge or hoovers when he should be sweeping or lightly rubbing with a damp cloth. (Also why I am not allowed to partake in housework. Only James passes strict entry requirements.)

3 p.m.
Mum and James have narrowed down her ideal career to three:

- accountant (i.e. what she is qualified for in first place)
- police officer
- head of emergency post-murder cleaning company.

Said there was not much call for latter in Saffron Walden, but James says they are including Harlow in catchment.

Monday 29
9 a.m.
Something suspicious is going on. Am sure have just seen Jesus Riley disappear around end of D Corridor in (hefty) arms of Fat Kylie. Possibly am hallucinating. Is flashback to Reuben Tull mushroom madness.

1 p.m.
Oh my God. Was not hallucination. Have had Riley summit meeting (i.e. me and James) outside lower school

toilets, (i.e. neutral territory as Scarlet is refusing to allow James and Mad Harry within a metre of Goth corner on grounds of their involvement in Ghost Hustlers). Anyway, according to James, who got it off Mumtaz, who got it off Damon, who got it off Nosey, who got it off Mrs Leech for a Tunnock's Teacake, Jesus is now fully enrolled in the Camilla Parker Bowles Memorial Crèche. Fat Kylie is bringing him in every day with Whitney, her brown baby sister. This is huge mistake. Not only is Jesus consorting with O'Gradys on official basis, but he is being educated by a host of former Criminals and Retards including Mark Lambert (owner of the 'Lamborghini'), plus Thin Kylie. It is like prison, where all the criminal masterminds pass on their illegal skills. He will be carjacking within a fortnight. Will tell Mum she needs to reconsider her resignation.

4 p.m.
Mum says Jesus can be taught by Reggie Kray himself there is no way she is having him back in the house. She has only just unclogged the sink with a crochet hook (residue included half packet of Shreddies, four dried apricots, and a Lego head). She will change her mind when he is on the front page of the *Walden Chronicle*, bringing shame on the Riley name. Although is possible that she will be doing that herself if her job hunt continues. She has filled in application to join fast-track police officer course. She will not get on. She is no good at

taking orders from hard-boiled, hard-drinking, chain-smoking Scots (Rebus) or hard-boiled, hard-drinking, chain-smoking Northerners (Gene Hunt).

Tuesday 30

Jewish New Year

It has already started. Mr Wilmott cornered me outside language lab to inform me that my 'brother' Jesus and his 'accomplice' Whitney O'Grady had managed to flood the Camilla Parker Bowles Memorial Crèche. Said *a*) he was not my brother, in fact, had no idea who he was talking about, and *b*) why had no one removed plugs as is elementary rule when looking after delinquents or toddlers (plugs on Mum's banned list during Jesus residence). Mr Wilmott said *a*) how odd, he looks just like me, and *b*) the plugs had been removed but Jesus and Whitney made cunning use of Jammie Dodgers and toilet paper then turned all taps on full to enjoy the lake effect. Said then can only blame operator error, i.e. Criminals and Retards, or Mrs Leech for choosing notoriously claggy jam-based biscuits as official snack. Mr Wilmott will have forgotten by tomorrow anyway as one of BTECers is bound to have tried to blow up, maim, or melt something. Plus he is still consumed by the mystery of his disappearing swively orthopaedic chair. Clearly the bat disguise works as Scarlet actually wheeled past him down A Corridor yesterday and he utterly failed to identify her bottom half.

147

School filled with gloom as well as water. It is Sad Ed and impending eighteenth birthday, i.e. tomorrow. He had planned to be dead musical genius with grieving groupies by now. Whereas he is very much alive, single, and singularly untalented music-wise. Plus is covered in layer of flour. He says is utterly depressing to be entering middle age with nothing to show for creative endeavours. Said *au contraire* he is in position of utter power and public acclaim, i.e. is head boy. But he says all that gets him is a daily shouting from Scarlet because he is not following her media strategy. Plus his head girl (i.e. Thin Kylie) looks like Paris Hilton as dental nurse. (Crèche uniform is, inexplicably, white coats. Which makes it look like cross between science lab and lunatic asylum. So quite appropriate really.) Have got Sad Ed Vampire Weekend album for birthday. He wanted limited edition 'Hatful of Hollow' on vinyl. But Woolworth's only does chart CDs so it was that or Pussycat Dolls.

October

Wednesday 1

Hurrah, it is utter landmark day, i.e. is Sad Ed's eighteenth birthday. Which means we now have stooge to purchase alcohol, cigarettes, fireworks, and porn. Although in reality have been able to buy alcohol off Mr Patel for several years by cunning use of hat and sunglasses disguise. Plus none of us smoke or require sparklers or *Big Ones International*. But is excellent grown-up occasion none the less. Sad Ed is not having party today. He says he is going to be too busy wallowing in failed untimely death gloom. We are going to defer until Saturday instead, and stake our claim on table in Duke of Wellington pub (squelchy carpet, well-stocked snack shelf including Cheese Moments, absolutely not favoured by beardy and potentially grassing teachers (aka Cowpat Cheesmond and Mrs Buttfield (aka Buttface)) who prefer folk night and pickled eggs at King's Arms).

5 p.m.

Has been successful older man-based day all round, i.e. *a*) Sad Ed very much liking his birthday presents. Although CD outdone somewhat by packet of condoms from Scarlet. Sad Ed says it is a token of her true affections for him. It is not. It is a freebie from Suzy's sex show. Also *b*) drama was excellent fact-based lesson on using theatre to resolve conflict. Mr Pringle made us choose sides in Middle East and argue our way to compromise. Sad Ed was Yasser Arafat and Reuben Tull was Ehud Olmert. I got

151

to be Saddam Hussein, who had cameo appearance as sort of evil *deus ex machina*. There was a fraught bit where Ehud Olmert tried to resolve crisis by having a game of musical statues, but in end, debate won the day and they joined forces and decided to populate Sweden instead.

On theme of older men/birthdays/anti-war politics, I have heard nothing back from Jack thanking me for fact-based birthday card. Maybe a goat has consumed letter, or postman, as well as postbox. On plus-side, think no news is good news, penis-fish-wise.

Thursday 2

There has been another Jesus-related incident in the Camilla Parker Bowles Memorial Crèche, i.e. a prison break. Lesbian PE teachers Miss Beadle (overweight, bulgy eyes like Joey in *Friends* and rabbits with myxamatosis) and Miss Vicar (stick thin, no breasts, facial hair) found Whitney burying him in the long jump pit, aka cat toilet. Is lucky they saw him before Whitney finished project. There is no way he would have survived Fionnula Flack (Year Eight, alleged 'gland' problem, actual cheese consumption problem) and her hop, skip, and jump.

I fear Jesus is being sacrificed for the sins of others though. I blame Whitney. She is the one who stole the spade from Cowpat Cheesmond's potting shed. Or Fat Kylie for failing to look up from article on Kerry Katona's

new haircut in time. That is what happens when you put power in the hands of the populace. They just buy *Heat* magazine and claim they were on a tea break.

Friday 3
1 p.m.
Am having fact versus fiction financial quandary. It is following revelation that JK Rowling now earns £5 a second, thanks to utterly fairytale (though non-happy-ending) Harry Potter. On one hand, is against all writerly principles, i.e. point of being writer is that is hideous impoverished existence whereby you are forced to live in bohemian squat and consume Marmite soup and cat biscuits. But on other hand, would quite like to be millionaire. Scarlet says am pathetic money-lusting capitalist who is swayed from political cause by chink chink of gold sovereigns and ker-ching of metaphorical till. I said that's as may be but I could have earned £25 pounds in the time it took her to say that and then spent it on leprous midgets or harpoon-threatened whales. Plus it is now up to £60 pounds. No £65 . . . £70 . . . £75 . . . At which point Scarlet hit me with a Grizzly Bar as she said it was like watching *Bargain Hunt*, including the absurd hairdo. Thank God is film club tonight, which will restore my faith in fact, and banish the Harry Potter money madness whence it came (i.e. BBC Breakfast News). Film is *Control*, i.e. about moany dead Manchester musician. Sad

153

Ed is mental with untimely death musical genius anticipation. Am mental with Mr Pringle anticipation. Am
wearing Joy Division T-shirt (borrowed off Sad Ed so
actually more of capacious dress) and will be nodding and
saying 'God, yes' at intervals to indicate agreement at
theme of wasted youth and Northern deprivation. Am
hoping Mr Pringle will be imbued with Northerny passion, or at least blinded by glare of fluorescent library
lighting, and fling me older manfully against stack of Enid
Blytons.

1.10 p.m.
Except that would be illegal.

1.15 p.m.
But all best things are illegal.

1.20 p.m.
But not murder, obviously. Or drugs. Actually most illegal
things are not good at all. Maybe that is why they are
illegal.

9 p.m.
Luckily Mr Pringle was not imbued with Northerny passion or blinded by fluorescent glare. In fact was too busy
arguing with Sad Ed about New Order and brilliance/
crapness thereof to even notice me 'God, yes'ing artfully
in utterly grown-up manner. Scarlet did notice however

and said, 'This is not *When Harry Met Sally* and if that is the kind of performance you give then you need to see Suzy.' Have no idea what she is talking about. Have seen film but Mum always fast forwards through a bit of it as she says there is a hideous murder which could psychologically damage both James and me. Plus the dog does not like Meg Ryan so by that point a lot of fast forwarding gets done to alleviate the leg/furniture chewing and frenzied barking at her inexplicably immovable hairdo.

Saturday 4

Have had driving lesson. Is utter torture. Would give up except that will need ability to drive in order to have life-changing road trip across America/transport first aid supplies to refugee camps/get job delivering pizza. Told Mum do not know what she ever saw in Mr Wandering Hands though. He has no patience when it comes to forgetting which switch is windscreen wipers and which is to turn left. Mum looked wistfully through Windolene-smeared door and said he can change from first to second as if he is cutting through melted butter, plus his hair smells of pine furniture polish. But then face of Dad loomed idiotically through glass and Mum returned to planet Janet and pointed out that these were objective observations and that in fact she did not see anything in him and their relationship was merely one of mentor and protégée. I hope she is not getting all heated about Mike again. It is

Dad's fault for letting himself go. He has been wearing the same trousers since 2002 (obviously not every day, he is not Barry Blade, just unprogressive fashion-wise). Plus he has no regard for his physical health, as Mum has pointed out to him on several occasions. He claims he weighs exactly what he did at age of 30. Mum said, 'That's as may be, but it has all redistributed itself to your stomach.' It is totally sad. I will never let self go in middle-age and take up golf or start drinking Horlicks. Will be utterly edgy Kate Moss-type (but with bigger hair, and body) until am ancient fifty year old when will turn into Vivienne Westwood. Except will wear knickers. But not waist-hugging M & S ones am currently limited to due to mysterious disappearance of black minimalist pair (potentially gone way of dog, or Mad Harry) and tiny Topshop pair (confiscated by Mum for contravention of lace/buttock coverage rules). It is so unfair. Scarlet actually has pants from Agent Provocateur. Although at least am not Sad Ed who I have seen in Power Ranger Y-fronts. Maybe now he is eighteen he will break free from confines of Mr and Mrs Thomas and their Aled Jones ambitions and assert his authority when it comes to underwear. It is inaugural Sad Ed/Scarlet/Rachel pub drinking outing tonight. Hurrah. By last orders will be hardened Duke regular with seat at bar and whisky habit.

11.45 p.m.
Or not. Was allowed in pub, but was not permitted to

purchase or in any way consume alcohol. Landlord 'Shorty' McNulty (former police dog trainer, half left ear missing, seven feet tall) is apparently stricter than Mum when it comes to serving underage drinkers. At least Mum lets me sip shandy on special occasions. Shorty limited me to a pint of soda and lime and a packet of Twiglets. Kev Banner's dog gets preferential treatment. It is allowed beer in a bowl and has its own stool at the bar. On the plus side we have staked a claim on a table in saloon, i.e. the wobbly one next to loos. It has advantage of clear jukebox access, but pervading odour of wee and Toilet Duck. Scarlet says it is swings and roundabouts and anyway we will be upgraded as soon as Wizard Weeks (beard, long hair, once came fifth in all-Essex Dungeons and Dragons marathon) goes into rehab again and we will have all-essential squishy seats and a view of the roundabout.

Was excellent grown-up evening though, i.e. had raging argument about minimum wage with Wizard Weeks (for) and Shorty and Kev Banner (and dog) (against). Plus now know all words to 'Here I Go Again' by Whitesnake, which was on jukebox thirteen consecutive times (is Kev's dog's 'theme tune' apparently), much to Scarlet's anger as she paid 50p for 'Oxford Comma' and it never got played. Shorty refused a refund on grounds it will get airing tomorrow around five and she is welcome to come back in for a listen then. She declined, but we are going in extra early next week to line up a better

playlist. Sad Ed also happy with coming-of-age pub evening due to free birthday crisps on the house. Shorty is like drug dealer—getting him hooked on Cheese Moments then charging him 70p a packet next week. He is still compromised on pant front though. Waistband of Rhino Ranger Y-fronts definitely visible above low slung combat trousers (not in hip way, in more 'can't get them over Cheese Moment and beer-filled stomach' way).

Sunday 5

10 a.m.

Called Sad Ed to check on his first legal hangover. He is racked with remorse. It is not due to shameful drink consumption leading to shameful behaviour. It is shameful snack consumption leading to not-at-all-vampiric stomach. He says he is thinking of taking up bulimia (he has already failed spectacularly at anorexia). Reminded him of sick phobia and suggested he could exercise off snacks by walking round here and watching documentary on coal miners' strike. He said he would but he has just opened a packet of Buttons and *Hollyoaks* is on.

How I pity him and his lust for third-rate fictional soap operas. Or third-rate fictional soap opera actresses. Instead will spend entire day consuming fact-based *Sunday Telegraph* from cover to cover, i.e. not just fashion supplement or cartoons, which is usual limit.

11.15 a.m.

May just go out for walk instead. And possibly purchase fact-based *Grazia* or at least borrow it from Grandpa Riley. *Sunday Telegraph* is sorely mistaken if it thinks Andrew Lloyd Webber or Archbishop of Canterbury of interest to general populace.

1 p.m.

Have abandoned walk without purchase or borrowing of celebrity gossip magazines of any kind. Is not due to sudden appreciation of frog-like impresario Mr Lloyd Webber. Is due to sudden appearance of utterly non-froglike, and in fact annoyingly handsome princeish, Justin Statham outside Mr Patel's. He said, 'So, Rach, you and Jack back together then?' Said, 'Uh, yeah.' (As did not want to encourage him trying to win war, even though had lost battle etc. Despite his hair looking totally halo-ey and definite visibility of six-pack through ripped Velvet Underground T-shirt.) He said, 'No you're not.' Said, 'Yes I am.' He said, 'No you're not.' Said, 'Yes I am.' He said, 'No. You're. Not.' Said, 'Is not bloody pantomime season, and how would you know if I'm not anyway?' He said Scarlet told Rosamund (works in Nuts In May, ailment-ridden, nits) who told Dean Denley (midget, meat mincer, works opposite Nuts In May) who told Stan Barrett (once saw Paul Weller in John Lewis) who told Barney Smith-Watson (white, dreadlocks, fake Jamaican accent) who is also on rock foundation at Braintree. Said, 'OK. Am not.

159

But does not mean am on market as am in fact totally anti-romance as am busy being grown-up and above all things pant-based.' He said, 'What's in my pants is pretty grown-up, Rach.' Said, 'No thank you, as have already proven we are chemically incompatible. Plus ICK.' And left before could change mind, or ogle pants area.

Only now have pants areas on brain and am being forced to read about Andrew Lloyd Webber as contraceptive measure. Is good tool as he is utterly repellent, pants and all areas wise.

Monday 6

Had special Upper Sixth assembly with fact-based, grown-up theme, i.e. the fact is that deadline for Oxbridge applications is in less than two weeks and it is time to grow up and think hard about future if do not want to eke out days on minimum wage stacking bean cans or sweeping up hair clippings. Mr Wilmott is minty because Emily Reeve (owner of Lola Lambert, knee-length socks (not in Japanese way), cracked nipples) has decided to train as Jo Jingles instructor which only leaves Ali Hassan and he is hell-bent on St Andrews. Scarlet says she is minded to apply so that she can subvert the idle rich from within. I said as long as it was that, and not rekindling of interest in Hilary Aneurin Bevan Nuamah, formerly ensconced at Pasty Manor helping inbred Cleggs clean toilet and restock freezer with Viennetta, now ensconced

in Fray-Bentos free Magdalene College, studying to become first-ever black Prime Minister. She said *au contraire*, she prefers Oxford as it has produced more politicians by volume, and anyway Hilary is too muscly to stir her vampire-obsessed mojo. She is going for pale and weedy, i.e. malnourished with possible scurvy/rickets, i.e. not Sad Ed, who, while he has potential scurvy due to replacement of oranges in diet with orange-flavoured TicTacs, is far from malnourished. (He has given up on bulimia already. He says it is too hard fitting fat fingers in mouth.) Sad Ed is not applying to Oxford or Cambridge. He says there is no point wasting money on a top-notch education as he will be dead by the time he's twenty-seven. He claims it is mystical age by which time all musical geniuses have written their best work and either die (Jimi Hendrix, Janis Joplin, Jim Morrison) or turn into tedious do-gooders (Bono, Chris Martin). He is going to try for Braintree Art Foundation instead. Am also not applying. Is not because want to die. It is because *a*) they do not do media studies at Cambridge and *b*) even if they did, there is no way I would get in as am not working class ethnic minority who has had to tramp twenty miles to school in freezing snow in order to educate self above lowly birth. Am not even from North. Why, oh why couldn't Mum and Dad be Newcastle Brown-swilling Geordies. Or at very least live in Harrogate. It is so unfair. Being middle class and Southern is utter curse.

· ·

Tuesday 7

Mum says there is no way I am doing media studies as it is a totally made up subject like BSc Golf Course Design and BA Surfing. Dad made fatal error of declaring that he wished he had done golf course design instead of accountancy as then he could be drawing water hazards and hanging out with Tiger Woods instead of spending eight hours a day trying to find out why Malcolm from IT needs twenty-five packets of Post-Its a week. He got despatched immediately from the Shreddies table without a second slice of toast and marmalade as punishment. But it is hollow victory as Dad just went round to Clive's where there is no limit on toast slices, and Nutella. James is fully backing Mum in her made-up subjects proscribed list (also banned: Stage Combat, Homeopathy, and Women's Studies). He says media studies will only qualify me to wear nobbish glasses and take cocaine. At which point he also got despatched, missing out on his second Marmite-on-granary. The dog is jubilant though. It was allowed the confiscated goods as a prize for not eating the wall.

But am now in complete degree subject choice quandary. Cannot do English literature any more as is utterly fiction-based. Nor can I do any of Mum's approved subjects, i.e. medicine, accountancy, or engineering, due to non-boffiny choice of A levels. Plus would rather die than do engineering. It is bad enough having to sit near the mathletes at lunch without voluntarily joining their betank-topped ranks. Maybe will not do degree at all, but will go to university of life instead. Is utter grow-up-fast experience. Will travel war-torn countries and document horrors with naive yet insightful authentic voice of youth. Hurrah!

5 p.m.
Mum says I am not going to the university of life. I am going to an actual university, with halls of residence, on-site canteen, and at least four stars according to the *Times* rankings. And not in London.

Wednesday 8

Told Scarlet and Sad Ed about thwarted university of life dream. Unbelievably Scarlet is on Mum's side. She says it is my duty as an underprivileged state-educated female to claim my rightful place amongst the elite ranks. She said I should be aiming for Durham, Manchester, or the LSE. Pointed out LSE is in London, i.e. banned, due to overinflated rent costs/potential to become crack whore. Scarlet said I can commute from Saffron Walden and live with Suzy, which is almost like being in student housing, due to abundance of incense sticks, marijuana, and cheap sex. Said that would all be over once the new baby arrives. But apparently there is still no news on that front and Suzy is back on the Merlot and funny fags. Sad Ed is more on my side. He says university

is only a back-up plan if his garage band fails to get signed. Said what band? And what garage? He only has a shed. He said is not real one, is virtual Garageband garage band. He is experimenting with a new sound and is confident of being the next Kate Nash. At which point had to vacate Goth Corner as thought of Sad Ed in vintage dress singing about sick on trainers too much to bear.

Anyway, have more pressing matter than the rest of my life. It is Mr Pringle. He has announced that instead of churning out mass-oppressing musicals like *Miss Saigon* or *Cats* (though surely this is cat-oppressing not mass-oppressing) at the end of term, we are going to write our own political documusical. We have to come up with a key historic event for a brainstorm next week. Sad Ed is mental with anticipation. Though pointed out that I do not think the death of Kurt Cobain is necessarily what Mr Pringle is after. Scarlet said since when do you know what Mr Pringle is after? Luckily at that point two Year Sevens started flicking tapioca at each other and she had to go and assert Sad Ed's authority for him. (Sad Ed has tried to do it on his own but he is too slow, and not at all scary. Mostly shoutees just roll eyes at him.) Though do not know why she is getting minty. She is utterly pro older men. Especially political ones. She had a crush on Neil Kinnock for years. Sad Ed said I am wrong and the death of Kurt has changed the course of music history and history history. Plus I could be Courtney Love. Was

swayed for instant as am totally like Courtney Love, i.e. prone to fashion mishaps. But then remembered *a*) am own person and *b*) there is no way would get part anyway as Daisy Devlin has fake tattoos, bigger breasts, and once overdosed on Junior Disprin. Will rack brain, or *Children's Illustrated History of the World*, later for genius idea instead.

8 p.m.
Hurrah. Have narrowed down docudrama suggestion to following (with aid of James, and his trusty companion Google):

- veteran BBC journalist John Simpson invading Afghanistan dressed as woman (has excellent transvestite theme potential)
- Anthrax terrorism scare (thus finding useful role for school sheep, who are renowned for carrying disease)
- infighting in Labour Press Office over giving Gordon Gok Wan style makeover (everyone loves a transformation scene).

Am total documentary fact-based genius. Though possibly not entirely grown-up. As list-making delayed by fight over who got the swivelly chair, plus James insisted on weighing our peanut and raisin mix snack to ensure there was fair division of spoils.

Thursday 9
Yom Kippur

Mum has been dealt a double credit-crunch-related blow.

1. She is still jobless. The police have turned down her application for fast-track detective status. The Inspector Morse dream is over before it has even begun. James says she should fight them on grounds of sexism. But apparently it is not that she is a woman. Just that her demands on flexible working (i.e. she will only work 9–3 in term-time) were too rigid.

2. A For Sale sign has gone up next door. Mum is mental with potential ASBO neighbour panic. She has gone round to Clive and Marjory's to demand a full explanation, and potential withdrawal of sign and moving ambitions.

4.30 p.m.

Mum is back having secured a partial victory. On down side, Marjory has refused Mum's demands to not move. She says Clive's job (have no idea what job is, but possibly something to do with pet food) is in balance, and they are downsizing before they get repossessed, in utter forward-thinking move (which Mum cannot argue with as she is all for forward thinking, and economizing). Sign is also still up. Marjory says it is not a blot on the landscape, or a threat to security, or a distraction to drivers causing potential crashing into low level wall and pea gravel,

which James had listed as bargaining tools. BUT, in ill-thought-out concession, she has agreed to involve Mum in choice of new occupiers. This is fatal. Mum's list of banned neighbours is vast, e.g: anyone from North, anyone with potential to hang Austrian blinds, and anyone vaguely related to an O'Grady. Marjory will be stuck there for ever. James is in agreement. Though he says it will not be because Mum and Marjory are turning the hordes away, it is that at £395,000, the house is vastly overpriced, considering the avocado bathroom suite, the ill-advised carpet in the kitchen, and the lack of all-important stormporch, and that in fact they will be lucky to get any viewings at all in the current climate.

Friday 10

Is my turn to be dealt a double blow. Is not credit crunch related. Is Jesus- and Criminal and Retard- and mathlete-related, i.e.

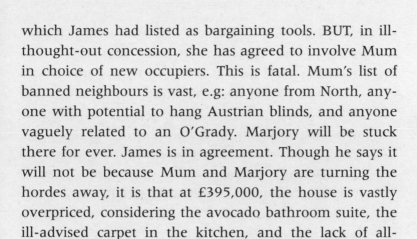

1. Grandpa fell asleep during *Diagnosis Murder*, and forgot to pick Jesus up from the Camilla Parker Bowles Memorial Crèche this afternoon. Fat Kylie tried to ring Mum but Mum does not converse with O'Gradys and put the phone down on principle. So Mr Wilmott nominated me to take Jesus home. Said James was more responsible (official declaration by Mum) but Mr Wilmott said he was well aware of that but James's many talents were needed

elsewhere, i.e. in a crucial chess-off against Burger King Sports Academy. Fat Kylie gave me Jesus's weekly school crèche report to take home. It said 'Weed in Wendy house and hit other child on head with hammer.' I blame Mark Lambert. He is the one who lent Jesus his toolbox.

2. Film Club has been cancelled tonight, i.e. there will be no Pringle-gazing. It is due to a domino effect of catastrophic events, i.e. an unnamed Retard (widely believed to be Kyle O'Grady) tried to overturn authority by gassing Mr Potter (Physics, underarm issues, beard with bits of food in it), i.e. leaving all Bunsen burners on, which meant that A Corridor had to be temporarily sealed off to avoid potential explosion, which meant that One Fenton's double geography lesson had to decamp to Mr Knox's audio-visual suite, but during journey Mad Harry bet Evan Fletcher that he couldn't drink a can of Nutriment in four seconds. He could, thus winning 45p. But bet null and voided after Nutriment made reappearance on audio-visual suite carpet five minutes later, which meant that library had to be sealed off until tomorrow to avoid vomit-smell moaning.

4.30 p.m.
I mean discussion of brain-stimulating cinematic experience. Not Pringle-gazing. Obviously. Though as didn't happen, doesn't matter. No one will know.

4.45 p.m.
Just got text from Scarlet. It says 'No Pringle gazing 4 U'. How does she do it? It is the throne of Davros. It is imbuing her with weird Dalek-like powers. And laziness. She actually used it to navigate beans queue at lunchtime. She will be commuting on it next.

Saturday 11
Hurrah. Have achieved older man cancelling karma, i.e. Mr Wandering Hands cannot do driving lesson today. According to Mrs Wandering Hands (who knew??), he has sustained a repetitive strain gear-knob-related injury. Dad says it is more likely a Mrs Wandering Hands wandering hands-related injury. Then Mum got all het up and said it was like talking ill of Jesus (churchy one, not uncle. She is all for talking ill of that one), and at least Mike took an interest in his physical health. But James pointed out that *a*) Mum is an atheist therefore Jesus is no more than a fictional construct; *b*) gear knob RSI is utterly made up, according to Google; and *c*) Mr Wandering Hands has previous. At which point Mum stormed upstairs with the Beastly binoculars to keep an eye on viewings next door. She is probably just minty about finding out there is a Mrs Wandering Hands. It has ruined her hopes of being driven off into sunset in an X-reg Fiesta. She is still trying to reduce Dad's calorie intake. He is only allowed one almond slice at teatime and no sugar on his Shreddies.

He says it is worse than wartime rationing. James pointed out that rationing ended in 1953, i.e. a full eleven years before Dad was born. But Dad said he meant the Falklands, when Grandma Riley got stingy with the corned beef in case Argentina stopped exporting cattle.

5 p.m.
James is jubilant with his real estate assessment, i.e. there have been no viewings at Clive and Marjory's. There was a near panic when Les Brewster and Ying showed up, but through cunning deduction (i.e. James being sent over to borrow cup of flour (wholemeal, i.e. utterly plausible, although Mum running out of anything not at all plausible)) it turns out they were buying a second-hand abdominizer (Marjory also selling off random household goods in financial crisis averting move). But Mum not so jubilant as is annoyed at bargain-missing potential as abdominizer could have been answer to Dad's stomach issues.

Thank God have got welcoming refuge of Duke to escape to. Is utter grown-up activity, i.e. sink sorrows in pint (of diet Coke) and relate family-based woes to world weary but sympathetic regulars.

11 p.m.
Or place bets on how many bottles of Pale Ale Kev's dog can drink before it falls off stool (answer five).

Sunday 12

Have remembered have appointment with destiny tomorrow, aka careers counsellor 'Bonkers' Batty (long hair, adult onset acne, obsession with obscure German heavy-metal bands). James says is like psychometric testing, i.e. they will delve into the murky depths of my personality to see if I am geared to working with people or should stick to hermit-like shelf-stacking menial labour. It sounds excellent, like diary room in *Big Brother*. Oooh. Maybe will find out am utterly meant to be tragic poetess like Sylvia Plath.

8 p.m.
Or fact-based Christiane Amanpour newshound type.

Monday 13

Careers meeting not at all like psychometric delving into personality nor in *Big Brother* diary room style mentalist suite. Was crap multiple choice questionnaire in library (now free of vomit smell—must find out recipe to pass on to Bob for sick-smelling Volvo), i.e. surrounded by Year Sevens trying to look up 'knob' in OED.

Plus, according to results, am not tragic poetess or newshound. In fact am ideally suited to being 'data processor', which have no idea what is, but sounds crap. Said test was utterly wrong. Bonkers Batty said Carol Ann Duffy and Christiane Amanpour not on listed options and

171

test is never wrong, is infallible judgement of character. Made him take test. It told him to be a careers adviser or premier league footballer. He said see, is accurate, except that test does not know about his rheumatoid arthritis. Said, whatever, there is no way am being a data processor, as despite having no idea what it is, it is obviously pants. Bonkers said maybe I should consider having a gap year until have made up mind about future. I said I would, except gap years are banned in our house due to risk of: *a*) catching dysentery, *b*) being sucked into cult by yogic guru/Operation Raleigh leader, and *c*) getting overused to amassing wealth from temp jobs and refusing to return to studies. And fish up penises (not on Mum's list, but will suggest it as amendment).

Scarlet got 'civil servant'. She is citing it as further evidence of her government potential on her Cambridge application. Said did not think the dons would be persuaded by the equivalent of a *Cosmo* sex quiz (question example: Do you prefer working with *a*) your hands, *b*) your brain *c*) children). But she says *au contraire* it is world-respected accurate test, and I would do well to consider its conclusions on my own potential.

Sad Ed is on my side. He got 'fisherman' (is because he said he likes gloom and solitude, and is not scared of dying). But he also found out twenty-four words for penis (Mad Harry, James, and the OED), so he says it is not entirely a wasted afternoon.

Tuesday 14

Grandpa Clegg has rung. There is devastating news from Pasty Manor. It is not that Granny has remembered she is progressive non-racist type, it is that Bruce has had a fight with Pig over a leftover chipolata and the neighbours are complaining about the barking (both Bruce and Pig, who claims he can 'talk to the animals'). Apparently Granny says one of them is going to have to move out. I said *a*) did not know Pig was permanent resident, *b*) if he is, who is looking after the pigs, and *c*) since when had Pig taken precedence over Bruce in Granny's affections. Grandpa said *a*) semi-permanent, i.e. he sleeps on broken Parker Knoll when *CSI* is on as he can't get reception on the farm, *b*) Mrs Pig (who knew!), and *c*) since Bruce took a dislike to Eamonn Holmes. Put the phone down. There is no way anyone can solve such an idiotic conundrum.

6 p.m.

Unless it is weird boffin boy James Riley. He has drawn up infallible mathematic equation that proves it is Pig who has to move out. He is ringing Grandpa with the joyous news as we speak.

6.15 p.m.

Equation redundant as condundrum already solved. Bruce is apparently taken with Dr Doolittle barking, or possibly hairy face and essence de pig, and is treating him as new leader of house. Granny says she does not mind as

Pig is in her thrall anyway so she is still in actual charge of them, and Grandpa does not mind because he is in charge of Granny, due to mere dint of owning a penis, so he is actual top dog. Is sorry state of affairs when top dog is a man who has Hammerited own face and thinks Cold War was fought with ice throwers.

. . . .

Wednesday 15

Mr Wilmott is jubilant. He has a record fourteen applications for Oxbridge including Scarlet, Alan Wong (son of sadistic dentist Mrs Wong, Mars Bar habit, rumoured to be in triads), and at least four Criminals and Retards. He says it shows how times are changing and positive attitudes to comprehensive pupils are encouraging high-flying academic ambitions. It is not that. It is because everyone who applies gets next Wednesday morning off to watch *Chariots of Fire* to introduce them to world of boffiny elite. Am unmoved by academic ambitions though. What is high-flying about moving thirteen miles up road. Or to Oxford, which is basically Cambridge, but with Inspector Morse location tours. Am thinking instead will form guerrilla (not gorilla) theatre troupe and travel bombed-out cities performing life-changing fact-based political drama. Have submitted all my ideas to Mr Pringle. Think he was utterly impressed by breadth of my fact-based (i.e. Wikipedia-based) knowledge. Though he did point out that John Simpson one was potentially

libellous (had changed character slightly to make him evil Western warlord). It is still better idea than Sad Ed or Reuben Tull though. Sad Ed is still clinging to his Kurt Cobain dream (despite being a foot too short and four stone too heavy to in any way play him convincingly). And Reuben Tull wanted to recreate Woodstock including hiring the Rolling Stones and making the audience take mind-altering drugs. He is moron. Anyway, Mr Pringle is announcing the result next Wednesday and we start rehearsing straight away. Hurrah.

Thursday 16

There is further proof that going out with older man is way forward. It is Madonna who is divorcing pseudo-cockney toy boy Guy Ritchie. According to Grandpa Riley (who got news from *Heat* Online—number three most popular website at Twilight Years Day Centre, after Times Obituaries and Viagra shop) she needs to focus her sights on someone at least ten years older, who will appreciate her dedication to leotards, instead of realizing she is rad-dled old has-been. Is true. Look at him and Treena. There is forty-something-year age gap and they still do it twice a week and extra on Saturdays if Treena has been watching *X Factor*. (It is not Simon Cowell. It is midget impresario Louis Walsh. Treena says he makes her 'go funny down there'. Said Ick.) Will refocus sights on Mr Pringle tomor-row night in film club. We are watching *The Doors* starring

Batman as Jim Morrison and Meg Ryan as a groupie with bad wig. Sad Ed is mental with anticipation. He says he is thinking of resubmitting a stage version for our play. Pointed out that *a*) Jim Morrison spent most of his life wandering around semi-naked and did he really want to expose his manboobs to the Year Nine Criminals and Retards, and *b*) on the subject of fighting the flab, what has happened to his vampiric ambitions as have seen him eat four Twix fingers and a packet of Monster Munch Flamin' Hot in less than an hour. Sad Ed said it is comfort eating. Scarlet's demands as Chief of Staff are getting absurd. She wants him to demand funding for lesbian and gay caucus minibus to ferry anyone afeared of discrimination around in comfort and safety. (She is mental. There is no way she will secure backing from head girl Thin Kylie, who is anti-all things lezzer, let alone Mr Wilmott.) Plus, according to minigoth Harriet Pucklechurch, who got it off Melody Bean, former head goth and lover of Scarlet Trevor Pledger is on verge of breaking up with Tamsin Bacon. Melody says they had a row outside the Co-Op about badminton being anti-goth due to white clothing requirement and she has given him his rat back (Hedges, inferior in every way to Benson, according to Scarlet). Sad Ed says it will be all over for him the minute she gets a whiff of Trevor's patchouli-ingrained vegetarian leather coat. I said to be fair, it had never really begun. Sad Ed sighed and unwrapped a Chomp bar.

Friday 17

Sad Ed is right about Scarlet. Mr Pringle had to shush her four times during *The Doors* due to her comparing Trevor favourably to Batman in terms of hair, nipples, and the way he leans on stuff. I told him is because Trevor is older man and it is the way of nature for me and her to pursue grown-ups. Sad Ed said he was utter older man. I said twenty days does not count, especially when backed up by evidence of childness, i.e. fact that he broke another spring on saggy sofa at lunch when he attempted to use as trampoline to reach the legendary flump that has been stuck on ceiling since 2002. Sad Ed said was not childishness, was rite of passage John Major tradition, i.e. totally grown-up older man. Then Scarlet overheard and demanded to know what was discussion about older men? I said is nothing. Just that older man is utterly way forward for fact-based grown-up style relationship etc. Scarlet said is true, plus they have cars and are better at finding G spot. At which point Mr Pringle demanded to know what was conversation about so we said trade unions and went back to concentrating on film, and eating Sad Ed's Revels (stealth chocolates, i.e. you think you have delicious Malteser but turns out to be ickky orange thing).

Saturday 18

2 p.m.

Something fishy is going on next door. There is a man in

a pinstripe suit with scary hair and a clipboard peering through Marjory's letterbox. Mum has got the Beastly binoculars out and is keeping an eye in case he is a burglar or a Mormon. The dog is also keeping an eye. (Although not with binoculars. It cannot control the focus bit. It is just staring menacingly out of the window.) It is its aversion to spookily helmet-like hairdos (Natasha Kaplinsky, Moira Stewart, Mrs Noakes. Even Granny Clegg has to be careful when she has a wash and set.) Dad says we are all overreacting and it is probably just a Cable TV salesman. James said they are more persuasive than the Mormons so the vigil was doubly necessary. Dad rolled eyes and and went back to putting golf balls into Nescafé jar. He should be happy. At least Mum is focusing her binoculars, and attentions, on potential criminals/religious fanatics, rather than Mr Wandering Hands. He was visibly disappointed at the lack of spying he got when he dropped me off.

2.15 p.m.
All signs point to helmet hair man being burglar. He has been joined on doorstep by Mrs O'Grady and several smaller O'Gradys. Mum is thinking of calling the police. Have pointed out that if they are planning burglary then they are not being very surreptitious, i.e. *a*) they are at front of house in full view of passers-by and the Beastly binoculars, *b*) since when do burglars wear pinstripe suits, and *c*) they have brought Whitney, who will surely only

be a hindrance in any crime situation. James says, *au contraire, a*) it is a cunning deceptive tactic to throw us off the scent and as we speak one of the Liams is probably shinning up a drainpipe and jimmying open Marjory's bathroom window, *b*) it might be a banker forced to turn to crime in the current economic climate, and *c*) Whitney is ideally suited to crime, they can funnel her into crevices and down chimneys and then she can undo doors from inside. Said he is mental. Plus Marjory has just opened the front door and let them all in, so either she is expecting them, or she is an accomplice in the crime, which is unlikely given her militant pro-*NYPD Blue* tendencies. James said possibly she is committing massive insurance fraud to avoid having to downsize and sell house.

2.45 p.m.
Marjory has just been over. Is not insurance fraud. Is bigger crime, i.e. potentially selling the house to the O'Gradys! Mum is mental with ASBO panic. She said it is bad enough having the Britchers opposite with their kidney-shaped pool (banned) and Union Jack flag (banned) but now it is as if *The Sopranos* are moving in as well. Pointed out that Mum had never seen *The Sopranos*, due to her own vigorous controls, and that if she had, she would know that comparing Mrs O'Grady to Carmela Soprano is like claiming Granny Clegg is Helen Mirren. Or so I had been told, as had obviously never seen it due to it being banned (did not mention *Sopranos* marathon

179

with Jack last year). Mum eyed me with suspicion but was too busy panicking with O'Grady menace to dole out punishment. Marjory says it is unlikely they will be able to afford it anyway, given their no jobs and penchant for gas-guzzling 4x4s. But James said they probably had a million stashed away in the microwave in used notes. He has been watching too much *Lovejoy*. Besides, there is no way they would keep it in microwave, it is only source of hot food.

. . . .

Sunday 19

Shreddies table was utter war zone this morning. Mum is still seething over anticipated O'Grady invasion, which is having detrimental effect on rest of house in terms of shoutiness. Dog got two for walking into door and licking genitals at mealtime, Dad got one for saying word 'genitals' at mealtime, and I got a stern talking to for cross-contamination of Marmite and marmalade. Only James remains shout-free. It is because he is in agreement with Mum. He says it is the beginning of the end for his 'manor'. Said *a*) he had said that about Thin Kylie and *b*) he is not Guy Ritchie, so please stop talking like a twit. He said *a*) Britchers are breeze compared to seasoned menaces the O'Gradys and *b*) the mathletes are adopting a 'street talk' stance in attempt to overhaul their public image and boost ranks. They are also going to be adopting a new look, which he will be unveiling tomorrow.

Said *a*) he was, officially, friends with foremost O'Grady menace Keanu, first toughest in the juniors, so he should be welcoming them to his 'manor' and *b*) please don't let it be waistcoats or cravats or will have to utterly disown him. He said, *a*) he may admire Keanu's skills as gang member, but he does not want a Daihatsu with a 'Honk if You're Horny' sticker miring Summerdale Road in chavdom and *b*) it is not cravats, it is much more ambitious and manly.

Monday 20
7.30 a.m.
Oh my God. James has revealed new look. Is not manly. Is moronic, i.e. is trousers halfway down bottom, revealing underpants (Marks & Spencer), tie undone, and back to front baseball cap (Mole Hall Wildlife Park) on abundantly gelled hair. He was right on one count though, i.e. is utterly ambitious. He is mental if he thinks he is going to get that past Mum.

7.35 a.m.
As predicted, James has been sent to his room to *a*) change and *b*) reflect on his use of the word 'ho' when referring to Mum, or indeed any woman. James said it's not his fault if the 'old lady is wigging about the 'hood'. Told him to quit while he was ahead, i.e. he may have lost the baseball cap and gel but he can pull his trousers down

as soon as he gets to school. Although, would not recommend it as it is tantamount to open invitation to get wedgied by a Criminal and Retard. He said, 'Props, blud.' He is idiot.

5 p.m.
Mum is in buoyant mood. It is the O'Gradys. They are not moving into Clive and Marjory's. Apparently the avocado suite is too 'minging'. Marjory is not so jubilant. It is having her interior design shunned by someone who wears velour. Personally I am with the O'Gradys. Green toilets are just wrong.

Also Mum has demanded to know why James is walking 'like he did the time he had a poo incident on the M5'. James says he sustained minor bruising from a rogue hacky sack in PE. He did not. He got three wedgies, and an 'up and over' (pants stretched to reach head—speciality of Criminals and Retards) in first break. Mad Harry got off worse. He had to see Mrs Leech for some Savlon and a glass of medicinal lemon barley. He is having difficulty sitting down at all.

Tuesday 21
8 a.m.
James's trousers are firmly back where they belong, i.e. covering his buttocks, with no visible wedgie targets. He says he is limiting his streetwise style to language only,

and then promptly got sent back upstairs for calling the dog a 'beeyatch', which is not only rude, but inaccurate. He also called Dad a 'dawg', which may be rude, but is at least genitally-correct. Dad took it as compliment anyway. They are both idiots. There is no way a man in a vest and Hush Puppies and reading the *Telegraph* is in any way 'dawg'-like. Mum is preparing herself for a summit meeting at Marjory's to discuss the housing crisis, i.e. the potential sale of Number 22 to unsavoury characters. She says she cannot be expected to live the next God knows how many months in perpetual fear that she is going to wake up to find Barry the Blade waving at her over the fence. Said that was unlikely given that Barry the Blade lives in an Austin Allegro, so his next step up the ladder is likely to be a Montego estate, not a four-bed detached with decking and a breakfast bar.

5 p.m.
Mum is utterly not jubilant. She says Marjory is unwilling to embrace change and move with the times. Said this was odd, as Mum is usually pro not moving with times, e.g. when Jif changed its name to Cif, when they turned Milky Ways white inside, and when Blue Peter stopped making Advent crowns in favour of hosting cheerleading displays. Mum said, *au contraire*, she is thoroughly modern, and cited acceptance of dark chocolate as potential health food, purchase of non-tapered trousers, and embracing of John Humphrys as Magnus Magnusson

183

replacement on *Mastermind* as proof. Did not retaliate, though have plenty of ammunition, as wanted to know what hoo-ha was about. It is that Mum had come up with genius scheme to avoid potential moving horror, i.e. renting out Marjory's spare rooms (two, as despite having four bedrooms, she and Clive have separate beds due to 'snoring issues', i.e. Clive's according to Marjory and Marjory's according to Clive). But Marjory says taking in a lodger is like inviting reclusive pervert into the house and they will be rifling your undies and eating all your HobNobs before the rent cheque has cleared. Marjory watches too much ITV. But, it is I who am (are/is?) genius, as pointed out that Mum could use own idea to avoid impending credit crunch crisis at Number 24, and save herself finding job (she has been rejected by Barclays, Saffron Walden Building Society, and, controversially, which cannot even begin to go into, Wainwright and Beacham in last few days). Mum says she is going to mull it over with Dad, i.e. tell him that she is doing it, and then ignore his objections. Is brilliant. Having a lodger is excellent for broadening minds and horizons, e.g. Humbert Humbert in *Lolita*, who is very much older man.

5.15 p.m.
And fictional.

5.20 p.m.
And potential pant-sniffing pervert. But still, it is good

idea. Oooh. Could lure Mr Pringle away from Chestnuts B&B. We have much more hygienic toilet facilities (i.e. Mum does not have bikini-line trimmer, let alone leave it on edge of sink). Although am not sure he could cope with the proscribed items list. Would be excellent to be in same house though. Then he could see how am utterly fact-based and grown-up. Think he may well be falling for my charms already. Bumped into him at fruit and nut dispensing machine at last break (or rather, had followed him down two corridors, using Sad Ed as visibility protection) and he said I would like the play announcement tomorrow. So he must have gone for my Gordon Brown makeover idea. Hurrah!

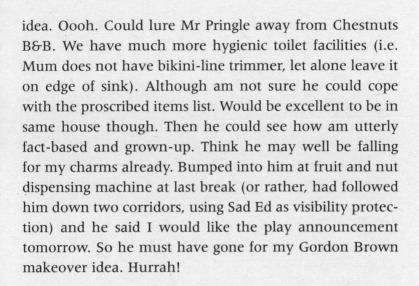

Wednesday 22
4 p.m.
Play is not Gok Wan Prime Ministerial makeover. Or John Simpson thing. But is better. It is *Secret Diary of Anne Frank—the Musical!* Which was no one's idea, but Mr Pringle said trying to re-enact the taking of Kabul in the lower school canteen would have proved problematic. Whereas this is smaller in actual scale, but bigger in metaphorical scale, i.e. is not just about Jews in hiding in a few rooms in Amsterdam, but about persecuted minorities everywhere, i.e. like me on my bed protest! I am totally Anne Frank! Caris Kelp (eats glue) says in fact she is Anne Frank, as she has been to Holland. But I

185

have hair like Barbra streisand, i.e. unmanageable. Plus, more importantly, I am diary-keeping, fact-based, sexual-awakening teenage prodigy type. Hurrah! As long as Sad Ed does not get cast as Peter. I am a good actress but faking sexual interest in him would be impossible. Anyway, is unlikely as his five a day (Mars bars, not fruit) diet is conducive to looking neither like a vampire, nor a ghettoized Jewish boy subsisting on cabbage soup and hope. Mr Pringle says at this stage no one is anyone, and we just need to read the book and get into the mindset of being effectively imprisoned. But I definitely saw him look meaningfully at me at that point.

4.15 p.m.
Unless he has lazy eye like Dr Braithwaite (huge hands, bottle of whisky in drawer) and was actually looking meaningfully at Reuben Tull in bid to stop him air drumming to theme from *Big Barn Farm*. Anyway, does not matter as am going to subsume self into book at half term so that Anne Frank's very aura transwhatevers into me then he will have no choice but to cast me.

Thursday 23
There has been another Jesus-related incident at school. He, and all other inmates of the Camilla Parker Bowles Memorial Crèche, have been banned from the school farm. According to Sad Ed, who got it off Mrs Leech,

Cowpat Cheesmond says the sheep have not been so terrified since the Criminals and Retards (yes, he did use that phrase, though is rich, considering his own swarthy and slightly backwoods tendencies) were allowed to try sheep shearing. It is Fat Kylie's fault. She was supposed to be supervising them, i.e. keeping them behind the fence at all times and ensuring sheep were only fed health-giving pellets. She said it is not her fault she is 'allergic to sheep shite', or that Whitney had concealed a packet of Hubba Bubba in her pull-up pants.

10 p.m.
Oh my God. I AM Anne Frank. Not only is she philosophical and poetic. But her mother is irritating stickler for rules! Oh, cannot wait for ending. Hope it is tension-fuelled *Sound of Music*-style night flit to Edelweiss studded green hills of neutral territory like Austria or Belgium. Or Isle of Man.

* * *

Friday 24
Last day of school

Scarlet says I am not Anne Frank, I am Rachel Riley. Not least because *a*) I am NOT Jewish. I just have crap hair, *b*) I have never been persecuted, and *c*) consistently painting oneself as fictional construct is not at all helpful mental-health- or Jack-wise. Said *a*) hair is not crap and she is utter anti-Semite for saying so, *b*) I live under

restrictive regime that makes Taliban look lenient, *c* i) Anne Frank is not a fictional fairytale construct but is actual dead real person, so conforms to all rules, not that there are any, and why does she care because she doesn't want me to go out with Jack anyway, and *c* ii) that's rich coming from someone who claims to be the lover of a fictional 106-year-old vampire (i.e. older man but with lithe body of youth, so best of all worlds, according to Scarlet). Then she whizzed menacingly round the table at me on the Davros chair so did not say anything else as she was armed with pot of Petit Filous, which is not only stain-making, but substandard apricot flavour. She is obviously not taking news that Bob and Suzy have passed all their tests to become adoptive parents as well as thought. It is utter miracle though. I bet they did not disclose the time they accidentally left Scarlet aged three in the John Lewis car park for four hours while they tested mattresses. Or the time Jack ingested an entire packet of Suzy's contraceptive pills and grew temporary breasts. Although there is downside to joy. They are not allowed to adopt a black baby. Mr Lemon is insisting that it is not culturally beneficial to either party. Suzy says it is utterly racist, and that they will happily adopt customs and native dress if necessary. Mr Lemon said that was utterly racist and then they got into a tit for tat 'who is more PC' fight, won marginally by Suzy for knowing Martin Luther King's 'I have a Dream' speech by heart. Anyway, they are not getting a black, or brown, or Chinese baby. They

are getting a much more whitish one, if and when one shows up.

11 p.m.
Have finished *Anne Frank*. And am somewhat disappointed by downbeat gritty non-fairytale ending. But that is reality for you—no snogging in flower-filled meadows, no making snow angels, and no comedy airport dashes. Maybe will persuade Mr Pringle to do alternative finale, involving Anne single-handedly overpowering Nazis and escaping with Peter to America where they become world famous literary commentators and also invent fat-free mayonnaise.

Saturday 25

A blow has been struck to general grown-upness. It is Mum (as usual). She has decided that going to pub regularly is potentially life-destroying and that I will end up with shaky arms, thousand yard stare, and compromised complexion of alcoholic if I do not tackle my addiction. Have pointed out that so far only addiction is Sad Ed's to Cheese Moments, which, though junk food, do contain calcium, so are not at all as lethal or chav-based as Wotsits. Mum says *a*) The only permissable pub-based snack is protein-rich cashew nuts (unsalted, unroasted), and *b*) she is no longer funding my sordid lifestyle through pocket money. Said *a*) What about Twiglets

189

(Marmitey so with folic acid) and *b*) yet you are content to fund James's penchant for Warhammer crap? She said *a*) Absolutely not, as Marmite level minimal and outweighed by preservative content, and *b*) that is entirely different, as Warhammer is mind-expanding and encourages concentration and is thus good for his chess. Was about to argue that in fact just creates unemployable nerds with no social skills and bad facial hair but then the dog managed to turn the Magimix on and whizzed eggs all over the ceiling, thus ending conversation.

It is utterly unfair. Going to the pub is mind-expanding (and stomach-expanding in Sad Ed's case). For instance, where else would I have learnt the ingredients of a Mudslide (anything, according to Shorty, including cherry-ade and Malibu, as the Baileys overpowers everything else), or the words to 'Crystal Chandelier'? Will just have to economize, e.g. no more Frazzles and tap water instead of lime and soda. Will still be excellent night.

11.30 p.m.
Have had utterly pants night, i.e. have been downgraded to leaning on toilet door or hovering on sticky carpet. It is gangly landlord Shorty. He says we cannot have custody of the sought-after wobbly table if all we are going to consume is a pint of cider, a Britvic, and some tap water. It is Sad Ed's fault for deciding to revive his vampiric diet. Otherwise we could have guaranteed at least £7.70 on Cheese Moments. Scarlet pointed out that he was being

anti-poverty, i.e. classist. But he said he was not being classist, he was being an economist. And Scarlet couldn't argue with that as it is uber-political. We are going to think of money-raising schemes instead so that we can oust Reuben Tull (drug dealer, so flush) and his enormous-haired cohorts from their new-found table of glory. I did suggest joining forces but Sad Ed takes up too much seat room and there is no way I am sitting on Reuben's lap. Scarlet says Shorty will get bored with them soon because they clog up the jukebox with Pink Floyd, which is not at all conducive to selling Bacardi Breezer, and it is statistically proven that Phil Collins encourages far greater alcohol consumption. Is possibly true. As would personally only suffer Phil Collins if was heinously drunk.

Sunday 26
British Summer Time ends

Mum is going mental with Russell Brand prank phonecall hoo-ha. She is very much anti-Russell Brand already, on grounds of height of hair, tightness of trousers, and indiscriminate nature of penis. But now he has apparently gone too far by insulting her favourite comedy racist Spanish waiter actor. She is writing to the BBC to demand an immediate ban on Russell and Jonathan Ross, who is also very much proscribed due to outlandish suits, large-breasted wife, and speech impediments. Mum does

not believe anyone with a speech impediment should be in position of public broadcasting, including a stutter, lisp, or Birmingham accent.

Have retired to bedroom to escape idiotic discussion and immerse self in *Diary of Anne Frank*. Oh how our lives intermingle. She reads great literature, I read great literature (or at least I did until became fact-based). She hates dentists, I hate dentists. It is like she is reincarnated in me.

3 p.m.
Ooh. Maybe she is reincarnated in me! Which would mean I AM Anne Frank, not Rachel Riley after all!

3.15 p.m.
James says she is not reincarnated in me. If anyone is reincarnated in me it is a plague-ridden haggle-toothed gypsy. Asked who was reincarnated in him. He said Nelson. Said Nelson Mandela not dead. He said Lord not Mandela, which is further evidence of why no one uber-intelligent is camping out in my body. He is wrong. Even if Anne Frank not in me, am still utterly at one with her plight.

4 p.m.
James has persuaded Mum to add Noel Fielding to her BBC ban demand letter, citing scary eyes, overlarge teeth, and revealingness of catsuits. Have told them that they are not to trouble me with such trivia any more, as am

persecuted Jew with deeper concerns than the petty-minded flippant whines of the overprivileged. Honestly. They do not know they are born.

5 p.m.
Oooh. Have had genius character-building fact-based idea. Am going to annexe self off from rest of world, and subsist on meagre rations, my diary, and an occasional news update from my helpers, i.e. James and dog. Although dog potentially not great source of news. But will be comfort in my incarceration.

5.15 p.m.
Unless it has criminal wind. I do not know why Mum persists in giving it health-giving vegetables. They are not at all good for health of anyone else within twenty-metre radius. Anyway. Is definite. Am going into hiding. Have instructed Mum that am only to be allowed war-based food from now on, which is to be brought to my room, in secret, by a sympathizer, i.e. James. Although he is not utterly sympathetic, i.e. he said am mental, but he is best I can do as dog cannot carry tray (James has tested this in past, it ended in Rice Krispy spillage and a level two shouting). Mum says I will not last past *Watchdog* tomorrow night. She is wrong. I am iron-willed in my determination to evade my Nazi persecutors. Plus *Watchdog* isn't on because of the snooker.

193

Monday 27

Half term

10 a.m.

Hurrah. It is Day One of Anne Frank annexation. Have consumed two bowls of Shreddies and stood in garden for ten minutes to boost Vitamin D levels in preparation. And am now back in room with diary and jug of tap water. Is utterly war-like. Except for possibly Chris Moyles's breakfast show (even Anne Frank had radio).

10.15 a.m.

And *Heatworld*. Was present from Grandpa Riley to sustain me in hour of need. Though have finished already. There is only so long you can look at Calum Best without gagging.

1 p.m.

Mum is wrong. There is no way am going to cave. Besides, is easier than bed protest as am allowed to use bathroom. Although will not flush toilet for authenticity. James is taking role very seriously. He has brought cottage cheese on jacket potato for lunch, which is not cabbage soup, but is still war-like in blandness. Plus he has reviving news of the outside world, i.e. Mum has made new clothes for naked Will Young out of old Action Man outfit, although now he looks like Prince William; Beefy (postman, dyslexic, notorious gossip) says Mr Patel got red gas bill (so obviously porn, junk food, and nicotine

patch empire not as lucrative as thought) plus Mad Harry has worms.

He is sending Mouchi, i.e. the dog, up later for some pet therapy. Plus he is going to test my ability to move about the house undetected by the Nazi enemy (i.e. Mum).

3.30 p.m.
Have sent Mouchi back whence it came. Watching it trying to eat piece of gum entangled in paw fur is not at all therapeutic. Am going to attempt surreptitious foray to kitchen in minute to secure rich tea biscuit (utterly povvy and warlike).

3.40 p.m.
Have failed foray test. James sprang out on me from under table and issued yellow card (actual yellow card, embossed with swastika). He says I will have to forego snack as punishment, and await austerity dinner instead.

5 p.m.
Am starving. Thank God is tea in half an hour. Maybe will be celebratory war-like casserole.

6 p.m.
Was not celebratory casserole. Was authentic dried bean soup. Mum is trying to flush me out with meanness. It will not work. She underestimates my Jewish resolve.

8 p.m.

Am going to sleep. James has issued authentic lights out warning. And cannot listen to any more Radio One as it is making nerves jangly. Being Anne Frank not as much fun as thought. Am starving and bored. Plus do not even have love interest to moon over. Sad Ed did offer but there is no way I am being incarcerated with his depression, or bowels, for any length of time.

Tuesday 28

10 a.m.

A new day dawns in the ghetto, and, despite my peril and persecution, am revived in my optimism for life. Plus got Edam sandwich for breakfast, on grounds that it is Dutch. Have made resolution to stop complaining and utilize time wisely, i.e. do homework.

11 a.m.

Cannot do homework in ghetto as am plagued by sound of *a*) stomach that is used to at least a bowl of Shreddies, a piece of granary toast and Marmite, and several rich teas by this time, and *b*) James and Mad Harry who are combining Beastly Boys and Beastly Investigations by singing 'The Lion Sleeps Tonight' on the landing, complete with dog howling the chorus bit. I bet Anne Frank didn't have to put up with this sort of hoo-ha.

1 p.m.
Have eaten lunch. Four crackers (dry) and an apple with a brown bit. Ate brown bit despite maggot potential. Think need protein as can feel muscles depleting.

3 p.m.
Have failed yet again in foray test. Was trying to liberate cheese (Edam, so legal) from fridge while Hitler, i.e. Mum, safely replenishing slug traps in garden but Mussolini, aka Mad Harry, had installed himself inside boiler cupboard and burst out, causing me to hit head on fridge door and sustain medium to severe bruising. Plus cheese confiscated.

8 p.m.
Another day closes. Feel like have been locked up for months. Maybe it will get easier. Deprivation will become second nature and I will be unable to rehabilitate into outside world, like lifers when they are released from Broadmoor. Hurrah.

. . . .

Wednesday 29
9 a.m.
Uggh. Deprivation is not any easier. Cannot be expected to survive on Edam and crackers. Only thing keeping me going now is prospect of visit from James. He is my Miep, bringing hope, joy, and digestive biscuits.

11 a.m.

Was not digestive. Was oatcake. Which is not biscuit at all but sliver of savoury concrete. Plus news from outside world is not at all hope-imbuing, i.e. Mum is bulk-soaking dried beans, Granny Clegg has rung to say Pig has got hand stuck in jar trying to retrieve liquorice allsort, and the dog has attacked Mad Harry which is utterly like when lions turn on their tamers. It is not, it is like when crocodiles eat annoying morons who jump into their zoo enclosures. Mad Harry is always pestering the dog.

James has brought me more fact-based reading though, as have exhausted the *Children's Illustrated Encyclopaedia* and the Penguin *Guide to Punctuation* (there is nothing I do not know about semi-colons now). It is Mum's hypochondriac's bible aka Dr Le Fanu's *Book of Family Health*.

7 p.m.

Am dangerously ill. Have looked in mirror and have definite look of concentration camp. Have checked symptoms and have narrowed it down to:

- Hepatitis B
- Yellow fever
- Bird flu (sparrows on windowsill looking bit sickly and may have sent germs through glass by osmosis)

Death is imminent. So am recording poignant, yet mysterious, last words for immortality.

198

7.15 p.m.
Cannot think of anything mysterious. Plus need a poo.

7.16 p.m.
But what if die on loo. Cannot have 'need a poo' as last words. Oooh. Will borrow meaningful phrase instead.

7.20 p.m.
Aha. Have got it. 'The World Is Not Enough'. Is utterly mysterious and deep. Cannot remember where comes from though.

7.30 p.m.
Did not die mid-poo. Which is lucky as have remembered it is name of James Bond film and not even good one as has Pierce Brosnan in who is neither retro cool (Sean Connery) nor postmodern macho (Daniel Craig). Is just Mr Wandering Hands with better hair and weird accent.

Am retiring to deathbed now, with following, final words: *No one understands me.*

. . . .

Thursday 30

10 a.m.
Am not dead. But wish was. Was not Edam for breakfast. Was authentic soused herrings. Feel sick now. That will teach Mum for trying to break me with pickled fish as

cannot flush sick away, thus breaking all sorts of cross-contamination rules.

3 p.m.
There has been reviving news from the free world. It is Mum. According to James she is mental with anticipation as her lodger advert is in the *Walden Chronicle*. Have begged him to bring me contraband newspaper to see joyous news for myself.

4 p.m.
Have read joyous news. And am less joyous. Advert says:

WANTED

Non-smoking, non-drinking, drug-free professional tenant to join our clean and comfortable household. Must uphold high levels of tidiness and hygiene and be dog-friendly. £70 a week, bills included. References, CRB check, and credit rating required.

She will not get any replies. Plus it is unfair as Mum is not at all friendly to the dog herself—I have heard her shout at it three times today for something to do with the washing machine temperature knob.

4.05 p.m.
Miep, i.e. James, says, *au contraire*, there have been two calls already and I am under strict instructions that this Anne Frank nonsense is to end by tea tomorrow as Mum does not want any potential tenants thinking she has a mentally deficient child on the premises as they could demand a rent reduction. Apparently James and Mum are showing them round on Sunday, when they will undergo a thirty-minute interview and written test. Is utter farce. No one will pass test as it is bound to include trick questions about Jif, and James's notorious general knowledge round. I am unmoved. Anyone moving to 24 Summerdale Road will have to take me as I am—i.e. fact-based, politically committed and utterly grown-up.

4.10 p.m.
And also demented looking. It is the lack of sunlight. I tried sticking my head out of the bathroom window to soak up essential rays but Beastly Investigations, i.e. Miep and Mad Harry, were busy in the side return and issued a red card and three-match ban. They are morons.

. . . .

Friday 31
Hallowe'en
10 a.m.
Breakfast has been reduced to oatcakes and margarine. Miep says enemy forces have commandeered the ghetto

food supplies. They have not. It is Mum employing CIA tactics to get me to give myself up to the occupying forces. But I am strong. My Jewish resolve will not falter.

2 p.m.
The toilet roll is missing. Have had to use several pages of Dr Le Fanu instead (concussion, conjunctivitis, and constipation, *quelle* irony). I do not mind. I am hardened to adverse conditions like this.

5 p.m.
Sad Ed has been round. Miep let him up on grounds he was Jewish sympathizer (he likes Matzo balls) and had essential news from free world. It is that Scarlet is having Hallowe'en party tonight. Said was not interested in non-Kosher goth-based celebrations as am hardened fact-based individual, but to hand over any contraband confectionery concealed about person immediately. Sad Ed said he would, but Mum had conducted a full body search on entry and confiscated two Picnics, a packet of Minstrels, and four Freddos. Have sent him away.

7 p.m.
Although do slightly wish was at Scarlet's party. Not only would be gleaning essential facts such as how many glasses of rum and blackcurrant can one drink without doing purple sick on Habitat rug, but there would be endless Waitrose mini snacks. Have begged Miep for

sustenance but he says he can no longer risk his life for mine. Said he was not risking life, just a shouting and potential limiting of biscuit privileges, but Miep says that is more than my life is worth. It is utterly like Anne. But will not give up. Am here to the bitter end, and the pounding of Nazi boots on the stairs. Or at least the shuffle slap of Mum's Marks & Spencer's slipper mules.

ID
RACHEL
RILEY

november

Saturday 1

9 a.m.
Oh. Am on sofa. And head hurts. And have no idea how got here. Maybe Nazis arrived in annexe after all and knocked me out with Dyson handle. Though do not remember shuffle slap sound. Will ask Miep.

9.15 a.m.
Miep says *a*) he is not called Miep he is called James, or Jimmy Boy (it is idiotic 'street' mathlete nickname) and *b*) there were no Nazi boots, or shuffling slippers, but that I attempted a foray to steal the Nazis' supply of Shreddies and dog got excited and jumped on me and in weakened state I fell backwards and knocked self out on cereal cupboard door handle. Asked if had been rushed to hospital. James said no. Mum made Dad put me on the sofa while they watched *ER*. I said what is point of consuming endless medical-based drama when they do not take hint from plotlines and call swarthy paramedics to give me mouth to mouth. James said they tried to check symptoms but the concussion page of Dr Le Fanu was mysteriously missing.

So ghetto dream is over. Like tragic Anne Frank, my number was up from the very start. But on plus side, James and Mad Harry have given me two Chupa Chups and a Boost bar from trick or treating. They went as Wolverine and the Bionic Woman. Plus my driving lesson is cancelled on grounds that I am bad enough at operating

heavy machinery at best of times let alone after sustaining head injury. Hurrah. Will luxuriate on sofa all day and appreciate the freedoms of post-war society, which hitherto have taken for granted.

10.30 a.m.
Mum has confiscated Chupa Chups, banned me from sofa, and issued instructions that I am to have shower, shampoo, and vigorous nit comb as according to Marjory, two O'Gradys were scratching vigorously outside Mr Patel's earlier. *Plus ça change*.

. . . .

Sunday 2
11 a.m.
It is D-Day for Mum's recession-busting, crisis-averting, spare room-clogging lodger plan. James has typed and printed their checklist of infallible questions, designed to root out perverts, evangelical Christians, and murderers, and Mum has set up an interview/torture area, complete with blinding anglepoise lamp and unnerving, or at least annoying, presence of dog to sniff out drugs, and chav-based snacks. Pointed out that they are trying to find kind, helpful, and hygienic tenant, not interrogate Al Qaeda suspect but Mum says you can never be too careful. Dad is not at all happy about the idea. He is worried his place as head of the household may be usurped by young dynamic intellectual who shares Mum's obsessions

208

with Jeremy Paxman, mung beans, and Cillit Bang. James has pointed out that *a*) he is not, and has never been, head of household, and *b*) it will mean the Cleggs can never again infest the spare room with their Spar bags, racist tendencies, and odour of Fray Bentos. Dad is marginally happier now. And has agreed to assume air of authoritative, yet benign presence, by reading boffiny *Sunday Times* (main section, not sport), and listening to Classic FM (not Radio 5).

Asked what my role was in grand plan. James says I am to go to Sad Ed's and stay there until at least 5 o'clock lest I put either interviewee off with my bad hair, appalling taste in music, or habit of engaging guests in crap philosophical discussions. He is wrong on all counts. But have agreed none the less. Do not want to witness mentalism that is Mum and James's bad cop idiot cop routine. Plus need to find out if Sad Ed snogged Scarlet at the Hallowe'en party. It is possible, given the strength of Suzy's uber-alcoholic punch.

5 p.m.

Sad Ed did not snog Scarlet. Apparently percentage proof of punch did not compensate for *a*) non-vampiric nature of bulgy tummy and bingo wings and *b*) presence of former head goth and current shuttlecock checker Trevor Pledger—twenty-eight inch waistband, upper arm fat quotient minimal. Demanded to know if Scarlet had locked fangs with bat boy, but Sad Ed said only plus point

was that while punch not strong enough to force Scarlet to fling self into his (flabby) arms, was strong enough to make her throw up on Tuscan tiled floor and pass out in hovery love swing. Said am surprised Bob and Suzy allowed such debauchery, given their newfound responsibility as soon-to-be adoptive parents. Sad Ed said they are getting the revelry in while they can. It is a shame I missed it. Although it wouldn't have been the same without Jack. I wonder if they have Hallowe'en in Chichicastenango. Probably not. Although goats are quite devilish.

Got home to unsurprising news that 24 Summerdale Road is still tenantless. Mr Garamond disqualified on grounds of wonky eyes and shifty legs and Mr Tennick on grounds of actually being Mr Whippy! Is utter relief. Thought of Fat Kylie testing his 99 in spare room potentially horrifying.

They will never find a lodger at this rate. Even Paxo would fail to make the grade. As would Dad. He is in trouble for losing the sink plunger. Plus he is still battling weight issues and Mum has never quite grown to love the mole on his right ankle. Thank God is school tomorrow so can escape fat and money-based tension that pervades every Cif-scented corner.

5.30 p.m.
Oooh. And see Mr Pringle. Will tell him of my excellent half-term annexization experiment. Then he will not

only immediately cast me as Anne, but also want to move into fact-based 24 Summerdale Road! He will totally pass test as his eyes are straight, his stomach is flat, and he has no discernible blemishes. Am genius!

Monday 3
3 p.m.

Am not genius. Mr Pringle said annexe experiment good, but he is operating a cunning Auschwitz-style casting system whereby we pull number out of hat to seal our fate. Said that was open to all sorts of horror, e.g. Nigel Moore (impetigo, not potato blight) as Mrs Frank or Sad Ed as the cat. Mr Pringle said the point is not to create beautiful art, it is to get the cold hard facts across. He will struggle if Reuben Tull gets a lead role. He thinks learning lines is too much pandering to 'The Man'. Whoever he is. But on plus side, he says he is totally interested in position as lodger as Chestnuts is not only overpriced, but Ying's breakfast is sliced Nimble and Nutella. Said it was health-giving granary all the way at 24 Summerdale. Have given him phone number and hints to pass James's hygiene and spillage test, e.g. count to fifteen elephants while soaping hands and red wine does NOT come out with salt, that is only adding insult to injury. Hurrah. May well be under same roof as Mr Pringle within days. Our age gap chemistry will pervade the air like a brace of Glade plug-ins.

Also school is mental with Barack Obama madness.

Scarlet says it is less than two days until America has its first ever black President. Said she shouldn't count her chickens as that other man (old, bit wrinkly, no idea of name) looks quite kindly, like benign grandpa, plus Sarah Palin has excellent glasses and a pregnant daughter, which is complete liberal vote-winner. Scarlet told Sad Ed to remove me from her vicinity before she did something she may well regret later. Said *a*) since when is Sad Ed acting as bodyguard and *b*) she never regretted any act of violence, not even when Tracey Hughes had to go to hospital in Year Seven with a pair of compasses stuck in her left thigh. Sad Ed shrugged and carried me to saggy sofa using one arm. He is quite manly really. Although he did have to stop for emergency deep breathing halfway down the Gaza Strip.

The mathletes table is also over-run with black president anticipation. I heard Ali Hassan call James 'bro' twice during Mrs Brain's fruit-based pudding (Spotted Dick). They have taken forty-eight bets on Barack winning, twenty-three bets on no one winning, and one bet on Sarah Palin actually being Ross Perot in a wig.

Tuesday 4
9 a.m.
Scarlet is still not speaking to me on account of my potential racist tendencies and general air of political idiocy. Have pointed out that am not racist, am realist, and am

not political idiot, just that I do not have advantage of
parents who spent 1980s stuffing envelopes in militant
wing of Bethnal Green and Bow Labour party, as well she
knows. Scarlet said well I had better shape up fast if I
want to attend her all-night CNN election vigil in the den.
Have bought an Obama badge for £1 off the mathletes' fly
trader market stall (behind the bins aka Rat Corner). They
are making them out of a copy of the *Observer* colour supplement and James's laminating machine.

4 p.m.
Scarlet has relented and agreed I can come to CNN vigil,
if only because it will educate me in the workings of the
American Electoral College. I wish we had an electoral
college here, I would go and stun Scarlet with my
prowess at naming marginal seats and swings to gain.
Mum is not at all happy as it is a school night but have
pointed out that is utterly part of history, e.g. where was
she when Kennedy was shot, or when Tony Blair swept
to power in landslide? Mum said *a*) inside Granny Clegg
(ick) and *b*) in the bathroom cleaning up James's sick
after he swallowed the Monopoly iron (ick ick, especially
as know for fact we are still using said iron).

8 p.m.
Chez Stone is infused with Obama/potential adoptive
baby madness. The kitchen is crawling with Saffron
Walden Labour Party members (all seven of them)

blogging via their BlackBerries and furiously checking Twitter. Suzy says she is utterly calling her new arrival Barack, even if it is white (which it will be) and a girl (quite possibly). Scarlet says this is without doubt the most seminal night of her life, beating even the time she saw Germaine Greer in Tesco and the time Trevor touched her right breast (under T-shirt but over bra). She is right, is utterly seminal. Although to be fair not much is happening at moment, and *Friends* is on E4 and would quite like to switch over.

8.05 p.m.
Scarlet says there is no way we are switching over and this just further illustrates why I am no more than a pretender, i.e. am Duffy to her Dusty Springfield.

8.10 p.m.
We are watching *Friends*. Is one where Joey wears all of Chandler's clothes. Genius.

11 p.m.
There is still nothing actually happening in America. Although Kay Burley is barking mentally with excitement at pictures of people at polling stations and milling aimlessly round a park in big hats. She will be hospitalized by the time somewhere actually declares. Thank God we don't have Sky. The dog could not cope with her hair or starey eyes.

12 midnight
Politics is time consuming and essentially dull. Wish the history part would hurry up. May just rest eyes a little bit. Will be fine for five minutes. They are still showing pictures of Arnold Schwarzenegger grinning manically at a polling station.

Wednesday 5
Guy Fawkes Night
8 a.m.
Oh. It is all over. Apparently Obama did win. Asked Scarlet what historic thing I was doing when this was declared. She said I was drooling slightly, but was not as bad as Sad Ed who was snoring and had hand inside pants. Will not mention that in future years. Will say I was opening bottle of vintage Krug in celebration. Or possibly carton of Ribena. At least am going to school in same slightly sweaty clothes as yesterday, which is badge of utter honour as indicates political commitment.

8.05 a.m.
Or night of debauchery with Mr Whippy's Rocket in Fat Kylie's case.

12 noon
Oooh. Mr Pringle is also in same clothes as yesterday! So

215

he is utterly politically committed. Asked if he had stayed up at Chestnuts to watch but he said he went to his friend Henry's up in London, as Ying was watching *Bid-Up* to get a Diamonique necklace set for £3.99. Apparently Henry works for BBC. Did not mention myriads of TV rules in our house. Or antipathy towards anyone who works in media. Cannot wait until drama though. It is well known fact that post-election atmosphere is hotbed for extra curricular snogging.

12.05 p.m.
Not that am hoping he snogs me, as is illegal.

12.10 p.m.
Or that am keeping mental note of Mr Pringle's wardrobe.

12.15 p.m.
Except that he does look good in chest hair revealing V-neck T-shirt.

4 p.m.
Drama was not hotbed of victory snogging. But was excellent none the less, i.e. I AM ANNE FRANK! Hurrah. Reuben Tull is moany Mrs Frank, Sad Ed is dodgy dentist Mr Dussel and Caris Kelp is Peter. Which adds interesting lesbian frisson to annexe.

On downside Mr Pringle not amenable to idea of incorporating Barack Obama as voice of Jesus on grounds

that *a*) play is JEWISH and *b*) there is no one in the group who is remotely black and the favoured John Major High method of portraying anyone of colour (i.e. boot polish) is not acceptable. Mr Pringle also not amenable to rewriting of ending to include uplifting escape scenario. He said that is the sort of schmaltz that has ruined the New Hollywood. He is utterly right of course. Although I do excellent terrified fleeing face (as practised in magnifying bathroom mirror).

Sad Ed is also mental with Anne Frank-based joy. It is not at not being minty Mrs Frank. It is because he and Reuben are writing the songs. He says it is the break he needs and could potentially lead to a concept album and slot on the Peel stage at Glastonbury. He is wrong. It will lead to embarassment and flying Criminal and Retard-related Skittles if his rendition of 'Eleanor Rigby' in the Year Seven All-Faith-Embracing Beatles medley concert is anything to go by.

Thursday 6

There has been a bitter blow to my fact-based grown-up older man stance. It is that film club has been suspended. It is because hairy librarian Mr Knox lent the DVD player to the Camilla Parker Bowles Memorial Crèche so they could watch *Underground Ernie*, and someone (probably Jesus but also possibly Mark Lambert) inserted two party rings and a chocolate finger into the slot. I offered to host the club in our living room but Mr Pringle says we can better use the time to work on the musical. He is right. Plus there is no way Mum would let us watch *Sid and Nancy*. Or let Reuben Tull over the threshold. He looks like a mentalist and smells like a badger.

4 p.m.
Not that have smelt a badger. But they look a bit ripe.

4.05 p.m.
James says that according to Beastly Investigations research, badgers are not foul-smelling creatures, but are in fact quite hygienic, like gerbils. Reuben Tull is more of a stoat.

• •

Friday 7

Oh my God. Mr Pringle has called to ask if lodger vacancy is still vacant! James has informed him that there is indeed an opening for a tenant at 24 Summerdale Road, and has invited him for interrogation on Sunday! Hurrah. So it is swings and roundabouts as far as fact-based film sessions are concerned as will be on John Lewis sofa discussing jump cuts, fade outs, and the seminal influence of the *Blair Witch Project* wonky camera technique within days.

• •

Saturday 8

11 a.m.
Ugh. Have driving lesson. Was hoping that Mr Wandering Hands would get domestically abused again by Mrs Wandering Hands, preferably fatally compromising his accelerator foot or gear-knob hand. But he is foot and knob-intact and due to guide me round the hell that is the Hockley one-way system any minute. Mum is also slightly disappointed. I think she was hoping he might be in need of temporary accommodation. He is her dream tenant: clean nails, bouffy hair, embracer of laws of all kinds. Dad would have gone mental though. He is still fully convinced that Mr Wandering Hands wants to embrace more than Mum's rules. Shudder.

2 p.m.
Why, oh why can I not learn to drive around nice quiet village, e.g. Catmere End (three houses and a bus shelter). Negotiating Bishop's Stortford on a Saturday is utterly worse than Oxford Circus, i.e. clogged with traffic impediments, 4X4s, and nine year olds high on Haribo. Pointed out to Mr Wandering Hands that I should not be penalized points-wise in my test for knocking over one if not several of these dangers to driving. He did not reply as was too busy using his emergency instructor brake to avoid a Jeep Cherokee. Maybe should give up lessons and use money instead for more enlightening activity, e.g. going to Duke tonight for political discussion and/or close

harmony rendition of 'The Gambler' with Kev's dog on percussion. Will suggest it. Is just redeployment of funds. Not actual extra money.

2.15 p.m.
Mum says there is no way I am redeploying £20 a week from the fluff-free pockets of Mr Wandering Hands to the filth-filled coffers of Shorty McNulty. I pointed out she could consider an increase in pocket money (still languishing around the £3 mark) given that she will be flush tomorrow with a rent cheque and hefty breakages/soiled goods deposit (contract includes forfeits for damages to soft furnishings, hard furnishings, and mung bean cultivator). But Mum said there is no guarantee Mr Pringle will pass muster, and even if he does, the money is earmarked for a mini Dustbuster and a new rotary washing line. (Old one broken due to repeated hanging off and whizzing round by Mad Harry and James. And me. And Dad.)

6 p.m.
Yet another evening of *Casualty* beckons. Poverty is utterly hampering my horizon-widening, philosophical pub ambitions. May well write to Gordon Brown to complain about mad-eyebrowed Chancellor Alistair Darling. His poor money management could compromise an entire generation, condemning us to hospital soaps and *A Touch of Frost* when we could be more usefully

keeping economy afloat by purchasing beverages and snacks.

8.15 p.m.
Oooh. Have found £2.30 down the back of the sofa. James claims it is his and that he got it off Mad Harry for successfully predicting that he couldn't eat more than two cream crackers in two minutes. (Is weird phenomenon. Have tried. Is utterly impossible.) Dad says *au contraire* it is his, because the right hand cushion is his *Lovejoy* viewing area and he has notoriously leaky pockets. Luckily Mum is round Marjory's looking at seed catalogues so am going down Duke to splurge it all on Cheese Moments and lime and soda before she can lay claim to it, under Rule 91 of household management law.

12 midnight
Hurrah. Have had excellent night in pub, despite still being relegated to the swirly carpet until we can prove our increase in Britvic and peanut consumption is long-term rather than a rogue blip. Scarlet is in agreement that Mr Pringle moving into house will be excellent, education-wise. She says my parents are restricting me with their *Telegraph* editorial outlook, and Mr Pringle will inject refreshing new views. Sad Ed asked if he could move into Scarlet's as he is utterly compromised by having to reside with two members of the Aled Jones fan

221

club and she can inject him with whatever she likes. She said no.

. . . .

Sunday 9
Remembrance Sunday
1 p.m.
It is less than an hour until Mr Pringle's interrogation commences. James is armed with his clipboard and Mum is armed with fleaspray (this is not for Mr Pringle, it is for the dog, who is scratching uncontrollably). Have begged them to look favourably on his position as pillar of community (i.e. teacher) and impeccable academic record but James says drama is not pillar-style subject and Stoke got no stars in *Times* guide last year so unless he has an MA from either Harvard or Yale, then he will have to ace his hygiene test to get through.

1.59 p.m.
Oh my God. Doorbell has gone. He is here, and is punctual, which is five points before he has even got over threshold. Hurrah!

3 p.m.
Oh my God. Mr Pringle is moving in. He got an unprecedented seventy-nine points out of a hundred, which is, according to the *Which* rules of consumer testing, a guarantee of customer satisfaction, and worthy of a coveted

Best Buy award. Hurrah! He is giving Ying and Les notice tonight and will be bringing his allotted two bags and a bicycle (with lights) round next Sunday.

Thin Kylie was sitting on the wall with Fiddy when I went to take dog out for a poo. (Mum claims he has been holding it in in bid to gain access to Bran Flakes, which I said shows remarkable intelligence, but Mum says shows new levels of idiocy. But it is not withholding, it is probably just stuck behind a sock or a stapler.) She demanded to know what business Mr Pringle had been conducting at 24 Summerdale Road. Actually what she said was, 'Oh my God. Are you, like, knobbing Pringle? He is a minger. Lambo saw his thing in the staff toilet and it is, like, totally ginger down there. And he wears Hi-Tecs. Knob.' I said *a*) No, he is our new tenant, *b*) what was Mark Lambert doing in staff toilet, and *c*) what is wrong with Hi-Tecs (which were, as far as I knew, de rigeur in world of chav). She said, *a*) 'Oh my God, he is totally, like, going to get in your knickers, Riley. Minging,' *b*) 'He had drunk, like, five cans of Fanta and it was leaking out. But he won £3.40 off Fat Kylie so he don't care about the stain,' and *c*) 'Oh. My. God. I, like, can't believe you just said that.' And at that point she flounced off dragging Fiddy out from under dog, who is still determined to mate her despite several feet in height difference and no testicles. It is hard to believe she is head girl. She is so not a role model for enlightened leadership. Last week she banned hummus sandwiches from common room on the grounds

it 'like stinks, innit'. Anyway, she is wrong. Mr Pringle does not want to get into my knickers.

5 p.m.
Does he? Oh. My. God. Maybe he does fancy me after all. It is totally possible. I am bohemianish, fact-based, and my hair is marginally less mental at the moment due to unseasonally clement weather conditions. Oooh, the Shreddies table will be boiling with sexual chemistry.

5.15 p.m.
Except that Mum is bound to add a million caveats to her already fourteen page banned list to include any lusting over the Marmite jar. It is so unfair.

5.30 p.m.
And also wrong. Have remembered that he is teacher and is out of bounds, no matter how potent our love for each other.

5.45 p.m.
Also am not sure he has potent love for me.

5.50 p.m.
And utterly do not have potent love for him. Love is fictional happy ending construct, and not in any sense fact based. Yes. Will think on him as benign uncleish presence.

6 p.m.
Or at least will try.

* *

Monday 10
12 noon
Think may have been wrong about Mr Pringle. Have just seen him in B Corridor (having discussion with Miss Beadle about who has to monitor the lower school playground on a Friday, i.e. notorious demob-happy day). Said hello and his gaze definitely lingered on my legs! Oh my God. It is totally potent love!

12.10 p.m.
Was not potent love. Was Dairylea cheese triangle that had somehow adhered itself to back of thigh. Possibly during emergency visit to Camilla Parker Bowles Memorial Crèche to separate Jesus and someone called Samson Judd who were locked in a no-win situation over a sticklebrick.

* *

Tuesday 11
Another milestone looms along our arduous passage to utter grown-upness, i.e. tomorrow is Scarlet Marjory Mowlam Stone's eighteenth birthday. James says from now on it is all utterly downhill and she needs to start doing stomach crunches and using Oil of Olay to combat

225.

the seven signs of ageing, e.g. fine lines, dark patches, and wearing criminal sandals. Have no money to purchase present, as spent it all in Duke on Saturday. So have written her meaningful fact-based poem instead.

The Lady in Scarlet (i.e. utter genius play on Granny Clegg's favourite crap ballad 'The Lady in Red' by monobrowed midget Chris De Burgh.)

> *You cloak yourself in black.*
> *The uniform of the Goth.*
> *Of the semi-EMO.*
> *Of every angst-ridden teen.*
> *But it shines through.*
> *Your true colour.*
> *You are Scarlet!*
> *Red like fire.*
> *Like menstrual blood.*
> *Like the corpses of slaughtered lambs.*
> *Scarlet.*
> *Bright and shining.*
> *Like the top off full fat milk.*
> *Like an old phone box before they replaced them with*
>   *plexiglass and aluminium.*
> *Scarlet. Scarlet. Scarlet.*

Scarlet will be moved to point of tears. It is utterly better than bottle of gin, which is what Sad Ed is getting her.

226

Wednesday 12

Scarlet says *au contraire* she would have quite liked another bottle of gin in order to drown her monumental sorrows. It is not fear of wrinkles. It is devastating news that Bob and Suzy have utterly forgotten her birthday! She says they are consumed with thoughts of their potential adoptive child and this is just a precursor of life to come where she will be forgotten, the abandoned middle child. And will possibly turn to crime or drugs or marginal political causes. Apparently even Edna, the non-Filipina Labour-friendly Rothman's-smoking cleaner remembered (she got her a box of Toffifee). Scarlet says she is thinking of adopting her as a new mother. Said that is the trouble with progressive parents. All the tantric sex and drugs have messed with their priorities. Whereas mine might wear vests and have not had sex since 1996 (James) but our birthdays are noted and highlighted in a WH Smith diary and checked on a weekly basis. Thin Kylie said *au contraire* (actually she didn't, as is too French, she said 'Yeah, well, whatever'), we are all wrong and pointed out that in fact it is brilliant as now Scarlet can totally blackmail them. Apparently Cherie forgot her birthday one year and she got £150 and a PS2 in compensation. Maybe she is more political than I thought after all.

Also Scarlet says it is semi-skimmed milk that has red top, and as a vegetarian she takes offence at the corpses line. Luckily had to go to drama rehearsal before she could deconstruct poem any further. Now I know how

227

poet laureate Andrew Motion must feel, having the words he has poured his soul into being pulled to pieces by cack-handed A-level students.

Rehearsals went well though. Mr Pringle said my Anne showed acute understanding of the torment of metaphorical entrapment, i.e. in the body of a teenager, with the mind of a young woman. It is so utterly true. I am mature beyond my years mentally, yet my breasts have only just grown to 34B.

Thursday 13

Thin Kylie is not political genius. Her solution to today's common room row over whether Mark Lambert had spilt Pepsi Max on Ali Hassan's iPod and was it deliberate, and possibly even justified, was to make them battle it out on sheep field with shaken up bottles of a carbonated beverage of their choice. She was right about the blackmail though. Apparently Suzy remembered last night, when Jack's email arrived from Chichicastenango (they have finally got reliable electricity and a twenty-year-old Dell). She was racked with remorse and has given her £100, two bottles of vodka, and a giant Toblerone. Scarlet is utterly jubilant. Said she should not allow them to buy her affections, and what about her new mother Edna? Scarlet said she has changed her mind about Edna. She may have left-wing credentials (husband was a miner), but she buys non-organic vegetables and has a fur hat.

228

Plus she thinks Penelope Keith is the greatest living actress. Asked if Jack's email mentioned me. It did not.

· ·

Friday 14

Went round Sad Ed's after school. He is utterly depressed about the Scarlet/mojo situation. He says his attempts at a *Twilight* look have not curried favour, and, to top it all, he is not even an older man any more. Said that skinny jeans was possibly a step too far in the vampiric fashion stakes for someone of his unique build, but that he will always be an older man, even if it is only by a crucial few weeks. He is marginally revived and is pinning his hopes on tomorrow night's celebration in the Duke. Scarlet has vowed to spend at least £75 of her birthday money on beverages and snacks. She says it is an utterly economic strategy to fiscally stimulate a valuable local business. It is also utterly economic strategy to win us back custody of the wobbly table. There is no way Reuben Tull can top that on a trolley-herder's wages.

· ·

Saturday 15

5 p.m.

Is shaping up to be excellent two days.

1. This morning Mr Wandering Hands said my three-point turn was down to five points, which is vast improvement on 13-point turn previously.

2. Tonight is Scarlet's utterly grown-up eighteenth party when she will finally realize that Sad Ed is her utter destiny, despite his non-batlike build and penchant for buffalo wings (i.e. chicken wings, not actual wings of buffalo, which was confusing for quite a few years).

3. Tomorrow Mr Pringle moves into the spare room, with his library of fact-based DVDs, wardrobe of fading nineties tour T-shirts and potential potent love for me.

Hurrah. Is recipe for weekend of utter success on grown-up front. I predict that by this time tomorrow, Scarlet and I will both be in the arms of older men, or at least in close proximity to them on the John Lewis sofa watching *Antiques Roadshow*.

· ·

Sunday 16
6 p.m.
Am in close proximity to older man. In fact, am almost in (flabby) arms of older man. But is utterly wrong one, i.e. is not fact-based media studies expert Mr Pringle. He is currently in dining room, going through a checklist of do's and don'ts with Mum (heavy on the don'ts) whereas I am in bed, with Sad Ed, glass of water and emergency sick bucket.

It is all Scarlet's fault for fiscally stimulating Shorty

230

McNulty. If I ever see another Cheese Moment will possibly die of anaphylactic shock. In fact feel sick again just
writing words. Yes, definitely sick coming.

6.10 p.m.
Have rinsed out bucket with bleach and anti-bacterial
spray concoction, according to Mum's instructions (typed,
laminated (to protect against projectile emissions) and
inserted under door). Oh. Sick is endless. Sad Ed also sick
(five times, beating my three and a half (no sick last time,
just weird green stuff)). It is not Cheese Moments though
for him. It is beer. He drank eight pints in bid to prove his
older man credentials but effect slightly lost when he did
the Macarena with Kev Banner and the dog. Had to get
Dad to fetch us at half nine in Passat (with Sad Ed hanging head out of window like giant St Bernard, to avoid
sick-smelling Volvo repeat). Dad wanted to deposit him at
Loompits Way but Sad Ed begged him to carry his addled
body upstairs as Mrs Thomas is under impression that
Saturday nights are spent drinking Ovaltine and singing
campfire songs and he did not want to shatter her illu-
sions. Mum was not at all happy with arrangement but
James pointed out that it gives her excellent trump card
leverage against future misdemeanours of mine. Credit
crunch is turning everyone into Machiavellian wheeler-
dealers. Or morons. Mum agreed but only if he slept in
my room as did not want Mr Pringle's contaminated with
sick, or sweaty Morrisey T-shirts.

Jack was right. This is typical Riley mess. Am not at all grown-up. Grown-ups do not eat twenty-four packets of Cheese Moments. And four pickled onions. And past sell-by pork scratchings that have been open for fortnight and are meant for dog. Cannot face Mr Pringle. Will stay in room, alone with shame, for ever.

6.30 p.m.
Except am not alone with shame, am wedged in junior bed with giant bulk of Sad Ed hogging sprig-patterned duvet. Will eject him. He is not at all conducive to penitent thoughts.

6.45 p.m.
Am alone. Will think pure Joan of Arc-style factual thoughts.

8.40 p.m.
There is funny noise under bed. Maybe my shame has taken on human form, like ghost of Christmas past, and is hiding like homunculus under bed to torment me.

8.45 p.m.
Was not homunculus of shame. Was dog eating one of Mum's shuffly slippers. Am giving up on today. Tomorrow will be better. Will be grown-up by then. Or at least vomit-free.

· ·

Monday 17

7.30 a.m.

Am revived. Have purged myself of childishness, with Cheese Moments sick. Am ready to take my place next to Mr Pringle at Shreddies table as utter grown-up. And if his potent love pervades air like steam off coffee, will rebut it with my penitent facty breakfast of granary toast with no butter.

8 a.m.

Did not take seat next to Mr Pringle (Mum has allotted him official place between her and James, i.e. where he is least likely to get mooned over by me or harangued by Dad over antipathy towards *Top Gear*), and did not notice potent love wafting around table as James too busy testing him on 'house rules', i.e.

- No shoes beyond doormat, but stack carefully, away from jaws of dog;
- No food to be consumed whilst walking around house;
- No biscuits to be consumed except at allocated snack time. Ad infinitum.

But on plus side, at least have not shamed self further.

8.15 a.m.

James has just returned my *Railway Children* DVD in full view of Mr Pringle. Said, 'Um, thank you. It is excellent

chance to observe the full workings of Britain's pre-nationalized rail system.' James said, 'And you always cry in "Daddy, my Daddy" bit.' Thank God am going to school. Common Room is utterly more grown-up atmosphere than 24 Summerdale Road. Plus can get gossip from Scarlet about what happened in Duke after Passat rescue on Saturday.

4 p.m.
Oh my God. Scarlet did snog an older man in the Duke! It is Kev Banner (26, works in BJ Video, owner of alcoholic dog). She said it is utter rite of passage and she feels no shame. She should. He shops in Next. On plus side, we have regained control of wobbly toilet table. Reuben Tull is in the car park due to suspicious herbal smell.

Also Common Room not entirely grown-up due to incident involving Thin Kylie, Mark Lambert, and jar of peanut butter. Part of West Bank (aka microwave corner) has been cordoned off and will remain a no-go zone for several days.

Tuesday 18
Mum has drawn up strict bathroom timetable. Said she need not worry about me walking in on Mr Pringle having shower as I am utter woman of world and have seen it all before. Mum said *a*) what exactly have I seen before and *b*) it is not me she is protecting it is Mr Pringle who

walked in on James having poo this morning, which is distressing enough but he was also trying to clean dog's teeth at same time. Said was talking metaphorically. Which is true. As Jack kept pants on, and was too drunk to remember what Justin's looked like. Which limits penis-memory to Grandpa's, James's, and Sad Ed's. Which is not at all worldly. Or pleasant.

Sad Ed is in agreement about his penis, i.e. that it is not at all worldly. Although he says it is due to underuse, rather than size or shape. He says he is thinking of joining me in my pursuit and redirecting his affections for Scarlet to an older woman as it is very rock-starrish to have Mrs Robinson-style experience. Plus then Scarlet will get all minty and jealous and beg him to bestow his penis on her.

Think he is overegging it somewhat as do not think Scarlet will be begging for his penis anywhere near her, whether it has been near an older woman or not, but agreed it is good idea to experiment, as cannot cope much longer with his mojo-related depression. Asked if he has set his sights on a lucky lady yet. He said no, but he is going to check out the market over the next few days.

. . . .

Wednesday 19

5 p.m.

Grandpa Riley has rung in panic. It is Jesus. Apparently he is lying on faux leather sofa in silent shock. Asked if it

was this morning's incident in Camilla Parker Bowles Memorial Crèche (he headbutted Samson for putting Whitney's Bratz doll in the soiled nappy receptacle). Grandpa said no, and what is wrong with that, it shows chivalry. It is news that hobbit-like political pundit John Sergeant has quit *Strictly Come Dancing*. Jesus has been glued to screen for weeks and is very much taken with him, particularly in his tight tango outfit. I do not know why, he looks and dances like Granny Clegg, but there is no accounting for taste. Grandpa says he does not know how to comfort Jesus, who has spurned all his usual tricks, including Wagon Wheels, Wotsits, and the Patrick Swayze DVD. Said there is nothing to do but wait. Jesus is grieving a significant loss, and time will heal his wounds, i.e. utterly grown-up answer, as Mr Pringle in room at time trying to rescue shoe from dog. Think it impressed him, especially when I threw in brilliant fact that John Sergeant was also actually a sergeant in Welsh Guard.

5.15 p.m.
John Sergeant not sergeant. James Googled it. Curse Scarlet and her propensity for evil. And my gullibility.

. . . .

Thursday 20

Went to see Jesus in Camilla Parker Bowles Memorial Crèche at lunchtime. He is still in mourning, i.e. is lying

on cushion in Wendy House while Whitney strokes him with a filthy Iggle Piggle. Fat Kylie said he even refused his snack-time Cheese String so things are really bad. Grandpa is writing to BBC to complain about the debacle. He is demanding reinstatement of John Sergeant, who he says is a role model for pensioners and the facially-afflicted everywhere, and a replacement of Arlene Phillips with Amanda Holden, who cries at anything. He will be waiting a long time.

Friday 21

Mr Pringle said an old man rang and went on about pigs for five minutes then hung up. Said did he sound a bit retarded and have a tendency to say 'arrr' a lot. He said yes. Said it was a wrong number. It was not. It was Grandpa Clegg. Cannot let Mr Pringle know I am related to inbred racist, homophobic, and Hammerited man. He will never bestow love, potent or otherwise, on me.

6 p.m.

Not that I want his potent love, as am utterly Paxman-like—i.e. only interested in facts.

Saturday 22

It is typical. Have utterly turned corner (real and metaphorical) in my grown-up pursuit of wheel-based

freedom (i.e. am finally allowed to negotiate Hockerill lights and notorious Sparrow's Hill), and driving lesson is cancelled so that Mr Wandering Hands can take Mrs Wandering Hands on a relationship-rekindling trip to Madeira. Mum is not at all happy. She says it is not the relationship-kindling. It is the lack of commitment to his pupils. She says she is minded to become driving instructor herself and offer her services as substitute teacher. Have begged her not to. It is bad enough she wears waterproof trousers in public without barking at half the teenage population of Saffron Walden about their emergency stops. Was hoping to spend time discussing Anne Frank's sexual awakening with Mr Pringle but he has gone to visit his friend Henry for the weekend. (They are going on an 'end the occupation' march. Not sure what occupation they mean. Could be Iraq. Or Afghanistan. Or possibly Isle of Wight, which I know for fact he thinks should be independent principality.) So am going to Waitrose car park instead to see if Sad Ed has found a potential Mrs Robinson for his unworldly penis.

5 p.m.
Sad Ed has narrowed the field down to three possible penis contenders, i.e. Suzy, Miss Mustard (lab assistant, not Cluedo piece) and Janine off Waitrose meat counter. Said that while Suzy was clearly the front runner, given her pro-sex stance and heaving bosom, she is also *a*) Scarlet's mum and *b*) Scarlet's mum and therefore utterly

238

out of bounds. Have also ruled out Miss Mustard on grounds of greasiness of hair and fact that she is engaged to Mr Waiting (economics, bad ties, distracting mole). Reuben Tull suggested Mrs Stimpson, who is wee-smelling white-flare-wearing lady tramp. But Sad Ed said he didn't want to tread on Barry the Blade's toes. Literally or otherwise. Or go near the source of the wee smell. So it is down to Janine off meat. Made surreptitious browse of ham and gala pie on way home in order to 'check out the goods'. She is at least 30, has a tattoo of Daffy Duck on her bicep and wields a meat cleaver with conviction. Sad Ed will be putty in her swarthy hands.

. . . .

Sunday 23

2 p.m.
Am utterly bored. Scarlet is giving Sad Ed assertiveness training, and James is round at Mad Harry's having a Beastly Investigations crisis summit. If only Paddy (i.e. Mr Pringle) was here. Have started calling him Paddy in head, now that our relationship has moved to a new more informal level. May actually try calling him it out loud at some point. Is utterly modern. And is less weird to think about snogging someone called Paddy than someone called Mr Pringle.

2.10 p.m.
Not that am thinking about snogging him.

2.15 p.m.
Although I bet he is excellent at snogging. Radical political types always are, according to Scarlet. Which would partially explain John Prescott. But not entirely.

3 p.m.
Mum not in agreement about 'modernizing' my relationship with lodger. Asked her when Paddy was getting back from Henry's. She said it is Mr Pringle to you and if I hear you call him that again you will be delimescaling the draining board for a week. She is just minty because Dad managed to beat her on golf driving range. Dad says it is his superior man strength, and eagle-eyes. Mum says it is not that, it is that she has tennis elbow from excess Cillit Banging. Am going round to Grandpa's to escape fraught atmosphere. And to comfort Jesus in his hour of need. Maybe he is political prodigy, i.e. he can sense John Sergeant's superior intellect.

6 p.m.
Jesus is not political prodigy. He is over his John Sergeant-based grief and has instead latched on to a new and improved celebrity. Was hoping it might be continuing with the current affairs theme, i.e. Trevor McDonald, but it is someone called Mister Maker who has unfeasibly large forehead and does stuff with PVA glue and buttons. Paddy still not back from Henry's, which has only added to tension as Mum had made meat loaf for

240

tea and his portion will be wasted. She has offered it to Dad, who has declined. As has dog. Do not blame them. There is nothing normal about meat masquerading as bread.

* *

Monday 24

8 a.m.
Mum is going mental with potential murder excitement. It is Paddy, who is completely absent from Shreddies table, and has not been in bed for at least seventy-two hours, according to James, who was sent to do forensic check. Mum is blaming Henry, who she thinks is crack-addicted anarchist. She thinks everyone who lives in London or works in telly is on drugs or about to blow something up. So Henry is utter evil overlord in her eyes. She is thinking of calling police. Or Marjory, who watches *Waking the Dead* and several *CSI*s, so is expert in all murderous matters.

9 a.m.
Paddy is not dead. He is in staff room with black coffee and funny red mark on neck. Sad Ed says it is lovebite. But he is wrong. It is probably a truncheon wound from a radical march. Anyway, have rung Mum before her and Marjory start serial killer scare. She sounded disappointed. It is Paddy I feel sorry for. She is bound to wreak revenge.

5 p.m.

Was right about Mum. She has removed Paddy's TV remote privileges for a week. She says she will not be treated like a hotel. Paddy pointed out that she was in fact a hotel of sorts. But then Mum made her lips go super thin and he said he had some marking to do and disappeared into dining room.

Tuesday 25

8 a.m.

Hurrah! Shreddies table is hotbed of political debate. Is like *Newsnight* live version with Mum as self-important Paxo and Paddy as ubiquitous Shami Chakrabarti. It is at news that first ID cards for foreigners were introduced today. Heated discussion ensued, i.e. 'It will end in insidious function creep' (Paddy) versus, 'It is small price to pay to stop Osama Bin Laden being able to wander around Waitrose willy-nilly and inject chemical weapons into tins of cling peaches' (versus 'Oh for heaven's sake, I'm going round to Clive's to listen to Terry Wogan' (Dad)). Scarlet was right. Having lodger is excellent for political enlightenment of Riley household. Although Paddy did not win argument. Mum will not be moved in her quest for more curtailment on personal freedom. She thinks everyone should have ID cards, and is fully in favour of function creep and invasion of privacy. It is why she likes this house so much with its panopticon-like

central hallway, i.e. she can stand in single vantage point and monitor all occupants with one sweep of her all-seeing eye. She says it is why Clive and Marjory's is not selling as it has a dogleg corridor that can hide a multitude of murderers or miscreants. It is not. It is the overpricedness. And the gnomes.

6 p.m.
The ID card row is still rumbling on. Mum only gave Paddy two fishfingers for tea and he got the potato with the brown bit on. Said it was excellent and house had not been this intellectual since Grandpa Clegg and Dad had the week-long argument about Tony Blair (to be fair, was not about policy, was about teeth, but was feisty all the same). James said that's as may be, but the smart money (i.e. him, Damon Parker, and five Year Nines) is on Paddy moving out before Christmas. He is betting obsessed. It is the mathletes and their illegal gambling ring. Anyway he is wrong. There is no way Paddy will move out before Christmas. He has to give a month's notice and it is the 25th of November already.

. . . .

Wednesday 26
5 p.m.
Oh my God. Sad Ed has got a date with Janine off meat! He says two days lurking by the brisket after school has utterly paid off. Asked if he was going to take her out for

243

romantic dinner and walk by river (or shopping-trolley
clogged Slade). He said no, duh, he is bringing her to
Duke, so that Scarlet can observe his manly pulling
power, then hopefully it will be straight back to hers for
lessons in love. Ick.

It is like miracle though. He is imbued with optimism.
Or at least is not dragging feet listening to German new
wave on iPod all day and thinking of new ways to achieve
untimely death, i.e. he has also written two songs for
Anne Frank the Musical, i.e. 'Beanfeast' and 'Dreams of a
Drilling' (thwarted dental theme). Paddy says they are
excellent. Although he has banned him from including
version of 'I Kissed a Girl' for Anne and Peter's pseudo
lesbian kiss. Pointed out that we will not actually be kiss-
ing anyway, as that is too naturalistic and fairytale. Plus
do not want to get superglued to Caris Kelp's mouth mid
performance. Instead we will be hugging and exchanging
metaphorical red paper roses as symbols of our love and
leftwingishness. Think am definitely going to apply to do
Drama and Politics at university. It is ultimate theatre of
debate combination of creativity and evil-minded genius.

5.15 p.m.
I mean philanthropical drive to create better world.

Thursday 27
Scarlet says Drama is not ultimate left-wing university

dream. Is self-obsessed wannabes with more ego than brain or talent. She says economics is the only real subject and we should be more concerned with the effect of the US subprime market than whether or not spirit fingers are the same as jazz hands. (Answer: not. Spirit fingers involves definite additional wiggle.) Said would be plenty of time for learning about that when I go to electoral college in America for my Masters degree and anyway Paddy said we are utterly Brechtian and world-changing. Scarlet said *a*) oh my God, you are so-o-o-o retarded, *b*) I think not, and *c*) since when do you call him Paddy? Said *a*) obviously not or wouldn't be going to electoral college in first place, *b*) whatever, and *c*) sorry, thought had just said it in head, did not know it had come out of mouth. Scarlet said Hmm. And wheeled herself off mysteriously in the Davros throne in direction of Mrs Brain's healthy jelly surprise (segment of tinned mandarin at bottom of pot).

. . . .

Friday 28

Oh my God. Have lost height. James did my official measurement before school and have gone down by a centimetre and is crucial centimetre as am now only four centimetres off being medical midget, according to James. Dad says it is because dog ate old John Lewis tape measure (semi-retracted—God knows how it got it down) and now we have substandard B&Q one. But Mum is not in

agreement. She says it is down to my louche teenage lifestyle and lurking in darkened bedrooms, which is renowned for depleting your Vitamin D. And possibly your height. She is putting me on extra protein for the next month and prescribing at least half an hour healthy outdoor activity a day. Have agreed to walk around sheep field at lunchtime. Do not want to deplete any more. It is utterly depressing. Am not growing up at all. Am actually shrinking.

. . . .

Saturday 29

1 p.m.
It is D-Day for Sad Ed and his unworldly penis. Tonight he will be snogging Janine off meat in the utterly grown-up surroundings of the Duke saloon bar, before having Mrs Robinson experience in her flat above BJ video. Had thought of inviting Paddy to come too, as potential inspiration, but he has gone to Henry's again. Although he has agreed to return by 8 p.m. on Sunday, and will have left-over tea of cold cuts and pickles. Have measured self again. Am still centimetre under height. But have styled hair in Amy Winehouse beehive do which has added five inches so am now relative giant.

5 p.m.
Have unstyled beehive. It would not fit in Mr Wandering Hands's Fiesta. Pointed out he should have more

246

capacious car for extra tall people and policy was possibly heightist, and racist as Somalians are renowned for being ultra lofty. He said he was not heightist, or racist, but that my hairdo was a danger to driving in case of partial collapse, thus obscuring my vision and potentially killing several pedestrians. He is so like Mum it is frightening. Anyway, am undeterred. Have put on ironic hat instead (is bowler from James's brief fling with tap dancing). Look like Kelsi from *High School Musical*, i.e. small, but with utter geek-turned-beauty potential. Will report back tomorrow on Sad Ed's coming-of-age older-woman worldly-penis moment. And Scarlet's raging jealousy. And will utterly not be eating any Cheese Moments. Will restrict self to ready salted crisps and one packet of peanuts for height-attaining protein content.

5.15 p.m.
James says I do not look like Kelsi, as she is ultimate in boffiny undiscovered-talent-and-beauty womanhood, whereas I am a hirsute midget in a hat.

Sunday 30
St Andrew's Day
Coming-of-age older-woman worldly-penis night has been disaster on several fronts.
1. Sad Ed did not get to snog Janine off meat or have Mrs Robinson experience at flat above BJ video.

She ended up in ladies with Kev Banner. And noises from wobbly table vantage point indicate they were not discussing pork belly. It is the dog I feel sorry for. It sat on its stool alone all night with no one to talk to except Wizard Weeks.

2. Scarlet not at all jealous, but now even mintier with Sad Ed for bringing rogue element into pub and ruining her older man snog potential. I pointed out that she does not even fancy Kev Banner unless she has had six vodka and blackcurrants but then she threatened to get Shorty McNulty to banish me to the car park with Reuben Tull so I shut up. It is true though. She only wants Kev because she can't have Trevor. He is back with Tamsin Bacon according to James who got it off Melody Bean who got it off the other Tamsin. Apparently they were all over each other by the Gayhomes mop display at lunchtime.

3. I ate five packets of Cheese Moments. Could not stop myself. Every time went to bar they were calling out to me in all their savoury deliciousness. They are utterly like heroin. I am pathetic addict.

Oooh. Maybe Cheese Moments have depleted height! Will get James to Google for potential side effects.

3 p.m.
James said it is not Cheese Moments that are making me a midget. It is my Clegg blood. I am destined to be

248

underheight. And of limited intelligence. Plus will have a moustache by the time I am thirty. Said that Mum did not have any of these symptoms but James said she is genetic throwback from the one generation when a Clegg mated with superior middle-class stock.

december

£20

PAPER ROSE →

TICKET

Monday 1

Am utterly depressed. It is not my height. Although am still nine millimetres down, according to the tape measure of doom (millimetre possibly gained from late night ham slice snack). It is the credit crisis, which has not only crunched me, but has chewed me up and spat me out, i.e. I have no job and no savings and not many shopping days until Christmas. James says it is always the low-skilled and mentally subnormal who fall victim first and I should just be grateful that Gordon Brown is pumping money into counselling services for the fiscally challenged. He is a moron. But he is a rich moron. He is making a fortune from the mathletes gambling ring. It is because he and Mad Harry persuaded Reuben Tull to take out a two-way accumulator on Mrs Buttfield's weight loss programme (she has gained at least a stone so far). Have begged him to lend me some of his amassed fortune but he says I have a history of debt, and it is people like me who brought the economy to its knees in the first place.

Tuesday 2

Scarlet has refused to lend me money as well. Pointed out that it is ultra left-wing to redistribute wealth to the impoverished proletariat, i.e. me. But she says that is outdated old labour attitude and new labour is all about doing business with business. Then she went into a lecture about negative inflation at which point

brain switched off as have no idea what any of it means.

. . . .

Wednesday 3

Thank God for Anne Frank and her Nazi persecutors to cheer me up and take my mind off my hideous misfortune and curtailed life. Paddy says we need to knuckle down though as only have two weeks left until the show and Sad Ed still has a finale to write ('Kinky Boots' and 'These Boots Were Made for Stalking' have both been rejected). Plus Reuben Tull is not at all convincing as Mrs Frank. Unless she was secretly smoking skunk in the toilet. We are having an extra rehearsal day on Sunday to 'nail it'. Hurrah. Maybe he will give me lift on his bicycle. Will be utterly romantic, but environmentally-friendly and economical. Is ultimate in credit crunch love.

7 p.m.

Will not be getting lift on left-wing bicycle of love. It is not because Paddy is against idea (though to be fair, have not actually asked him). Or Mum. Though she would be, on grounds of peril, common-ness, and fact that no bike helmet stays on on huge hairdo. It is dog, who has chewed through the front tyre and now has head entangled in spokes. Mum is leaving it there for an hour to teach it a lesson. She is wasting her time. You

cannot teach an old dog new tricks. Or anything for that matter.

. . . .

Thursday 4

Mum is in a fiscal crisis panic. It is James's grave news (gleaned from Radio 4) that interest rates could dip below zero, meaning in theory she would be paying Barclays to look after her millions. He has offered to investigate off-shore potential, but her non-throwback Clegg genes have reared their (criminally) ugly heads and revived the shoe-box under bed might be better idea. James said she is wrong as dog is renowned for consuming cardboard of all persuasions (he is still mourning the loss of cereal packet robot from four years ago). Mum said she did not mean an actual shoebox, but a metaphorical one, possibly in the shape of an iron safe with two combination locks and a potential anti-theft attack device. James says he will see what he can do. He was right after all. Mathletes is like the mafia. There is seemingly nothing he can't procure.

. . . .

Friday 5

Mum is writing to the BBC again. This time it is financial guru Robert Peston who is the object of her ire. She says his constant talking down of the economy, plus ferretish features and faulty turntable drawl, are potentially responsible for shoebox dilemma, if not entire credit

crunch, and that they need to bring back baby-faced business reporter Declan, who may have been Irish, but at least he had benign look of shoe salesman. Paddy pointed out that Robert Peston in fact has stutter which he controls with his unique declamatory style, but Mum says that it is even more reason to get him off our screens. She is still reeling from the Gareth Gates debacle.

Mum is sounding more like Granny Clegg every day. Maybe it is true, and we do all turn into our mothers. Oh God. Is bad enough have got her knees. Let alone inheriting her hygiene obsession and ferocious parental controls.

8 p.m.
Crisis averted. Granny Clegg has just rung to ask if veal comes from rabbits.

. . . .

Saturday 6
8 a.m.
Have woken imbued with new-found economic optimism. It is thanks to dream involving Robert Peston, Barack Obama, and Fern Britton (who was irrelevant, but did save Saffron Walden from tidal wave with power of magic microphone). Anyway, point is Obama did not let his colour stand in way of success. He rose against prejudice to ultimate triumph. So am utterly going to take leaf out of his book and not let my background (shortness and bad hair, rather than blackness) hold me back. Instead am

going to write list of transferable skills and tread mean streets of Saffron Walden hawking myself to traders until someone gives me a job.

10 a.m.
Have written list of skills:
1. Have maths GCSE, i.e. can add up using calculator.
2. Thanks to months of experience on Nuts In May till of doom, am unafraid of perilous or baffling mechanical equipment (though have slightly mis-shapen right index finger).
3. Am adaptable to new and complicated shelf stacking systems thanks to Mum's patented alphabetized, height-co-ordinated and in use-by-date order method.

James says I should add that have experience caring for the elderly and infirm, i.e. Granny Clegg last year, and see if I can get work at the Twilight Years Day Centre. Said no. It is not that am ageist. It is that would have to work with Treena and go on pub crawls that involve her cousin Donna who is 'double mental'. Anyway, am aiming higher, for job that involves monetary responsibility, or at least avoids the smell of bleach and endless Jeremy Kyle. Oooh. Have had excellent idea. Will offer skills to Mr Wandering Hands. I could run office and be in charge of booking out the fleet of Ford Fiestas! Is all phone-based so hair and shortness not in any way impediment. Am genius.

1 p.m.
Am not genius. Mr Wandering Hands says he does not have office, he has Mrs Wandering Hands and a week-to-view A4 WHSmith diary and no I cannot wash the Fiestas for £5 a time because he has it on good authority that my cleaning skills leave a lot to be desired. Curse Mum and her honesty is the best policy policy. Will have to tread mean streets after all. Am like Oliver Twist. Or Dick Whittington. Or someone who had to walk a long way in cold, rain, and endless dog poo.

5 p.m.
Have beaten credit crunch and ferret-faced Robert Peston and have got job! On downside, it is in Woolworth's, which requires *a*) crap overall wearing and *b*) willpower to stay away from pick-and-mix lest I put on two stone in violet creams by New Year, but is job none the less and means will be able to purchase presents, and go down Duke on regular basis (to reinvest in local economy). I start December 19 (said cannot do before then due to the-atrical commitments). Anyway Mr Luton (trousers an inch too short, hair in ears, dandruff) could obviously see my excellent potential as he said that was fine, as long as I could do Christmas Eve, because that's when it gets totally mental.

Mum says my joy is ill-founded as according to her sources (James and Mad Harry) Woolworth's is in dire financial straits and could be about to 'go to the fence'.

Said *a*) it is 'go to the wall' and *b*) she is wrong, the atmosphere there is positively festive (tinsel hats all round) and she will be eating her poorly chosen words when I am furnishing her with lavish seasonal gifts. She is such a doom-monger. As is Sad Ed. He refused to even ask Mrs Noakes (bad perm, calls trousers 'slacks', notorious gossip) to put me back on the waiting list for trolley-herding. He says he and Reuben are barely clinging to their jobs as it is in this climate, and they do not need fresh-faced competition. Pointed out that if he and Reuben did more herding and less crashing then they would not be on final warnings. But at that point there was distinctive crunch of metal on metal and Sad Ed had to go and untangle Reuben and a Ford Ka. Anyway do not care. Am no longer one of Brown's jobless millions.

7 p.m.
Paddy has pointed out that was never one of jobless millions in first place as, being under eighteen, I am not included within official statistics. He said he and Henry are fighting to get people like me the right to be counted. Which just proves that in his eyes my age is no barrier to being grown-up. Oh God. I think I love him.

8 p.m.
Scarlet has rung to demand to know why I am not seated

at the wobbly toilet table in the Duke. Said I was feeling a bit below par and needed to conserve joules for tomorrow's all-day Anne Frankathon. She said but Sad Ed is not conserving joules, he is at very minute at bar securing Cheese Moments. Did not tell her he is only following the demands of his unworldly penis, i.e. trailing Scarlet wherever she goes. Nor that I am following mine. (Not penis obviously. Do not have one, unworldly or otherwise, despite recurring nightmare at age of eight. More my heart. Or head. Or possibly pants.) Anyway, am staying in so can watch telly with Paddy. Atmosphere of fact-based love marred only by fact that he is on other side of room whereas I am wedged in on sofa between dog and James who are both taking advantage of Mum and Dad being at Mr Wainwright and Mrs Wainwright Mark II's for wine and nibbles by eating crackers with no crumb-catching plates.

10 p.m.
Think it is definite and Paddy is potently in love with me, i.e. there was discernible atmosphere of tension during *Midsomer Murders*. Will assess situation further tomorrow. Am going to call him Paddy to face. Is time we were on first name terms. It will be last barrier to be broken down before he flings me against wardrobe department (i.e. broken wardrobe) and snogs me in left-wing fact-based grown-up manner. Hurrah!

Sunday 7

Paddy has not flung me against wardrobe in fact-based or any other manner. He has been too busy trying to rescue *Anne Frank the Musical* from current state of disaster. It is utterly Caris Kelp's fault for making herself sick on Pritt Stick in the Beanfeast number. And possibly mine for slipping on sick and elbowing Mouchi in eye. Paddy said he has no idea how we are going to be ready for Thursday. I said, 'Don't worry, Paddy. We'll pull something out of the hat. That's showbusiness!' He said, *a*) we had better do, *b*) it is not showbusiness, it is docudrama, which is utterly different, and *c*) please don't call him Paddy, it is Mr Pringle.

It is a bitter blow. But I understand. It is school rules, and we cannot let our love compromise his job in the face of Mr Wilmott's oppressive (though ineffectual) authority. We must bide our time before revealing our relationship to an un-understanding world.

10 p.m.

And actually have relationship.

Monday 8

Scarlet summoned me to Davros throne at lunchtime. Thought it might be to discuss her plans to persuade Sad Ed to persuade Mr Wilmott to have a goths-only toilet but it was not, it was to discuss my 'erratic behaviour'. She

says as my first best friend she demands to know why I would turn down an opportunity to consume savoury snacks and sing 'Crystal Chandelier' to spend an evening watching John Nettles, who do not even like, with my brother, who is an irritating mathlete, the dog, who is just irritating, and Mr Pringle, who I must surely be sick of the sight of, given that I am in rehearsal with him every day. Said I do not know what she was talking about and oh my God, is that Robert Pattinson in the apple pie queue? It was not, it was Sad Ed with a voluminous hairdo and too much eyebrow pencil (he is relentless in his bid to win Scarlet's bat-based love). But it gave me time to hide behind the mathletes. Cannot let her know about Mr Pringle. Our love is a secret. Forbidden, like Eve's apple. Or Ribena in the vicinity of oatmeal wool carpet.

5 p.m.
And not actually real at the moment.

. . . .

Tuesday 9

The crapness of *Anne Frank the Musical* does not seem to have reached the public arena, i.e. the rest of John Major High, yet. Tickets have officially sold out and the mathletes are touting them on the black market (i.e. nicotine patch corner, i.e. behind the bike sheds) for double face value. Oh my God. Is like when Prince played the O2.

5 p.m.

James says it is not like when Prince played the O2. It is like when Bobby Helmet plays the Miners' Arms in Goonbell, i.e. the public love a good car crash.

. . . .

Wednesday 10
9.30 p.m.

James is right. *Anne Frank* is utter car crash. In fact is three-lorry pile-up with oil spillage, minor injuries, and sheep all over the carriageways (Criminals and Retards, again). It is Mr Pringle I feel sorry for. This is his life's ambition—using popular drama to change politics. And what he has got is a load of teenagers in black T-shirts and tights singing about beans and falling off edge of stage (Mrs Frank aka Reuben Tull, due to 'compromised sense of perspective'). Oh his grief is unbearable. I long to comfort him in his hour of need. To stroke his hair. And whisper gentle nothings. And then gasp as he kisses me gently, yet masterfully, in the staff toilets . . .

10 p.m.

Oh. Had funny turn there. Am revived now. Thanks to Mum who burst into bedroom to demand if had eaten last Fruesli bar. Said no, was dog on fibre mission.

Must not fail Paddy though. Will channel grief and anguish into critic-silencing performance of lifetime. This time tomorrow I will be etched on everyone's memory as

263

the definitive Anne Frank. Vulnerable, yet assured. And beautiful, despite Barbra hair.

* *

Thursday 11
10 p.m.
Or as Rachel Riley, the girl who got a paper rose stuck in left nostril during Secret Lover routine (is Caris Kelp and her Uhu residue).

On plus side, there was catalogue of other misdemeanours i.e.:

- Mrs Frank aka Reuben Tull fell asleep in soup.
- Mr Dussel aka Sad Ed accidentally drilled hole in Mouchi's cardboard cat ears with Black and Decker (couldn't get actual dental drill due to unfeasibly high price demanded by potential triad Alan Wong).
- Nazis missed cue due to argument about Wayne Rooney in green room and Mrs Frank (with soupy face) had to go and remind them to come and arrest us all, which kind of ruined the surprise effect.

Is not good. Actually saw Mr Pringle bang his head on trophy cabinet in despair several times. But it is first night. And first nights always go wrong. He is hardened theatre professional and used to such setbacks. I predict he will be back in upbeat mode giving us director's notes first thing tomorrow.

* *

Friday 12

10 a.m.
Mr Pringle is not in school. Which is odd as he left house at usual time, i.e. 8.17 a.m., according to James's infallible timings, following a health-giving, if silent breakfast of Alpen (original, not luxury, variety). Although he was not wearing his usual school outfit or even suitable coat. Oh God. Maybe he is like Captain Oates, i.e. has gone out into the snow and ice (or at least drizzle) to seal his fate. Is all my fault. And possibly Reuben Tull's. And definitely Caris Kelp's for eating glue in first place. Her thirst for adhesives has sent grown man to his death.

1 p.m.
Scarlet is still mental with suspicion. She demanded to know why my eyes filled with tears over my cheese and chutney bap at lunch. I said it was the astringent pickle. Cannot tell her I am grieving for my lost dead forbidden love.

4 p.m.
Have informed Mum of my Oates theory. James says Mr Pringle would have to be naked for at least two weeks to sustain hypothermia and ensuing death, given the clement temperature today. He is wrong. At this very moment Mr Pringle is probably lying blue-lipped in a waterlogged ditch. Or behind the meat bins at Goddards. But we will not fail him. The show must go on.

4.15 p.m.

Unless Lou (school caretaker, former Criminal and Retard, once ate school rabbit) has forgotten to replace the safety curtain, which accidentally got wrapped around Sad Ed and fell down during attempts to extricate rose, in which case it can't due to fire regulations.

5 p.m.

Mr Pringle is not in a ditch. He is at the dining table consuming pre-show salmon fishcakes, and his lips are not blue but are pink and smiley. Though tight, i.e. he is not revealing where he has been. It is probably hell, metaphorically speaking (unless he actually did get as far as meat bins). But think he has had some kind of Saul on Road to Damascus revelation and is renewed in his commitment to fact-based theatre as he is definitely coming to supervise show. Hurrah!

5.15 p.m.

Though it would have been utterly brilliant if he had been dead. I could have wept at his grave, not for my personal loss, but for the greater loss to the worlds of theatre and politics, perishing slowly from grief and malnutrition like Greyfriar's Bobby. God, life is so unfair.

11 p.m.

Tonight's show marginally less fraught with crapness, i.e. no one got glued to anything, got things stuck in orifices,

or fell off the stage. Although at one point three Year Eight Criminals and Retards climbed on it to try to stop the Nazis storming up the staircase. Sad Ed had to use his bulk to intervene. Which was successful, but confusing storyline-wise. Mr Pringle was over the moon though. He said it showed that the play was so powerful it moved the audience to intervene in history. It did not. It moved some fist-happy mentalists who know a good opportunity for a fight when they see one.

. . . .

Saturday 13
4 p.m.
Thank God it is the last night tonight. Have decided am not even going to after-show party. It will only compound my frustrations—artistic and forbidden-love-wise.

4.30 p.m.
Oh my God. Think may not be frustrated after all. Have just bumped into Mr Pringle at fridge. He said, 'Listen, Rachel. I know the show isn't how we planned it, but I just wanted to say thanks. Your commitment is unquestionable. You ARE Anne.' At which point coughed milk on his Che Guavara T-shirt as was in shock from *a*) being caught in act of proscribed drinking from carton and *b*) use of 'we' to indicate our shared theatrical vision. But he obviously did not care, or possibly notice due to potent love (or presence of dog trying to reach cold meat

container), because then he said, 'You are coming to the party, aren't you?' Said yes. He said, 'Good. I really want you to meet Henry.' Then he went back to his room with two rich teas and a Müller Fruit Corner. He flies in the face of Mum's 'food only at the table and to be consumed with cutlery' rules. We are united in our artistic dream, our disregard for authority, and our forbidden love! Oh it is so obvious now. He wants me to meet his best friend so he can get official approval. And possibly an audition to their guerrilla theatre company. Hurrah! I will not need to apply to college after all. I will be travelling the world in a camper van, fuelled only by creativity and love. And lead replacement petrol. Am going to confess all to Scarlet immediately. Can leave her out of loop no longer. She must share in my joy.

5 p.m.
Scarlet says it is no surprise as her bat-like powers had detected my fatal attraction to Mr Pringle weeks ago, but she was waiting for me to come to her, rather than scare me with her supernatural abilities. (Being Head Goth clearly imbues holder with over-inflated sense of power. It is like when Trevor Pledger actually thought he was a vampire and tried to fly off bike shed roof.) Anyway, she is all for it, as, being an older man, he will tutor me in the 'art of love-making'. Said will be nice just to snog him first, before any penises get involved. Ick. Although will have to get used to penis potential as he is older man

268

and unlike Sad Ed's his will be utterly worldly. Oh my God. Maybe tonight will be night, i.e. will not only be in love with older man but will finally do 'It'. Will be utter meeting of minds and bodies. As opposed to twenty seconds on a bag of potatoes at the back of the Co-Op (Fat Kylie). Yes will do it. Must think of Anne Frank, i.e. cannot turn down opportunity in case tomorrow I am imprisoned in an annexe and then sent to concentration camp and certain death. (Which is exactly what will happen if Mum finds out. Although will not be concentration camp. Will be Auntie Joyless, who makes Mum look lenient.) Anyway, I am a grown-up, after all. And grown-up love is not about romance and happy endings. It is about the facts of life. And I'm pretty sure I know all of them now.

11.30 p.m.
Some facts I did not know:
1. Henry is short for Henrietta.
2. She is not working-class left-wing anarchist. She is daughter of evil Tory MP for Saffron Walden and environs Hugo Thorndyke.
3. She does not work on *Newsnight*. Or even *One Show*. She is runner on *Masterchef*.
4. She is Mr Pringle's fiancée.

On the plus side, at least he does not know that I was in love with him.

269

11.35 p.m.
Scarlet has texted to say she has told Mr Pringle he is a menace to young hearts and minds and that he had better keep his evil, dream-shattering penis away from me in future.

Oh God. Wish was dead. In fact am going to beg God to strike me down in my sleep. Preferably with a plague of frogs. As that would be utterly literary. Though do not know how frogs could actually kill you. Unless they are those poisonous blue ones. Although James's Ninja ones were quite perilous. Maybe a bolt of lightning would be better. Yes, will pray to be burned alive by electrical storm.

11.40 p.m.
In non-painful way.

11.45 p.m.
That does not singe bedding, or Mum will be extra minty.

Sunday 14
9 a.m.
Am still utterly alive. And utterly depressed. What is the point of God if he (or she, or the laser-eyed dog) will not smite you down in your hour of need. On the plus-side Mr Pringle did not come home last night. According to Mum he stayed at the Thorndykes' mock Georgian

mansion in Steeple Bumpstead. I hope he chokes to death on his class betrayal. Or at least on one of Mrs Thorndyke's overly chewy macaroons.

3 p.m.
Mr Pringle did not choke to death either on own hypocrisy or almond-based biscuits. He is very much alive and is moving out. He is going to stay at Thorndyke Towers aka enemy lair instead. He told Mum it is because Henry finished filming early, and he would rather respect Mum's 'not under my roof' wishes. It is not. It is because he is horrified at my 'definitely under my roof' wishes. Am praying for death again. Will sob on bed until the Lord hears me in my hour of need.

3.15 p.m.
Ooh. Is knock on door. Maybe it is grim reaper.

3.30 p.m.
Was James. So fairly grim. He demanded to know why I was so depressed. I said it is credit crunch, i.e. we will be destitute now that Mr Pringle has gone with his rent cheques and it is only Mum I am sorry for. James says *au contraire* Mum is quite happy as she was getting quite tired of the heated anti-John Humphrys atmosphere at the Shreddies table plus Mr Pringle has paid up through the whole of January anyway. Said cheque will bounce as he is impoverished teacher and Mum has been defrauded.

James said that is unlikely given that his great-great-grandfather invented diamond-based golf knitwear. Said why did I not know this essential fact. James said it is because I am not a fact-based person. Said he is wrong, I am utterly fact-friendly. And anyway why is he so cheery. He said it is because he 'got some' at the after-show party last night. It is with Wendy Shoebridge who is in Year Nine and is leader of the Forget-Me-Not Patrol at Fifth Guides (Baptist). This is typical. I am being out grown-upped by an eleven year old. My life is officially over.

. . . .

Monday 15
8 a.m.
Except that, typically, it isn't. It goes on in all its predictability, i.e. Mum is refusing to let Dad have a third slice of toast in case it redistributes more leg fat to his waistline, James is singing 'Up Where We Belong' and the dog is wandering aimlessly around the hallway with what looks like a toothbrush in its mouth. All of which only emphasizes the huge Mr Pringle-shaped fact-based left-wing hole at the Shreddies table.

4 p.m.
School is unbearable. Had to spend most of day lying on saggy sofa being fed reviving Maltesers by Sad Ed. Every corridor is replete with the possibility of bumping into

Mr Pringle. Scarlet says it does not help that I spent most of first break lurking by the drama studio. I said it does not help that she was the one who had gone there in the first place to get shouty at him and I was only there to arbitrate. Think I may have very slightly overplayed the exact nature of my relationship with Mr Pringle to Scarlet as she is definitely under impression that bodily fluids of some sort have been exchanged and that he is a two-timing pervert-in-school pseudo-socialist love menace (her words, not mine). Sad Ed is in agreement. But it is hollow support. He is only doing it to lure Scarlet towards his bodily fluids.

Thank God school is over in four days and with it my daily torment of being so close and yet so far from my older man dream.

5 p.m.

It is also good for Mr Pringle as I do not rate his chances against Scarlet. She has just texted to say she is thinking of reporting him to the *Guardian* as this is the sort of scandal that could being down the entire Tory party. Have texted her to hold off until David Cameron's poll ratings go up in order to achieve maximum effect (I learned this off Suzy). She has agreed. Thank God.

6 p.m.

Have just seen Gordon Brown on News. Think it may have been a mistake to pin my happiness on the reviving

273

fortunes of a man with no neck, giant head, and Vosene-compromised hair.

· ·

Tuesday 16

There is good news on the David Cameron/Mr Pringle downfall front. It is utterly bat-related, i.e. the film of *Twilight* comes out on Friday and Scarlet is too consumed with potential vampire-lust to bring down the Tory party. Goth corner was awash with excitement. In a sort of subdued, corpse-like way.

The mathletes table was also awash with lust. It was James, who spent the whole of lunch with his mouth full of Wendy Shoebridge's tongue instead of his ham and tomato sandwiches. Have pointed out to him that he is in danger of compromising himself nutritionally but he said he does not need food, he and Wendy will subsist on each other's love (he is wrong, I have tried it, you just get dizzy). Plus they shared a packet of yoghurt-coated blueberries in the computer room at first break. It is a match made in heaven. Or PC World.

Did not see Mr Pringle. But it is only temporary relief. Tomorrow it is drama and will have to share airspace with his treacherous Tory-snogging lips once again. May have to plead illness. The dog is looking a bit peaky at the moment. Will claim I have what it has got.

· ·

Wednesday 17

8 a.m.

Mum says I do not have what the dog has got, unless I have also swallowed a tube of Aquafresh and a dozen organic eggs (large), and I have to go to school as I am collecting Jesus from the Camilla Parker Bowles Memorial Crèche as Grandpa and Treena have got Christmas lunch at the Twilight Years Day Centre and will be too compromised by Linda Ronstadt and sherry trifle to be in charge of a minor.

4 p.m.

Oh God. It was worse than I could have possibly imagined. Even the scenario in which Mr Pringle shot me with Mark Lambert's air rifle and then opened fire on rest of drama class. It started off OK, i.e. was merely pale and shaky when Mr Pringle came into room, but that could have been low blood sugar because I had given half my turkey roll to Sad Ed out of pity because Scarlet had just told him he is waste of head boy space and makes Mr Wilmott look effectual. But then Mr Pringle revealed devastating news, i.e. that he is leaving school totally. And instead of realizing this is probably a good thing, as *a*) it will alleviate my pain and *b*) it will alleviate his pain, and potentially David Cameron's because there is less chance Scarlet will remember to bring about their downfall, I stood up and, before I could stop it, my mouth had said something like 'No, but you can't. Not because of me.

275

It was pathetic. I'm totally over it.' And Mr Pringle said, 'Er . . . actually, Rachel, this isn't about you. This is because I've got a part in *EastEnders*. That's where I was on Friday—at an audition.' And yet still mouth did not shut up, it said, 'Oh my God. You are an utter charlatan. You said soap operas are the opiate of the masses, even though Scarlet says it is religion, but whatever. I thought it was about facts, not fiction, about raw, political, life-changing conflict, not whether or not Peggy should marry Archie.' And Sad Ed said, 'She shouldn't, because he is much better in *Gavin and Stacey* and should leave and concentrate on edgy BBC3-based comedy.' Mr Pringle said, 'It *is* about the facts, Rachel. But it's also about following your heart.' So I said, 'What, and your heart lies in playing a cockney wide boy with a heart of gold who gets his girlfriend's best friend pregnant only she turns out to be his long-lost sister?' And he said, 'Actually I'm going to be a market inspector but the point is, I'll get paid four times what I do here and then I can fund me and Henry to make real, political stuff.' At which point thank God regained control of mouth and legs and stormed out, which was utterly dramatic, except when I had to storm back in to remind Sad Ed that he should be storming too.

So now am not only not snogging older man, but entire drama A-level knows about my torment. (Although Sad Ed says that to be honest, half the class were trying to unstick Caris from the fire exit and Reuben Tull was stoned and at that point thought he was an albatross so

my secret is still fairly safe.) But, worse, Mr Pringle has let down fact-based fans everywhere. He has no staying power and has fallen prey to the lure of money, and a fairytale happy ending. Or a grim one involving an explosion at the Queen Vic. But it is utterly not real. I will show him. I will remain strong in my political convictions. And be happy to work for less-than-minimum wage at Woolworth's.

5 p.m.
Mum is writing to Mr Wilmott to complain about the standard of teaching in the Camilla Parker Bowles Memorial Crèche. It is because Jesus is very sad about his namesake's having to sleep in a manger because there were 'no crisps for a bed'. It is Fat Kylie, she has Wotsits on the brain. And 99s in the pants. It is lucky Mum did not also hear Jesus's version of 'Jingle Bells' involving a 'one-whore open sleigh'. The mind boggles.

Thursday 18
8.30 a.m.
Woolworth's is closing. Mum informed me over my Shreddies, having been informed by John Humphrys, from whom she has also acquired an irritating smug tone. She is not at all sympathetic and says it is just 'winnowing the wheat from the chaff' and leaves room for potential expansion of quality establishments like John Lewis.

Pointed out that now she will have to fund me or no one will get any Christmas presents at all and the house will be utterly like Bob Cratchit's with James as the crippled one and her as Scrooge. She said she will think about it. She will not. Being compared to Scrooge is not an insult in her book. God, there is no end to my misery. It is so unfair. Everyone else is basking in festive spirit and I am condemned to walk in perpetual misery, with nothing but cold, hard truth flowing through my veins. Even Sad Ed is uncharacteristically merry. It is because Scarlet has agreed that he can go to see *Twilight* with her. But only on condition that he does not do the eyebrow thing, or the hair, or attempts at brooding sexuality, which in fact only make him look mental.

4 p.m.
Oh my God. Am not alone after all. Someone else is about to get injection of cold hard truth, i.e. James. Have just witnessed treachery first-hand and it is a double betrayal, i.e. his best friend and girlfriend. Mad Harry and Wendy were locked in lust outside the mobile science lab (they are locust monitors). James is going to be devastated. Is Mumtaz all over again. Will break grave news to him gently. Have got emergency reviving Marmite sandwich and a Glade Plug-in (could not find smelling salts).

4.15 p.m.
James has eaten the sandwich and his room smells of

pine forests. But he is not in slightest devastated. He says he is fully aware of nature of Mad Harry's and Wendy's relationship and they are conjugating with his full blessing. Said why is he not mourning the loss of his older woman computer-based geek love? He said, *au contraire*, he has not lost love, he and Mad Harry are sharing Wendy on a one day on/one day off basis. It is a grown-up modern arrangement and I couldn't possibly understand. He is right. She is mental. One of them is bad enough, but two. She has strong tonsils.

* *

Friday 19

Thank God it is the last day of school for two weeks. The sooner this term, and this year, is over the better. It is utterly not the season to be jolly. Christmas is for children, not grown-ups. Am beyond wearing tinsel headbands or lingering under Mrs Leech's mistletoe. And if Thin Kylie puts 'Hallelujah' (crap Alexandra Burke version) on the common room CD player again then will break Middle East peace accord, storm the Um Bongo cushion and overthrow the government myself. May well spend day in library instead ingesting facts. That way will also avoid Mr Pringle. By the time I emerge at quarter past three, like boffiny butterfly, he will be gone from my life for ever.

1 p.m.

Except that did not anticipate Mr Pringle would be in

library having argument with Mr Knox about suspicious bitemarks in a copy of *Mother Courage*. It is the dog. It does not like books. Especially ones with ugly old women on the cover. Tried to hide behind revolving Jacqueline Wilson display but it got whizzed by a Year Seven (still at age when revolving doors, display cases, and chairs are open invitation to spin mentally) so was revealed every few seconds behind whirling Tracey Beakers. He said, 'Can I have a word, Rach?' Said, 'No, this is library. Is illegal. Shush.' He said, 'Outside, in private.' Said OK. Then ensued utterly humiliating monologue, i.e. 'Rachel, I just wanted to say that I'm sorry if I somehow gave you the impression that I was in any way interested. I mean, you must realize that it was just never on the cards. I'm too old for you. You need someone your own age. You see that, don't you?' Except that I didn't, because at that point Sad Ed whizzed past pushing Scarlet on the Davros throne (festive version, i.e. with battery controlled fairy lights around base) and singing 'Bat Out of Hell'. But I didn't say anything. I just shrugged and walked away. Because am grown-up. And do not cry in front other people. Or hit them.

3 p.m.
Unlike Scarlet. According to Sad Ed Mr Pringle is in Mrs Leech's office nursing a black eye and bruised genitals. Scarlet claims it was an accident and that she lost control of the Davros throne. She did not. She never loses control

280

of anything. She is like Stalin. Sad Ed says on plus side he found out (through judicious use of a finger of Twix) who is taking over drama next term. It is Mr Vaughan. According to Mrs Leech, Sophie Microwave Muffins has left him for her Natural Sciences professor and he is utterly heartbroken. So it is one in, one out, on the pervert front.

4 p.m.
Not that Mr Pringle was pervert after all.

4.15 p.m.
Which is typical.

. . . .

Saturday 20
11 a.m.
Am still in bed. What is point of getting up when you have no job to go to. Now I know how long-term unemployed feel.

11.15 a.m.
Am up. Is not Mum and her anti-malingering/pro-laundry stance. Is hideous sound of James and Wendy through wall next door. It is obviously his day on. Have no idea what they are doing but there is a lot of 'Oooh'ing and 'Oh my God'ing. Ick. Am going to see Sad Ed instead to beg for sublet trolley work, i.e. he can pay

me to mind the herd while he spends quality time pestering Scarlet. Is mutually beneficial grown-up arrangement. Hurrah.

4 p.m.
Sad Ed not in agreement at all about arrangement. He says it is utterly against company rules and he could face the sack or prison and anyway he is seeing Scarlet tonight at the cinema where it will be dark, and she will be utterly in the mood for love having eaten aphrodisiac pick-and-mix and got all clammy over Robert Pattinson. Said *a*) since when did he care about rules, he is utterly against The Man, even though The Man is actually a woman, i.e. Mrs Noakes and *b*) cherry cola bottles are not aphrodisiac. He said *a*) it is utterly rock starrish and anti-The Man to do menial labour as a youth so that you can then rebel against it and write about it on critically acclaimed albums before killing yourself and *b*) it is the sugar, it makes you lick your lips, which makes you think about sex. He is going to empty some Silver Spoon into bag for good measure. Said is good thing am too broke to go as would not want to be luring random goths with my liking for Jelly Tots. Then Reuben said if I was looking for work then he would give me £2 to deliver Christmas 'present' to Wizard Weeks. Said what is in present? He said is herbally organic thing. Declined. I may be desperate, but I am not being his drugs mule.

9 p.m.

Being fact-based is utterly detrimental to love gone bad, as what I need right now is twinkly vampires and white-toothed werewolf boys. Or at very least Colin Firth in a wet shirt. Plus no one else understands my plight. They are all too busy engrossed in festive *Casualty*. Even dog is glued to screen. (It is the ITU. It likes the bleeping.) If only Jack was here.

11 p.m.

Sad Ed has texted. He did not get to snog Scarlet by the power of Silver Spoon and pick-and-mix. But she did fall asleep on him in sick-smelling Volvo and he has her sugary spit on his shoulder so he is happy. He says he will never wash it. He doesn't anyway. It still has Turkish Delight residue on it from October.

· ·

Sunday 21

Predictably 'Hallelujah', the tedious Alexandra Burke, Thin Kylie-endorsed version, as opposed to utterly brilliant untimely death Sad Ed-endorsed Jeff Buckley version, is Christmas Number One. James is jubilant. It is because the mathletes will rake in at least £87 in profit next term, as they had somehow managed to convince most of Year Seven that Golden Wonder would triumph, despite not actually having a single out. Or being a real band.

Am also in the money. Ish. Mum has agreed to my
request for emergency funds. Though she is not issuing
credit due to my subprime tendencies. Am going to have
to earn it instead by helping with festive chores. Asked
how much she was offering an hour. She said £2.50,
including a 15-minute juice and biscuit break and an
hour for lunch. All meals provided. Tried to bargain her
up to £2.75 but she has clearly been watching *The
Apprentice* as she immediately dropped her offer to £2.25
and I can buy my own health-giving snacks. Have
accepted first offer. At very least it will take my mind off
the utterly Eliotian wasteland that is my world.

Monday 22

Is torture. My hands are raw and have Cillit-Bang-
induced headache. Am like prisoner of war. But with
endless Radio 4 in background. Which is tantamount to
mental cruelty. Meanwhile James is up in his bedroom
with Wendy *and* Mad Harry. Mum is mental. They are
probably having some hideous three-way love orgy.

3 p.m.

They are not having hideous three-way love orgy. They
are playing Warhammer, in full costume, i.e cloaks
and random hats (one Harry Potter pointy wizard, one
cycle helmet, and a swimming cap). Which is possibly
worse.

5 p.m.

Cannot go on any longer. Have now: hoovered under beds, hoovered in beds, made twenty metres of paper chains and decorated (environmentally-, carpet- and dog-friendly) tree—TWICE—because apparently my eclectic, inspired 'place decorations in any available gap' method does not fit in with Mum's rigid 'only green and blue baubles, no tinsel and for heaven's sake don't clump them at the top the weight ratio is all wrong, Rachel' method. Have informed Mum that am leaving her employ forth-with due to artistic differences. She threatened to with-hold pay as am breaking terms of contract. Pointed out that had not signed contract so therefore she owed me £20. Mum said *au contraire*, *a*) I had signed contract sev-eral years ago pertaining to household chores, which was still valid until my eighteenth birthday and *b*) no one gets paid for their lunch hour so technically she only owed me £17.50. Have agreed compromise. Am doing hour of babysitting this evening while Mum and Dad go to Terry and Cherie's festive warm Baileys and prawn ring party and will get full £20 and no-blame redundancy. Is bargain as they will be back within twenty minutes feigning headaches. There is no way Mum will consume prawn rings. It breaks rules pertaining to seafood, overambition, and Coleen Nolan.

11 p.m.

Mum and Dad are still not back from the Britchers'. Am

285

torn between keeping quiet so can amass fortune as babysitting pay will go into time and half past midnight (have checked original contract) or going over road to rescue parents from potential hostage situation. There can be no other explanation as to why they can have been detained so long except under duress.

11.30 p.m.
Except 'accidental' consumption of eight Tia Marias (Dad) and heated debate as to whether or not Tia Maria is actual person (Mum and Cherie). For once am in agreement with Thin Kylie, i.e. 'Your mum is, like, worse than that winking woman.' (i.e Ann Robinson. At least assume it is. Not Mrs Dyer (fat feet, smells of Yardley, nervous tic).) Have removed parents and sent them to bed, but not without securing agreement of extra £5 for duties beyond scope of contract. So now have £35. Am rich beyond compare and will be able to buy family and friends utterly luxurious Christmas gifts. Hurrah!

Tuesday 23
9 a.m.
Except that Scarlet has just texted to demand presence in Duke tonight for wobbly toilet table pre-Christmas celebration. And will need at least £20 for purchasing of beverages and snacks and another £5 for jukebox in order to prevent Reuben torturing pub with the entire

Tangerine Dream back catalogue. Which only leaves £10 (am excellent at maths, is Riley family gift, like Redknapps with football) but have run out of hair products and cannot possibly go to pub resembling puffa-fish head so in fact have exactly no money for presents. Need Plan B.

9.15 a.m.
Have got Plan B. Am going to blackmail James into handing over his mathlete money by threatening to tell Mum that he is having inappropriate relations with Wendy Shoebridge in at least one proscribed area (bust, pants, and back of neck all banned until at least age 18).

9.20 a.m.
James says I will have to do better as *a*) in fact he has not technically breached any proscribed areas due to double vest protection and *b*) in any case he will match my threat and raise me a 'But Rachel got naked in bed with Justin Statham' (thus breaching several areas, including snogging people who live in mock tudor mansions). Need Plan C. And possibly Plan D as well.

10 a.m.
Have got it. Am going to utilize talents and write everyone fact-based festive-themed personal poems. Then when am famous they will be able to sell them on eBay for fortune so is utterly gift that keeps on giving. Will

start with Mum as she is notoriously hard to please, poetry-wise (she does not like limericks, religious iconography, or whimsical robins playing in snow).

1 p.m.
Mire of gloom is compromising, talent-wise. Am giving up on Mum and trying Sad Ed instead. He likes anything that rhymes. Will be a cinch.

Hmm. Will just possibly watch bit of *Ice Age* with James and dog though. Is for cheering up purposes, to aid poetry. And full of mammoth facts, so legal.

3 p.m.
Ooh. And *Brave Little Toaster*.

6 p.m.
Am not cheered. Am devastated and weepy at scale of braveness of toaster. Am going to pub. Will write when get back later. Hopefully mire of gloom will be ousted by festive spirit instead (though not actual spirit, as that would be illegal).

11.30 p.m.
Mire of gloom not entirely ousted despite consumption of several spirits. Is because Scarlet discovered brilliant method of confusing Shorty McNulty, i.e. purchasing two tonic waters and one double Malibu (retro drink thus utterly cool and tastes like liquid Bounty bars, i.e.

coconut, i.e. utterly health-giving). And then pouring Malibu into tonics thus creating two alcoholic drinks from one. Is brilliant. And am completely inspired to write poem, despite ongoing misery. Am like Coleridge, racked by depression and writing by candlelight (or John Lewis angle poise, but with energy saving bulb so fairly gloomy and underpowered) under influence of narcotics. Perhaps will do 'Rime of Ancient Mariner' style thing and be youngest ever Poet Laureate.

. . . .

Wednesday 24
Christmas Eve
10 a.m.
Ow. Why does head hurt? Malibu is sneaky drink and not at all conducive to health arrangements.

10.15 a.m.
Or poetry. Have read last night's work back and is not 'Rime of Ancient Mariner' literary genius. Though is definitely under influence of narcotics, and inexplicably written in Tippex:

Festive Feast

> *Christmas is coming.*
> *The goose is getting fat.*
> *So we can eat it.*
> *Except Scarlet who is vegetarian.*

*And Sad Ed because they are having duck because
Aled likes duck.*

But it will have to do as think may be sick if try to use
brain this morning. Will put in envelopes with instructions to read in secret as is personal. No one will ever
know.

2 p.m.
Am marginally revived after not-at-all festive lunch of
salad. It is because Dad is in charge of catering temporarily while Mum and James go shopping for a present for
Wendy. And he is not allowed to use the cooker, toaster,
freezer or microwave.

3 p.m.
Granny Clegg has rung to say Happy Christmas. Dad
pointed out she was a day early (unprecedented, usually
she is three days late) but she said she had a full social cal-
endar tomorrow and so would be unable to spend time
gassing on the phone (also unprecedented as there is
nothing Granny Clegg likes more than gassing on the
phone: favourite topics—Why are oranges round? and
Why don't bees develop gluier bottoms to keep the stings
in?). Dad asked what wonderment was compromising
her ability to pick up phone. She said she had fifteen people for lunch including Pig, Denzil, Hester Trelowarren,
Maureen from the Spar and Auntie Joyless (she actually

called her this) and her puritanical offspring Boaz and Mary. Dad asked what she was cooking. Granny said Turkey Twizzlers with Smash and a choice of Viennetta or Butterscotch Angel Delight for pudding.

3.30 p.m.
Mum and James are back from shops (with Warhammer figurines and a GCSE maths textbook for Wendy) and Dad has recounted latest Clegg mentalism. Mum said on plus side at least her idiotic relatives (she actually said this) are at least 300 miles away this year, and have no means of transport now that Hilary (one l, penis, future black Prime Minister)'s environmentally friendly Nissan Micra has a broken gasket, so there can be no surprise visits. That way we can have a brisk lunch and it will all be back to normal (i.e. decorations down, Quality Street consumed, and crap Clegg presents in recycling) by Boxing Day. For once am utterly in agreement with Mum. The sooner this charade of childish cheerfulness is over the better. Am going to watch News 24 instead to fill self with facts and combat Christmas creep.

8 p.m.
Oooh. There is potential terrorist situation at Stansted airport. Apparently bearded man has been arrested for carrying inflammatory material (though is unclear if they actually mean violence-inciting or just packet of firelighters). Mum says it is definitely Osama Bin Laden.

Although James has pointed out that chances of him arriving in Essex on an easyJet flight from Sciathos are slim to say the least. Mum says that's what he wants us to think which is why it is utterly cunning. Only not so cunning now the police have seen through his plan and have the world's most notorious madman in custody in Bishop's Stortford.

9.15 p.m.
The police do not have the world's most notorious madman in custody in Bishop's Stortford. PC Doone just rang to ask if we knew of a James Riley. Mum said yes indeed and he is at this very minute doing advanced Sudoku with the dog. PC Doone said no he isn't he is at this very minute locked in a cell talking about marigolds and rocking gently. Mum said is not James, is Osama, pretending to be James. At which point a confusing argument went on for three minutes while Mum and PC Doone argued over how Osama would know James, and the implications of the marigolds (Mum's theory: gloves, to hide fingerprints) until James came to phone to assert his official nature and managed to deduce identity of criminal suspect. Is not Osama Bin Laden. Is Uncle Jim, i.e. Dad's brother (full genetic match one, as opposed to soon to be three-year-old baby Jesus who is half Riley, half Boltoner) who has been living in Tibet for several years with his girlfriend Marigold (and who we had all forgotten about). Anyway he is not being charged with terrorism after all as

292

the inflammatory material turned out to be 'inflammable', only it wasn't. It was a bottle of rank alcohol. PC Doone said the sooner he is out of the station the better as he is annoying everyone with his sitar, and clearly needs mental help. Mum said PC Doone should call emergency psychiatric care. But apparently they are at their office party at TGI Friday's. Dad has gone to fetch him. Mum is mad with crossness. Not only was she sorely off the mark with her marigold glove theory, but she is being invaded by an idiotic relative after all, i.e. the black sheep of the family. Pointed out that black sheep is racist and anti-ovine but at that point she made her lips disappear so went for situation-diffusing wee instead.

9.30 p.m.
James has rung Grandpa to inform him of impending return of Prodigal Son. He said 'Who?' No wonder Uncle Jim has issues.

11.45 p.m.
Uncle Jim is in house. But is out of bounds to all contact with impressionable members of family, i.e. me and James. Pointed out I was utterly grown-up and in fact used to dealing with drug-addled mentalists, i.e. Reuben Tull. But Mum said I can wait until breakfast when he will have slept off the ouzo (Mum's forensic breath test) and been washed and shaved. (Mum does not allow beards in house on grounds of being untrustworthy and

unhygienic. How she puts up with dog is miracle.) James says Uncle Jim has definitely come to right place and Mum's diet of tough love and high fibre will sort him out in no time. She is better than Prozac any day. Said he has not come to right place. He will be begging for prescription drugs within minutes when he finds out Mum's regime is more restrictive than *Celebrity Fat Camp*.

Thursday 25

Christmas Day

Is Christmas Day, i.e. season of goodwill and forgiveness (possibly) to all men. Yet instead Riley household is imbued with mintyness. Is not over credit crunch nature of presents. (Although James has already broken his hole puncher and is blaming Mum for purchasing from Gayhomes instead of superior WHSmith. Mum is blaming James for trying to punch holes in trousers, brussels sprout, and dog.) Or personal poems, which received high praise, e.g. 'Gosh' (Dad) and 'It is the thought that counts' (Mum). It is over impromptu presence of Uncle Jim. On plus side, he no longer looks like fundamentalist, i.e. beardy, in robes, with rabid expression in eyes. Instead is relatively fresh-faced and wearing pair of Dad's corduroys. Although freshness does not extend to breath which is definitely still of ouzo variety. But as only words uttered so far are 'please God no' when Mum tried to

clean out his ears, is hard to tell for sure. James says it will all be fine when Grandpa comes over with Treena and Baby Jesus for birthday tea and Uncle Jim will be moved with love for his infant brother, and estranged father. Said *a*) do not think Jesus and his health- and brain-compromising antics will move anyone except Mum and her bottle of Cillit Bang, *b*) Grandpa Riley is not estranged, just strange, and *c*) oh shit, had utterly forgotten that is birthday of other Jesus (i.e. not at all spiritual and with no ability to turn water into wine) and have not got him present. Oooh. Maybe will write him poem. He can put in box of treasures until he can read, i.e. in about ten years.

3.15 p.m.
Ugh. Brain obviously being sapped by atmosphere of non-festive gloom, and possibly excessively brandy-soaked Christmas pudding (due to slippage of wrist according to Dad, and latent alcoholism, according to Mum) as have utter writer's block. Will listen to soothing music for inspiration.

3.20 p.m.
Have had utter Newton moment (i.e. pain of apple falling on head eased by discovery of gravity) i.e. put on CD player, and realized had accidentally left in nausea-inducing Christmas Crackers album (dog likes East 17 'Stay'—it finds it soothing) BUT first song was 'Mary's

295

Boy Child', i.e. all about Baby Jesus, so have basically stolen it and rejigged lyrics, i.e:

> *Now Ernest and his wife Treena came to Addenbrooke's*
> *Hospital that night,*
> *They found no place to bear her child, not a single bed*
> *was in sight.* (Due to ward closures following
> outbreak of Norovirus)

> *And then they found a little nook on a trolley all forlorn,*
> *And in the dermatology wing cold and dark* (actually
> heated to standard twenty-one degrees but
> that doesn't scan), *Treena's little boy was born.*

> *Hark now hear Beastly Boys sing, Jesus was born today,*
> *Yes, Treena's boy child Jesus Riley was born on*
> *Christmas Day.*

Hurrah. Is not plagiarism, is cunning satire. And is just in time as can hear unmistakable sound of small child trailing feet through pea gravel in utterly banned manner (even coverage needed for maximum security effect).

5 p.m.
As predicted, presence of Baby Jesus did not move Uncle Jim to wordy confession. Particularly given that Jesus seemed convinced he was Craig Revel Horwood and the whole John Sergeant thing reared its ugly head again

until Mum put on CBeebies. On plus side, he did seem to bond with Grandpa, particularly over their mutual (if silent) appreciation of Pinky Dinky Doo. Jesus's birthday poem did not go down as well as hoped either. Gave Treena envelope. She said, 'Christ on a bike, it's not bloody book tokens is it?' Said 'No' (although you can never have enough book tokens). Treena said 'Thank flamin' 'eck. Your mam gave him a tenner's worth last year and we still an't spent them yet, I mean how many books does a kid need?' Did not answer. Let poem speak for itself. Though not sure what it said to Treena as she was stunned into silence.

6 p.m.
Prodigal relation returning thing is spreading like wildfire. Scarlet rang to say she has got email from Jack. Apparently he is coming home for New Year. Suzy is mental with excitement and says it is best Christmas present ever, except possibly for when she got a bottle of House of Commons whisky from Charles Clarke. Said yeah, is brilliant present. Scarlet said why do you sound so minty about it then? Said was not Jack. Was that dog had just eaten my Quality Street golden penny.

But was not dog (although he had eaten seven golden pennies and four purple nut things). It is Jack. Why hasn't he emailed me to tell me he is coming home?

6 p.m.
Not that I care. Because I'm grown-up and I know there are no happy endings and knights in shining anything.

6.30 p.m.
But the thing is. Maybe I do. Care I mean.

7.10 p.m.
Oh God. Maybe should email him and tell him.

7.30 p.m.
No will not email him. Am grown-up and fact based and above all affairs of the heart. Or pants.

7.35 p.m.
Oooh. Will email him and tell him that instead. Then is like am getting cake and eating it, i.e. contacting Jack, but also reasserting my commitment to adulthood.

7.40 p.m.
Have sent email as follows:

> I hear that you are coming back for New Year. Which was shock as in fact had utterly forgotten you even existed, have been so busy with my studies of economic crisis etc. Am utterly changed person, you probably won't even recognize me.

PS Although hair is still mental.

Is completely nonchalant, i.e. he will think have not been thinking about him at all. Which have not.

7.50 p.m.
Well, not often anyway.

8 p.m.
Until now. Is like he is camping out in brain. With fully secured guy ropes and a week's worth of calor gas. All can think about is Jack. Nothing can move him.

8.30 p.m.
Except James. There is nothing like sight of idiotic eleven year old in a hole-punched swimming cap trying to do splits to banish thoughts of former lover from head.

8.35 p.m.
Except that am now thinking about not thinking about him which means am actually thinking about him. Damn.

8.40 p.m.
Maybe will just check email to see if he has replied. In nonchalant way.

8.45 p.m.
No email. But am utterly nonchalant.

9 p.m.
Will just check again.

9.10 p.m.
No email. And Mum says to stop turning computer on as is non-festive anti-family activity and if I want something to do I can watch *The Vicar of Dibley* with everyone else.

. . . .

Friday 26
Boxing Day
Have checked email (Christmas officially over in Riley household, i.e. tree may still be up but fairy lights are off, chocolate boxes in recycling, and last of turkey has been chopped, curried, and frozen in meal-sized portions, to avoid waste and poisoning issues) but there is no reply. Think it is because Christmas clogs up ether and my email possibly still hovering somewhere mid-Atlantic waiting to get through cloggy cloud of round robins and online sale shopping transactions.

2 p.m.
James says emails do not hover above oceans and I am sounding more like Granny Clegg every day. Said that was unfair as Granny Clegg thinks the internet works by giant invisible cables but James said, 'How *does* the internet work, Einstein?' and had to admit did not know

300

unless it is by microwaves. Although maybe Granny Clegg does know actual answer now. Maybe bang on head has knocked sense into her.

3 p.m.
Granny Clegg rang. Asked her how internet worked. She said giant invisible cables. On plus side, she said Christmas at Pasty Manor was utter success, despite Hester's pet chicken Dale mysteriously disappearing in 'Bermuda Triangle' in scullery, leaving only three ginger feathers behind as reminder of his trusting eyes. Eyes not trusting. Eyes beady and menacing. But did not say that. Instead asked her if Bruce had eaten much today. She said no he has been mysteriously off his food and she is taking him to vet in case he is also being affected by the Bermuda Triangle forces, sapping his appetite.

Told her about Uncle Jim coming home. She went mental with excitement. But it turns out she thought I meant her Uncle Jimmy who died of syphilis in 1936. She is not so excited about Uncle Jim. It is because he is embracer of alternative culture. And Cleggs are very much anti-alternative or indeed any culture. They do not even buy olive oil as is too left-wing.

I feel sorry for Uncle Jim. No wonder he is not talking to anyone when they all think he is a criminal or mental or a 'filthy commie'. He is utter non-racist black sheep of family.

Saturday 27

Both Jack and Uncle Jim are resolute in their silence, i.e. there is no email from Chichicastenango and Uncle Jim is mute on sofa watching *Tom and Jerry* with dog on his lap and bottle of Waitrose Belgian lager in hand. Said was amazed Mum was letting him consume alcohol in house, and at eleven in morning, but she says it is minimal alcohol by volume and is clever ruse to make him need to wee so that she can commandeer sofa and turn off TV without plaintive wailing (both Jim and dog).

2.10 p.m.

Oh my God. Have had complete revelation. I am also (non-racist) black sheep of family. Uncle Jim and I are at one. We are both depressed. We are both misunderstood. And we both have compromising hairdos (he has freak-ishly low hairline which gives him slight air of Cro-Magnon man/O'Grady). Am going to show solidarity by sitting on sofa and watching cartoons.

2.15 p.m.

But without the bottle of Belgian lager. I did try but Mum says I am not Amy Winehouse, much as I like to think I am, and I can have a glass of water or a small orange juice. She is wrong. I do not think I am Amy Winehouse.

302

2.20 p.m.
Although we do share poetic talent, cheating ex-boyfriends, and voluminous hair.

3 p.m.
Cartoons are off now. It was not the weeing. It was the falling asleep. Mum is now panicked that overfull bladder will give way during sleep and he will seep onto sofa. That will teach her. Or more probably mean we have reinstatement of plastic sofa covering (usually only brought out during presence of Bruce and Grandpa Clegg, neither of whom have complete control of urinary tract).

* *

Sunday 28

Still no email from Jack. It is good thing he is 5,466 miles away as Mum has decided enough is enough when it comes to silence and she is determined to break Uncle Jim. It is like Guantanamo Bay with Mum and James (who is assisting her in matter) as evil CIA agents. I do not rate Uncle Jim's chances. They are using the dining room as their torture chamber. James is already inside researching tactics on the internet.

10 a.m.
Mum has rejected waterboarding, sleep deprivation, and slapping. But is allowing mild threat (sectioning, or

withdrawal of all alcohol) and menacing stares. They are starting after lunch, and Dad and I are under instructions to leave table subtly after consumption of pudding course. As pudding is banana split asked if could leave before but Mum said would arouse too much suspicion. She is wrong. Is more convincing. Who voluntarily eats warm bananas?

5 p.m.
Uncle Jim has caved. It took two hours and forty-three minutes. And six bottles of Belgian lager. It turns out he has been in a trauma- (and possibly drug-) induced catatonic stupor after the love of his life, i.e. Marigold, left him halfway up a Himalaya for an accountant from Chipping Sodbury. Apparently she says he is a grown-up. Said Uncle Jim is a grown-up, i.e. he is 37. But Mum is utterly on Marigold's side, despite her being *a*) hippy and *b*) called Marigold. She said *a*) an accountant is a sound financial bet for the future and *b*) no man who still reads *Asterix* and *Tintin* can be classed as a grown-up.

Poor Uncle Jim. We are both victims of anti-fiction ageist policies. It is further proof that there are no happy endings. In fact do not know why I am wasting my time waiting for Jack to email. Love is utter charade and cold hard facts (and BBC) are only dependable constant in life. It is utterly depressing. In fact may join Uncle Jim in drowning sorrows in dining room.

6 p.m.

Mum has barred way to dining room. She says I do not need any alcohol to loosen my already overactive imagination or voicebox. Am going to drown sorrows down Duke instead. Although admittedly in non-alcoholic beverages. And possibly not in drowning quantities due to funding issues. Have traded book token with James on a crippling twenty per cent interest deal, i.e. I got £4 in return. Pointed out that interest rates were currently in fact languishing around the one per cent mark, but he said not for the likes of me they're not and went into a lecture on credit risk, so snatched money before he either changed mind or bored me to death. On plus side, Sad Ed will be there and will totally understand my plight. Plus hopefully he has had colossally awful Christmas so will feel somewhat smug. Scarlet is not coming. She says she is too busy preparing for return of Jack, i.e. repainting his bedroom walls black and getting his drum kit out of attic. Apparently Suzy had boxed everything up and Farrow and Balled everything off-white during mental premature nesting phase. Asked where baby will go if they ever get one? Scarlet said it is going to share with Bob and Suzy so they can fully bond as a family. It is baby I feel sorry for. I have seen what goes on in that bedroom and it is not savoury. Or even legal.

11 p.m.

At least in scheme of things I am not as sad as Sad Ed

(who actually got a packet of vests for Christmas, which he says just accentuates his non-worldly penis issues). Or as Uncle Jim. Whose penis, it turns out, is very much worldly. In fact it is possibly worldly penis, and its straying too close to someone called India Britt-Dullforce, that caused Marigold to fling self into arms of accountant. (Have just overheard him telling Mum ins and outs (literally) of relationship.) On plus side, at least he is still talking. It is over six hours of ceaseless confession now. Mum must be jubilant.

· ·

Monday 29
Islamic New Year

Mum is not at all jubilant. In fact she is very minty, due to lack of sleep and abundance of talking. Apparently Uncle Jim kept her up until three banging on about Marigold's golden aura and how India Britt-Dullforce had bad 'chi'. She says she is like boy with finger in dyke (dam thing, not butch lesbian person) and she should have jolly well kept it in instead of letting in flood of psychobabble and unsavoury sexploits. He is back at it already this morning, only James is taking role of sympathetic listener. Said this was risk given James is underage and already quite cult-based (Lord of the Rings, Warhammer, Ninja Turtles) but she says it is better than Dad as James is utterly moral when it comes to adultery, and Dad is still in doghouse for siding with Camilla

in Princess Diana debacle. Did not tell her about the James/Mad Harry/Wendy Shoebridge love triangle. They are all meeting up later at Mad Harry's to swap presents. I dread to think what he will come home with. Possibly 'cooties' (definitely real, as Googled by James).

5 p.m.
James got a book of Greek myths and a keyring spirit level. Which is marginally better than cooties. But only marginally.

. . . .

Tuesday 30
There is yet more prodigal child 'good' news Chez Stone. Scarlet has rung to say Suzy and Bob have been allocated a baby. They got a letter this morning telling them it is being despatched within weeks. Asked what kind. Scarlet said it is mainly white, with a hint of exotic, i.e. its mother is Irish. Said actually meant is it boy or girl. Scarlet said it is a girl, called Aoife. But they are definitely going to rename her Obama. And that tomorrow's fancy dress New Year's Eve party is utterly in her honour. Asked what theme was. Scarlet says it is heroes and heroines, as Obama is modern hero. She is going as Bella Swan, obviously. Said am not coming as am me, i.e. my own hero except that am utterly non-heroic. And am peed off. Scarlet said does not have to be fictional. Suzy is coming

as Harriet Harman and Bob as Nelson Mandela. Said do not let him near boot polish. Scarlet said as if, that is utterly racist. He is going to just hold symbolic copy of *Economist*. Am still not going. New Year's Eve parties are just childish excuses to drink dubious punch and snog dubious guests.

. . . .

Wednesday 31

New Year's Eve

Thank God it is New Year's Eve. The sooner 2008 is over the better. It has been utterly the worst year ever. Both the world and my life have been racked by ill-fortune and economic mismanagement. Plus am still one centimetre down on last year (millimetre gain was blip caused by rogue hair matting). The only consolation is that next year cannot possibly get any worse.

Am utterly resolute in decision not to partake in Scarlet's hero-themed welcome home Jack and Obama New Year's Eve party. Sad Ed has already been round to reveal his outfit of choice. It is Batman. Pointed out that this is mistake on several grounds, i.e. *a*) is utter lie as his heroes are all miserable/dead musicians, e.g. Jim Morrison/Morrisey etc. and *b*) tight and shiny bat suit is very revealing of bulges, including non-worldly penis and bingo wings. Sad Ed said am right on both counts but is all ploy to win over Scarlet as Batman is ultimate goth superhero, plus he knows for fact she is going `as

308

Catwoman, who everyone knows was doing Batman on the side. Plus on positive side, lycra is girdle-like and he has lost several inches off waist. He is mistaken if he thinks that outfit will win Scarlet over. He does not look at all batly. He looks like a crap transvestite. Sad Ed has begged me to go with him, preferably dressed as Robin, but said it would compromise all my anti-hero ideals. Plus am needed at home to babysit Jesus and Uncle Jim. Grandpa and Treena are getting drunk in Queen Lizzie, Mum and Dad are going to play Jenga at Clive and Marjory's and James is at a Warhammer mathletes ner-dathon with Mad Harry and Wendy. They are mental with potential debauchery. Apparently Damon Parker is bringing a can of shandy and Ali Hassan has a Kanye West CD. They are morons. Sad Ed says I will regret it later when he is doing utterly grown-up things like put-ting his penis to good use and I am watching *Lark Rise to Candleford*. Said *a*) ick and *b*) it is *Road Runner* actually. Jesus does not like Julia Sawalha. Nor does the dog. It is static hair issues again. Yet it is not afraid of meep-meep-ing emu creature. Anyway, he is wrong, I will not regret my decision.

10 p.m.
Oh God. If have to watch idiot Wile E. Coyote blow him-self up again am going to potentially steal Sad Ed's thun-der and engage in untimely death. Why does he not learn? Even Jesus has fallen asleep. May just go upstairs

and text Sad Ed to check on progress. Is just being caring. Am not actually interested in gossip.

10.05 p.m.
Have got reply. He is all minty as there are three Batmen, and both of them have proper suits as opposed to leotards borrowed off their mums and cardboard masks. Plus they do not have tails. Have pointed out that did think tail was mistake as do not recall bats actually having them.

10.10 p.m.
He says he has removed tail but it has left gaping hole on buttock, revealing birthmark shaped like Gary Lineker's head. Have told him to get felt tip and colour buttock black and no one will be any the wiser.

10.15 p.m.
Sad Ed says cannot find felt tip but has stolen goth eye-liner from Scarlet's bedroom. Said that is good.

10.20 p.m.
Sad Ed says he is now in trouble for leaving black bottom prints all over Habitat sofa. Have texted back to say am losing interest in his buttocks and what else is happening please.

10.30 p.m.
Oooh text beep. Will be gossip from Sad Ed. Not that

need gossip. Is purely philanthropical, i.e. making sure all friends have not drowned in eggnog punch.

10.31 p.m.
Was not Sad Ed. Unbelievably was Justin Statham asking if had changed mind about his grown-up pants area. Said NO. AM ANTI-PANTS. KEEP CONTENTS TO SELF. ICK.

10.32 p.m.
Ugh. Text beep. Is probably Justin again. When will he get message that am utterly not interested in content of his pants.

10.35 p.m.
Was not Justin. Apparently he got pants message after all. Was Sad Ed. Whose pants content I have seen and rejected outright. Anyway, he says no one drowned in punch, but that is not eggnog, is new experimental gin, pineapple juice, and chocolate sauce variety. Which is all very interesting. But notice that Jack is not mentioned. Not that care about him. Or contents of his pants. Am just concerned that he has made it home safely and is not caught up in actual Osama Bin Laden Al Qaeda bomb plot at airport (as opposed to drunk beardy uncle plot).

10.40 p.m.
Although would be good if he was caught up. I could steal the Fiesta, drive to airport and infiltrate aircraft and talk

311

terrorists down with my negotiating skills, and utterly rescue Jack. Hurrah. Will text Sad Ed to check if Jack in peril.

10.45 p.m.
Sad Ed says he not at party but not in peril. He stuck in traffic on A11 in Nelson Mandela's sick-smelling Volvo. Never mind. Is probably good thing. Do not want to rescue ungrateful Jack, who has not even told me he is coming home yet. Plus rescuing only works in fiction. In real fact-based life I would crash Fiesta on mini round-about and end up in hospital with gear stick where gear-stick should not be. Will check on Uncle Jim and moronic coyote (dog, not Wile E) instead.

11 p.m.
Oh God. Uncle Jim is having sobbing breakdown due to turning off of *Road Runner* and reading of *Tintin in Tibet*, which just reminds him of Marigold. Is all my fault. I should have followed Mum's instructions (A4, magneted to fridge) and monitored him at all times. Will check list to see what have to do in this situation.

11.15 p.m.
List has no instructions for weeping uncles. Although it does tell me how to relight the boiler pilot, make an emergency escape rope from bedsheets, and perform Heimlich manoeuvre on dog. Will use initiative and tell

312

him some simple facts of life, i.e. there are no happy endings, love does not exist, and the sooner he grows up the better.

11.20 p.m.
Uncle Jim is not at all in agreement with fact-based stance. Said he of all people should understand, given utterly non-happy ending of love life halfway up a Himalaya. He said *au contraire*, it has only fuelled his conviction that love is everything, and that if you don't believe in happy endings then there is no point to universe. Told him if he had any Riley sense, he would grow up, and read some Stephen Hawking instead of the *Asterix* and *Tintin*. He said where's the fun in that? Said life isn't meant to be fun and stormed out before he could baffle me with any more yoghurt-knitting alternative nonsense.

11.25 p.m.
Oh. Have got text. Is probably Sad Ed with more buttock-related hoo-ha.

11.26 p.m.
Was not Sad Ed. Was Jack. It said, 'Just got email. Must have got clogged in Christmas ether. Where are you, Riley? Want to see the new you!' Have not texted back. Cannot even be bothered to reply. Especially as the new me is wearing no make-up, is all red-faced from getting minty, and is in perpetually vile mood.

11.27 p.m.
Actually, is true. Am always in vile mood these days. Why is that?

11.30 p.m.
Oh God. Have had revelation. Is thanks to yoghurt-knitting Uncle Jim. He sat outside bedroom door (refused to let him in as was all red-faced from mintyness) and said 'Do you know who you sound like, Rach?' Said 'Sensible grown-up.' He said, 'Yeah. Like your mum.' And then stomach did hideous enormous heave thing. And realized do sound exactly like Mum. Although with slightly less use of phrase 'I told you so'. But none the less, have utterly morphed into low-fun, permanently minty Janet Riley. Was about to utter strangulated cry but Uncle Jim clearly on one of his confessional rants and got in first with 'Don't grow up yet, Rach. In fact don't grow up ever. Happy endings aren't just in books. You just need to believe in yourself. And in love.' And then he started going on about believing in rainbows and pots of gold so switched off at that bit because James spent a year trying to deduce the possibility of pot of gold and has established beyond reasonable doubt that it does not exist. But he is right about happy endings. That they're worth aiming for. Because even if you fall down, half the fun is in trying.

I want my happy ending. I want to be a princess. I want my knight in shining whatever.

And I don't need rescuing. But maybe I can rescue him

instead. And tell him that I might not be grown-up. And I might make mistakes. Colossal ones involving magic mushrooms and naked ex-boyfriends. But that it doesn't mean I don't love him.

11.35 p.m.
Because I do. I love him.

11.45 p.m.
Oh. I really love him. I have to go and tell him. I have to rescue him right now. Jesus will be fine. He is asleep on dog and dog is asleep on washing machine. What can possibly go wrong there? And anyway, Uncle Jim is here. And he might not be grown-up in Mum's eyes. But he's clever. And sober, for once (Belgian lager out of bounds now floodgates opened). And he knows more about life than anyone else I know. Oh God, have only got quarter of an hour of year left. Why, oh why did I wish it away. I have to get there before midnight. I have to tell him before he snogs Hillary Clinton or the Invisible Woman.

11.46 p.m.
OK. This is it. I'm going to get my happy ending. Not as a heroine. Mostly because I don't have the time to make authentic Sylvia Plath costume. Instead am going as me. Because Jack was right about one thing. Being me is enough. In fact, it's utterly brilliant.

Or at least it will be. In about fourteen minutes . . .

Joanna Nadin was born in Northampton and moved to Saffron Walden in Essex when she was three. She did well at school (being a terrible swot) and then went to Hull University to study Drama. Three years of pretending to be a toaster and pretending to like Fellini films put her off the theatre for life. She moved to London to study for an MA in Political Communications and after a few years as an autocue girl and a radio newsreader got a job with the Labour Party as a campaigns writer and Special Adviser. She now lives in Bath with her daughter and is a freelance government speech writer and TV scriptwriter. She has written five books for younger readers, several of which have been shortlisted for awards. *The Facts of Life* is her sixth book for Oxford University Press.

Have you read Rachel's first diary yet?

ISBN 978-0-19-275526-1

I need more **tragedy** in my life.

Why is life never like it is in books?
Nothing Jacqueline Wilson ever happens to me: I am not adopted,
my mum is not tattooed, I am not likely to move to the middle of a
council estate or be put into care. My parents are not alcoholics,
drug addicts or closet transvestites. Even my name is pants.

In other words, my life is
earth-shatteringly **NORMAL**.

This cannot go on. Something deep and life-changing has to happen.
This year I shall befriend more exotic and interesting people, learn
to drink coffee (tragic heroines do not start the day with Cheerios
and lemon barley) and capture the heart of Justin Statham with my
vintage clothing and knowledge of all-time great guitar solos.

It's time for my **so-called life** to be
brought up to speed. Starting now.

Rachel's diary
continues in . . .

Joanna Nadin

the life of Riley

My Utterly Hopeless Search for THE ONE

ISBN 978-0-19-275527-8

My quest to find
THE ONE starts right now!

This year I will utterly not snog random posh boys with congenital acne but will save myself for long-haired creative type with interest in tragicness and with musical potential i.e. Justin Statham. Though am not sure Justin has realized yet that I am THE ONE for him. Maybe he has heard I am rubbish at snogging.

I need to learn to
SNOG properly – and fast.

Though perhaps I am just generally unlovable. As well as tongue technique issues I have hopelessly untragic relatives and a dog who eats furniture. Plus I am practically a medical midget and my hair is mental.

Maybe I should just give up
on boys altogether . . .

Rachel's back in . . .

Joanna Nadin

the meaning of life

Rachel Riley's (not) DOING IT diary

ISBN 978-0-19-272833-3

Am ready for year of utter LOVE!

It is official. I am going out with rock god and part-time meat mincer Justin Statham. Am certain that he is **THE ONE** and will prove it by having excellent relationship on every level.

Oh no. What if he wants me to do it?

Have only just got to grips with art of snogging so will need to get help fast. Or at least by 16th birthday. If it happens it needs to be earth-shattering and meaningful as it is, after all, the **Meaning of Life.**

Thank goodness I have definitely found **love of my life** and am not hung up on Jack any more. **Not** at all...

Catch up with Rachel in . . .

Joanna Nadin

my (not so) simple life

Rachel Riley goes back to basics

ISBN 978-0-19-272834-0

Am racked by torture and loss!

But am making plan with Scarlet to deal with **post-break-up trauma.** Must channel anger into something positive, so have new mission statement:

1 Not to moon about over exes but to embrace single life.

2 To stay away from all men (Sad Ed excepted as he is not actual man).

3 To remain true to our friends, forsaking all others.

Scarlet is right. Life will be so much easier without the complications of love. It will be utter Simple Life and am completely committed. Am starting now.

Join Rachel
as she goes . . .

ISBN 978-0-19-272922-4

**Life is what you make it.
And am definitely going to make
mine fabulous. Starting right now.**

Have decided that in order to find **THE ONE** and have
meaningful and fulfilling life I must **seize the day**. Who knows,
THE ONE could be out there right now, right under my nose.

**Will need to kiss a few frogs
before I find my prince though.**

This means utter **experimentation** as far as snogging
is concerned. Am never going to find **THE ONE** if just keep
having accidental liaisons with Jack or ill-advised flirtations
with Justin. **THE ONE** is out there somewhere.

I just need to be **open-minded.
And open-armed.
And possibly open mouthed** ...